# INTEGRITY
## *of the*
# Headless Woman

*To My Sister*
*Joyce love you*
*Carlero Emil*
*9/12*

# INTEGRITY
*of the*
# Headless Woman

*Contessa Emanuel*

InspiringVoices®

A Service of **Guideposts**

ISBN: 978-1-4624-0085-0 (sc)
ISBN: 978-1-4624-0086-7 (e)

Library of Congress Control Number: 2012934638

Inspiring Voices books may be ordered through booksellers or by contacting:

Inspiring Voices
1663 Liberty Drive
Bloomington, IN 47403
www.inspiringvoices.com
1-(866) 697-5313

Printed in the United States of America

Inspiring Voices rev. date: 06/12/2012

# ACKNOWLEDGEMENTS

I thank my Lord and savior Jesus Christ for his guidance and entrusting me with this body of work. Empowering those women who have been denying their future its rightful place in their lives, by being trapped in their past.

Integrity of the Headless Woman is being dedicated to all my battered sisters around the world those with multi- colored and colorless (mental) bruises. Also in memory of those who did not survive the abuse may they rest in peace and their Integrity lives on.

I want to thank the women who bravely shared their stories with me of being unloved. And those wives who knew without a shadow of a doubt God has put them together with their husbands so they fought for their marriage commanding their head to come back. (Thank you, Clara).

To my best friend and prayer partner Sheila Wright, who for many years has been the one I could express my foolish thoughts to and not be judged for it, but rebuked in love when needed. We all need a friend we can be painfully honest with and who knows your honesty has been honored not judged thank you so much. To Annie Revere for her intercessory prayers for me and the book, thank you so much.

To my family, my granddaughter Tiera Haley, for her help and input, you encourage me by letting me know this book will transcend matters of the heart to all generations from teens to seniors. Also to my children Terry, Tracey and Princess for their love and support thank you Princess and Tracey for the time they have put in with the editing. Thank you, Paul Mabry for your words of encouragement.

# A WORD FROM THE AUTHOR

We trust the head of our household (husband) to keep our headship intact in all matters. Why should we be concerned? We did all the right things as a wife and mother, why should we ever entertain the thought of a cheating husband? After all they are our soul mate the one to be our cover and our lover till death do we part.

Did we ever once question the matter of their soul? The ones we referred to as our beloved soul mate.

The soul is said to be a place where a person's emotional and moral nature is kept, a place where our most private thoughts and feelings are hidden. How are we to know what other matters are attached to his soul? How are we supposed to know who else has claim to his soul and will stop at nothing to regain it? It has been a rumor for centuries that the soul is something that God and the devil battles for. It's also rumored that as soon as a child is born it arrives on earth with a Guardian Angel.

Therefore when our so called "soul" mate decides to remove his headship from our home, what else can this thing called divorce be but an execution? the death of a marriage? The other woman now has the head of our household, what is a more fitting name for her than the Headhunter. Sometimes it's not always another woman there are times when it is the other man.

Then the great word, which is so underrated, takes its place in our life "choices." That is when the battle of good and evil comes to play in this story. You are going to be introduced to a woman named Abigail Emanuel Monroe, her family, friends and the choices they surrendered too. These women will not deny their future its rightful place in their life by being trapped to their past

The guardian of Abigail's soul is an Angel named Gabriela, she is assigned to stop Satan and his demonic powers from wrongfully executing Abigail's marriage.

# CONTENTS

# The Imposer

From the beginning of time Satan has religiously been a misogynist, one that hates the institution of marriage. He roams around daily like a bloodhound seeking out marriages to terminate causing many to quote this famous line "life as we have known it has been stolen from us". His taste of this hatred began with the world's first couple, Adam and Eve.

In the 3rd chapter of Genesis, Satan introduces Eve to the sweet flavor of lust, which made it easy for him to persuade her to eat from the tree of knowledge, the same tree God told Adam "do not eat from".

Eve reached for the fruit. She could not resist the sweet appearance or the delicious aroma of disobedience. After carefully caressing the fruit she inhaled and bit into the fruit as she exhaled. It was like nothing she had ever savored before, 'ecstasy' rushed into her mind, causing a rush of power and knowledge. The curtain of innocence had been ripped from her sight she was now able to recognize nakedness. This caused her to look at Adam through different eyes. Like a drug addict, she needed him to experience her high. She then persuaded Adam to do the same just as Satan had persuaded her too. It only took a few seconds for Eve to part her lips and bite into the sweet fruit of disobedience, those seconds will cause a lifetime of bitter misery. This one act of disobedience shifted things in the atmosphere between men women and God, forever causing the Almighty to say to Eve "what have you done? From this day on you will obey your husband" Gen: 3:16. I truly believe that is when men were granted the Headship.

In spite of what Eve did, many women after her existence have committed similar acts of disobedience but God still had mercy on them, we find this proof in Proverbs: 18:22. *Whoso findeth a wife finds* a *Good Thing* and obtains *FAVOUR from the LORD*... *A Good Thing* is referring to the wife in the bible. Women you are a "G.T." a Good Thing, when those words are echoed, "Who gives this woman to be wed" you my dear will not be presented to your husband empty handed. You come with a gift, the Favor of God. That makes you a priceless gift but like most priceless things there is always the threat of it being stolen or destroyed. Thousands of years later the husband is still considered the HEAD and protector of his wife.

The sweet taste of disobedience still lingers in the heart of the adulterer. Take warning when the adulteress materializes to commit her crime she comes armed with a chainsaw attached to her heart. If she is successful in cutting the man away from his family then the wife has just been beheaded and left to 'bleed out,' then divorce becomes the final execution. Hell cheers these adulterine women on. Satan has named these women "Hells Headhunters". I refer to them as the "P.7.W"... Proverbs 7 women

Proverbs 7:21:27

*With persuasive words, she led him astray; she seduces him with her smooth talk. All at once, he followed her like an ox going to the slaughter, Like a deer stepping into a noose' until an arrow pierced his liver, Like a bird darting into a snare, Little knowing it will cost him his life. Now then my sons listen to me, pay attention to what I say. Do not let your heart turn to her ways or stray into her paths. Many are the victims she has brought down; her slain are very strong. Her house is a highway to the grave, leading down to the chambers of death.*

'Adultery' this crime of passion that is being committed against women is planned in the realm of Hell and executed here on earth by women or should I say Headhunters.

# A VISIT WITH THE IMPOSER IN HELL

Satan has just returned from the gathering of angels he was summoned there by God to report his actions on the earth. He lavished being the accuser of God's people day and night. Rev: 12-10. "Demons I am back from the gathering of angels. (Job: 1:6-7.) Even after he kicked me out of heaven he still expects me to report my actions to Him. I was so bored, God's lecture was "It is not good for man to be alone". Give me a break! I have heard this for centuries. They are never alone, they stay in packs. He also mentioned about us butting into their marriage. He must still be holding a grudge about the 'Eve thing'. I did not force Eve to open her mouth and I surely did not have a word with Adam, that was all on her. God referred to the one called Abigail Monroe we are to stay away from her if she resists me. Hmm not happening! How can he order me to stay away from my collateral? I own her! Which part of the word misogyny does he not understand? I hate woman! Especially Abigail Monroe, with the exception of my 'proverbs 7' women (Hell has no fury like a woman scorned) those delicious things keeps us entertained in HELL.

Abigail's father has sworn an oath to me his first-born shall be mine and that is Abigail. She will come to me you will see. I will turn her from God just as I did her father in return for all the wealth I have imparted unto him. It is a done deal. She's my collateral! I kept my word he has become filthy rich. Now it is time for me to collect. I have owned this family for generations all the others have complied, why shouldn't he do the same? Give me a freaking break! God really thinks one woman is going to make a difference? I own the best part of man's nature, the desire to sin. I make wrong feel 'so right' making it almost impossible for him to resist it… or me."

(Persuasion the demonic angel asked) "Satan, was the angel Gabriela present? "Yes, that meddling freak was there. I wish Gabriela had joined us. By the way Persuasion I hope you have your demons in check... Persuasion replied, "They are ready to persuade even you Satan, believe me on this one, ha, ha!" Satan smiled and rubbed his hands together "It's on Demons let's do this. He can't instruct who I may or may not destroy. Those so called "saved women" all start off strong, but sooner or later they call on us. May it be through Anger, Hatred or the cousins, pride and self pity, Everyone, do not forget the top cat in HELL! Who is it? 'Un- forgiveness' "Hella!" chimed the demons in unison. Satan continued: "They ought to give us more credit. When a lie is needed, who is always there to help them out? We are of course; I am the Prince of the air. 'I am the ACE in Space', so they had better stay out of my way".

# ABIGAIL

Dr. Abigail Emanuel-Monroe is blessed with beauty, grace and integrity. She is unwavering as the green is to the evergreen. Her spirit is compared to the great ancient Abbeys; where silence is empowering. She admires the beauty of nature but is aware of its destructive side, especially early autumn when things start to change before its time.

She defines the power of an early autumn, manifesting frequently, attempting to disturb her true nature, challenging her integrity season after season. Abigail is resilient to her seasons of life. She embraces the bitter winter moments of her life with warmth and passion. The summer heat does not scorch her cool way of handling temporary over heated situations. Spring arrives with its marvelous bouquet of blossoms which causes her, to second guess her nature as one with the evergreen. She does not get envious of their blossoms for she knows it's all temporary. 'They too shall pass'.

Abigail is one that loves deeply with all her heart. She totally emerges into a relationship. She does not believe in 50/50 but each person should be producing 100% towards the relationship. She believes her soul mate should be the head of the household, her lover and her cover.

She is true to God, her marriage to Bishop Sean Monroe, their three daughters, Jordan her first born followed by Savanna and Olivia and her career as a physician. She is happy and feels protected by her husband. He being un-faithful to her is the last thought that would ever enter her mind.

Her burning desire is to fulfill her purpose as a Life Coach to endangered women. Abigail helps women to regain their integrity which had been brutally stolen from them. Her accruement for L.I.F.E. is living in full empowerment.

She is aware of the satanic influence that is present all around us every day. Knowing sometimes you can walk into an empty room and the hair on your neck or arm has risen. You see nothing unusual with the natural eye but there is an invisible 'force' that is letting you know "I am here". Causing us to wonder is it good or is it evil?

There are those who would want to attain the benefits of Satan's wealth and be giving some of his limited powers. It does not come cheap, they must obey his creed which reads *"Destroy and kill everyone and anything that gets in your way, be loveless, ruthless and depend on nobody. Integrity is so overrated, use every one to your own advantage, forgive no one and reject everyone. My formula never fails. God said he gave humans free will. Well he lied. Nothing is free. It costs for you to play on my grounds".* And so reads the evil creed of Satan, Prince of the air.

Abigail's father, Montgomery, is in massive debt to the Monarch of Hell. This debt is yet to be paid. He has acquired great wealth and Power from Satan all with the collateral of the soul of his first-born child Abigail.

Fortunately, there exist a few obstacles with Satan's plan to destroy Abigail's destiny. One is Mona her mother, who is a powerful praying woman with friends in high places (heaven.) Her effective intercessory prayers are felt in a great way in the spirit world of good and evil. Her target is the world in which principalities and rulers of darkness abides. She is aware that the airways do belong to Satan. The bible refers to Satan as the *'Prince of power of the air'.* Ephesians 2:2.

In time of trouble, Mona is the ultimate Intercessor you would need on your side. She effectively bombards the airways with prayer. She is a great enemy of Hell.

Abigail's guardian angel, Gabriella's assignment is to guard Abigail from Satan and his demons so she will be able to reach her destiny.

When Gabriella appears she does not come to assist she comes to take over and defuse whatever situation Satan has thrown into Abigail's life. Gabriela's presence commands attention in a powerful way. When she appears, even Hell has to recognize she is a messenger you 'cannot shoot'. It is rumored, she reports directly to Michael the Archangel of heaven.

Then, there is the one and only Cousin, Montana. Of the well-established Montana Emanuel law firm. She is as gorgeous as any runway model. Her six-foot frame is held up with legs like Tina Turner. She does not believe in love and really does wonder "what love has to do with it." She is often heard saying "Men are for playing with darling, not loving". She believes Satan's price is too high and God comes with too much guilt, therefore she has declared herself a "free agent."

Hell has declared that anyone who is aligned with Abigail is also an enemy of Hell and will be treated as such. But, even Hell at times is confused about Montana!

The sins of Abigail's father are in route to visit her. Satan's objective will be to remove the headship of Abigail's household and try to get her to turn her back on Jehovah, the God of her mother, persuading her to pledge allegiance to him.

Satan and the evil spirit Persuasion, who is one of the highest-ranking demonic spirits next to Death, looks in daily from Hell observing Abigail's every move.

They will not stop until they have successfully carried out the execution of Abigail's marriage. Causing her to be headless, it will not be a clean cut. The axe will be extremely blunt, causing cruel and unusual punishment of passion. For the first time she will feel and taste the poisonous side of passion that abused women are experiencing daily.

It is imperative that Abigail survive this attempted execution. Her survival is crucial to the thousands of wives who are slowly bleeding a death of betrayal caused by their husbands who have summoned the headhunters into their homes.

# TEEN BEAUTY CONTEST

The hour has arrived. The tension in the majestic ballroom is as thick as the mysterious fog, which has rapidly announced its presence to the magnificent beauty of the Yorkshire dales in northern England, covering the city of Bradford.

I believe if a fly were to have landed on one of the thousands of crystal petals that dangle from the magnificent chandelier that illuminates the grand ballroom, perhaps one would have heard it land. The Brits are used to the fog in England, but nothing like this had ever taken over the city this pasty and this thick. No formal announcement from the weather masters was ever given. Like an unwanted guest, it crafted its way into the city to disturb the order of things. None of the buildings were visible. One could only imagine the comeliness of the rolling lush green hills that surrounds the out skirt of the city, or the beauty of the daffodils that makes us smile, and of course the extraordinary beauty of the English roses that compels us to say "wow". We cannot forget the fragile but relentless forget-me-not flowers that blanket the country side. Their delicate blue petals, reminiscent of mouse ears, didn't even hear the news of the unexpected fog.

There they are, ten beautiful girls who have worked so hard for this day, the Miss Yorkshire beauty contest. Abigail was the smartest and the prettiest one but would that be enough?

With only one more category left to go, there is no doubt in Abigail or her friend's minds that she was the winner. She has had the highest points in all categories so far and now it is time for the final walk.

Abigail's appearance for the evening gown segment commanded a boisterous round of applause. She had gambled on everything, all the money she personally owned went to the spectacular green beaded dress that fitted to her like a second skin. She resembled a live Barbie doll.

She took each stride on the runway with such pride as a fully bread Arabian stallion. The sparkles that reflected off of her emerald beaded dress were magical. She did her turns with such confidence, she could taste victory. The crowd went wild as she smiled and glided off the runway.

For Abigail this was more than a local contest, it was part of her survival plan for her new life. She must win if she is to help her mother escape a life of misery from her satanic wealthy father. It would take almost a plan of war as good as America had when they won their independence from England thought Abigail, but all she has right now is the contest prize, a fully paid scholarship to your school of choice anywhere in the world.

Abigail's mind drifted to the terrible fight she had with her father Montgomery just a few hours before the contest.

# Father Dearest

"Just learn from your mother Abigail, how to be a good wife and get that rubbish from your head about going to college. Why do you need brains? That is why God created men, we are your heads! I am not going to pay good money to teach you how to be one of those feminists! The next thing you will be saying is that you are a lesbian! Now if you were a boy it would be different but you are not. A good wife is priceless Abigail, priceless! If you're going to work, then be a good nanny to someone's children or an au pair girl, better still, be a nun and get locked away somewhere.

Those Pakistanis and Indians have the right idea. I may not like them but they have the right idea. Pick a wife and make them marry no ifs or buts. The man is the head of the house and that is that."

Abigail took a deep breath. It felt like she had swallowed a can of molasses in a room that already lacked oxygen. Her head felt like a merry go round spinning out of control. She made the sign of the cross as she had thousands of times in her eighteen years. It did not help her words from being slow and heavy. "Father" she slurred then cleared her throat. Her voice became louder. "Father I want to go college for law or medicine". Montgomery was fuming. Bradford still has chimneys from the wool mills that blow gigantic smoke clouds, however today her father was blowing harder and louder. Montgomery said "And how do you expect to pay for this". A scared Abigail muttered out "The youth club is having a talent and beauty contest in town and the prize is a scholarship to any school of your choice" Montgomery growled. "Over my dead body you will". Poor Abigail, she did not expect this to be so hard, she replied "It is being held at the Midland Hotel, Father". Montgomery firmly said "I do not care where it is being held, it could be at Buckingham palace for all I care. If you do this Abigail, you are dead to me! You will be beheaded and cut off, have I made myself clear Abigail?!" Abigail wept "Yes father". "Then what is your choice? Abigail glanced at her Mother Mona, watching as she inhaled and placed her hand over her forever-chapped lips, while exhaling, for it was not time.

The Monarch of Hell looked down at the situation and smiled. The demons that he had dispatched to aid Montgomery in his life of wickedness and wealth were all ready to pounce on Abigail. Satan stretched out his hand and motioned them to stop. He was amused, Satan remarked *"let's see how far the stupid girl thinks she can go, Oh hold on she is not our problem. Keep an eye on the mother"*.

Abigail knew this was it, whatever she declares she would have to reap the consequence good or bad. She inhaled strength and exhaled weakness as her mother has taught for years which made place for her first taste of power as she says.

"I choose my life father, I choose life" Abigail said firmly "If I am to be headless then let it be".

She could see her mother from the corner of her eye. Mona lips were moving rapidly, Mona was standing in a position as one of authority. Abigail had never seen this before. She knew she had her mother's blessing. One of Mona weakness is she was sickeningly submissive to Montgomery. She is like Archie's Edith in the sitcom all in the family. *"Yes Archie" "OK Archie"*. Mona had never been encouraged to think for herself and she chooses not to.

Mona was not educated so she depended on her husband for almost everything. They reside in a country which had a history of women being the property of men and nobody interferes with a man slapping his wife around.

"You have no head on you woman I am your head without me you are like a headless corpse remember woman, I am the ACE in this place and this is my house" Montgomery would echo those words to Mona daily.

They lived in a very strong catholic community where fathers know best and women knew less. Montgomery did not believe in women working or having an education or a life they were to be servants. This day Mona will change for the future of her daughter.

"Get the heck out of my house not a farthing (a ¼ of a penny) will you get not a farthing!" growled Montgomery.

The tears rushed out of Abigail like a shaken bottle of soda pop she was quickly wiping her eyes trying to hold back the rest of the tears as one trying to put the top back on the bottle but it was too late the explosion had happened .

"I will leave father and Hell will stay here with you" blurted out Abigail. Montgomery raised his hand to slap her. Mona interrupted him. "Montgomery you stop right now I have never said a word about how inhumane you have treated me but I will kill you if you touch a hair on her head. Abby go and do what you have to do love go to the contest may the blessing and protection of Jehovah be with you always before you go wait a minute Abby", Mona ran out to the garden and came back with a small bouquet of For-get-me-not flowers and gave them to Abigail. She took the flowers and wept.

Abigail walked out of her father's house and went to compete in the contest.

She would not turn her back on her mother. As Abigail walked out backwards, Mona gave her an assuring nod that she will be ok.

Mona knew Montgomery could not do anything but growl at her child. She and her God had this under control. After all, God did not want her to be imprisoned for murder. Mona believes strongly that God never sends us into battle without first developing our knowledge of mastering the art of choosing your battle…

Abigail had always seen her mother as a lamb, always being led to the slaughter of humiliation by her father. Today she did not look into the eyes of a lamb, this day she looked into the eyes of a roaring lion. She got strength from her mother's eyes while walking back wards out of her father's house. Yet by faith, she was stepping forward into her new life ordained by God.

Meanwhile, Hell froze for a moment to hear from the Monarch. He was a little shaken. Satan whispered "*So our little lamb is not a lamb after all. She has protection. We will see about leaving hell with your father. Darling we will be following you, ha, ha, ha. You are mine. My collateral, Property of Hell and I will not forget*".

# AND THE WINNER IS

There was no doubt in Abigail's or her friend's minds that she was the winner when she walked on the stage as one of the three finalists. Every one wowed but that was not the wow she is waiting for. Abigail needed the judges to be wowed. And "the winner is…" it was not Abigail. It went to the one of the girls who everyone knew was sleeping with a couple of the judges. Abigail was a devastated runner up. The same manner the fog had concealed the beauty of Bradford Yorkshire that spring day, is the same manner the power of lust had masked the judges.

"Wow Abigail you should have won, are those judges blind?" that's what all her friends were running up to her saying.

She could not take the pressure of the rejection. The disappointment was over whelming. Abigail turned around to look at her friends; Abigail's mascara had run down her cheeks unto the emerald gown. The white of her eyes was so red that her green eyes looked as stunning as a pure emerald but behind those emerald colored eyes was a pain that would manifest itself for years to come. You could clearly hear the pain in her subdued voice as she said so sadly "ta love (thanks love) for everything but your wow was not the one I was waiting for". She took a deep breath, gave a distressing half smile, and almost in a whisper, she said "what do I do now" and walked away out into the mysterious fog that blinded the city that afternoon.

The seed of rejection buried itself in a deep place in her heart with plenty space to expand its roots.

Montana, Abigail's cousin and their best friend Sir James Kingsley who they mostly call Wellington ran out to meet her. "Hang on Abby!" screamed an out of breath Montana. "We heard what happened with your dad, that's all right Abby you do not need him. We can use my inheritance from my mum's death. I will be getting it in a fortnight (two weeks) then we will go to school in America". Abby buried her face into Montana's shoulder. "I lost Montana, because I respected my body. I wouldn't sleep with that dirty old chap. I will never use my body as a bargaining tool as the rest of those girls did Montana never, never!", sobbed Abigail.

Wellington felt helpless. He loved Abigail so much, he has never kissed Abigail as a lover would but his passion for her confirms to his heart he is indeed in love. He had never ever considered anyone else to be his future wife, however in his dreams every time he reached in to kiss her she would disappear, and now his worst fear might be coming true. Wellington's passion was as Mr. Beckham's was for Lizzie in Pride and prejudice. By Jane Austin

"Come with us" said Montana to Wellington "I cannot, Montana, my father has great need of me. I have to attend to his estate." a sad wellington replied. Wellington reached for Abigail's hand and says. "Abby I will find you if you ever need me. Just call me". Montana sarcastically snorted "I guess the press would have a great time with that story "Sir James Wellington runs away to America with two barmy Yorkshire lasses". Abigail looks into Wellington's eyes and said "I am not worth waiting for. I am a loser. Find you a nice Yorkshire girl of breeding, Wellington". Abigail pressed two fingers on her lips then rested her fingers on Wellington's lips and ran away leaving him and Montana standing in the fog. "The keys Abby! you can't get in to the flat (apartment) without them". Montana threw the keys to her flat at Abby.

From that horrible day on Abigail never saw herself as a beauty again. She began on a low self-esteem diet guaranteed to shed away every ounce of love she once had for self. The fight was to begin, the boxing ring was prepared, Abigail weighed in, the scales showed she was overweight; she was to be placed into the heavy weight division. She became top heavy because of rejection, worthlessness, bitterness, hatred and self-destruction all had weighed in heavy on her heart.

Dear Abigail, she was to enter into a battle where the odds are against her. With Abigail's new diet there also came a new coach/ trainer. His name is Lucifer of Hades', his fee did not come cheap. The spirit of bitterness and an unforgiving heart had sprouted from the root of rejection to grow and control her emotions. So much so that everything she will do or say from now on will be well- orchestrated by the spirit of rejection. Her head will not have any say so. Satan has temporary custody of her head.

All through college in America Abigail chose to be friendless. Only Montana would she converse with. Almost three decades later which seemed more like three centuries to Abigail, she kept her promise to herself and her body by never becoming a barging tool (Satan had other ideas for her and her body). Sadly she never kept in touch with Wellington. Satan had convinced her she was unfit to be in such a nice man's life.

Abigail and Montana excelled in all their classes. Abigail kept her life private, success was all that mattered with Abigail. Montana… well she knew her professor's quite well.

# SEAN MONROE

Abigail is now a wealthy doctor in America married to the Bishop Sean Monroe they have three daughters, Savanna, Olivia and Jordan. Sean has been preoccupied more than usual. Abigail cannot put her hands on it. It has been twenty plus years since she met Sean, she had been in America only a few years before they met.

Hell had maneuvered Sean into her life. He was a patient at the hospital where she was doing her internship. He had survived a deadly plane crash, he suffered with many broken bones and his body was badly burnt he also suffered with amnesia he remembers some things. Plastic surgeons assigned by Hell worked miracles on him. They were never sure how he should look, but one thing for sure he was handsome now.

The plane was coming from South America he was returning from vacation but there were those that wonder, was he really? He thinks his destiny was divinity school in America. His story did not make any sense to many but his alluring charm covered all the confusion. His father was also in debt to Satan, Sean was his first-born. Sean was in trouble and his father turned to his satanic group to summon help from hell to get his son out of England. One of hell's agents had been assigned to reprogram his mind and convinced Sean that he is the one that had fought about his calling for many years. It also meant him leaving a jet style life that he had been faithful too. Soon he will surrender to his new style of life. His destiny to serve God has been sealed. The question became which God had called him? Sean had to learn to walk again. He was on a fast path to recovery, he was proclaimed a miracle but he was suffering with a slight case of amnesia. Seventy percent of his memory has returned to him, that is all Hell wanted him to retrieve for now, the other thirty would return in Hell's appointed time.

It was love at first sight for Abigail. She did not care about his past, just who he was now. He swept her right off her feet. Montana however, did not like or trust him from the beginning. Nevertheless, she was happy to see Abigail happy for the first time in years. Two years later they were married. It was a small private ceremony. Their lives were magical, for a few years they were inseparable. Their bedroom exploded with passion and love, but things are different know. Three daughters were born to them in their twenty-two years of marriage, Jordan being the first born.

Abigail was happy beyond her wildest imagination until a strange mysterious creature of the night was dispatched from Hell. It came to entertain her husband. It brought with it, a dark mystique. Lately, Sean's dreams would over take him with a passion that caused him to call out to a woman pleading for her not to leave him because he could not live without her. The worst would be when Sean would utter these heart-slicing words "it is you I want not her, she is just the mother of my children that is all, my arms are useless without you in them, my heart is keeping a corpse alive without your love. I am nothing without you do with me as you please but don't ever leave me". Whoever the woman is in his dreams, Abigail knew she could not compete with her. The dreams have been coming on and off for the past five years. For five long years Abigail has kept this secret of this nameless creature who shares her bed. Sean and Abigail have just celebrated their twenty-second anniversary. They are now preparing for their eldest daughter Jordan's wedding. Abigail knows something is very wrong with her marriage. Reality was finally coming in and it was coming with a price. How do you fight the mysteries of the night? How do you compete with a woman who gives your husband so much passion in his dreams that his groans causes your heart to feel like it is going through a paper shredder and even if you unplug it from the wall it still keeps shredding, how do you survive this?.

# CAVIAR POND

It is early summer, Abigail has taken time off work to be with the family and spend some time with her girls. They are coming in from Europe, bringing with them the wedding dress they had purchased in Milan, Italy for their older sister Jordan. Abigail also wants to have an intimate dinner with her husband. Finally, she wants to confront this demon. Satan is not in anyway threatened, he has sent out his best from Hell to begin torturing her. Abigail first visits her favorite place in the whole world, a body of water she calls the Caviar Pond. It is a mere fraction in size compared to the Lake District in Yorkshire, where she has left behind her most cherished moments, including memories of Wellington. "This is not like any other pond," Abigail will tell you she has become one with this mysterious pond. She takes a seat on the stone bench, the rays of the sun rest on her face. It feels like a warm sip of hot cocoa on a mild winter's day on her face. She removes her sandals and puts her feet into the pond to join the ripples which emulate millions of caviar shimmering upon the surface of the pond. At first it feels as refreshing as a cool glass of ice water that rushes from her feet to her warm cocoa face, she tilts back her head to welcome the much needed breeze that has joined them. She whispers, "Pond, it's been a long time since we first met".

Abigail's mind drifted to that bizarre summer day that drove her to the pond. She had only been married for 7 years. She remembers this particular day very well and so does Hell... She had given the cook and housekeepers the day off. Abigail worked hard preparing the dinner on that dreadful hot June day. It was almost twenty minutes before the children would arrive from summer camp. The table was set, it does not look like a table for a midweek dinner, more for a Sunday dinner.

The aroma of homemade bread and cake fills the house; she had made New-York strip steak with sautéed mushrooms and onions, scalloped potatoes, brown gravy, Greek salad and homemade strawberry milk shake for the children. Dessert would be trifle. She looked out of the dining room window saw that her children were coming off the private bus. They were a few minutes early and that irritated her. The table was not the way she wanted it to be. She runs and locks the door so the children would not barge in.

She quickly rearranges the table to her satisfaction. Presentation had been everything with Abigail in those early days. Since that awful foggy day, everything she does is on display, just as she was. She makes sure it is always a winning moment in other words a guaranteed WOW moment.

The children are screaming "let us in mommy! Let us in!" She takes a final look at the table and smiles. She then slowly opens the door and hugs the children robotically as they put their book bags down. They charge to the bathroom to wash their hands for dinner. As they approach the dining room, Abigail raises her hands at the dinner table just as a maestro would to his orchestra, and here came the music, the children say's "wow mommy this is a winner". She smiled as an understudy would, who had just received applause at rehearsal, grateful but wanting more.

Four hours later, the children are in bed, she has showered and changed her dress just as one would for the next act of a play. She prepared the table for her husband. This time she added candles and flowers. The Milk shakes have been replaced with red wine. The aroma of *Oscar de la Renta* perfume lingers from their bedroom into the dining room. Her coach, Lucifer and his demonic team have prepared her for this night since the beauty pageant. They expect a TKO. The bell rings, round one. She hears her husband unlocking the door. Sean is not aware that he has been elected to be the lightweight contender for Abigail's big fight. Lucifer of the Hades' is sponsoring this.

The door unlocks, her heart is pounding, anxiety and all its encounters are cheering her on as Sean makes his way into the house. She takes a quick look into the mirror, but she is not sure who is looking back at her. The demonic forces are taking over. She slowly walks down the hallway to the dining room, but in her mind the hallway is now the runway she walked on all those years ago at the beauty contest. She greets Sean and smiles at him just as she did for those judges on that horrible foggy day of the contest.

He looks at her and says "I am so hungry". (No greeting of any kind) In Abigail's mind Sean has just thrown the first blow. The fog has returned to make her invisible. They enter the dining room. She takes her place but remains standing as she pours the wine. She spreads out her hands in the same manner at the table as she did for the children.

Sean sits down and starts to eat without saying a word. [No wows] Her hand slowly goes down and tightly wraps around her waist. He has just struck below the belt. She sits and gently begins to rock forward and backward. The all too familiar lump in her throat has announced its presence. She is trying desperately to swallow but it is getting larger. Her green eyes are trying so hard not to tear as she awaits a wow just as she had hundreds of times since that horrible foggy day. She raises herself from the table Sean is too busy eating to notice his wife's eyes have just turned hunter green, surrounded by an island of red hot lava. Abigail stares at her husband as he is giving the dinner more attention than he is to her. Every time the knife and fork touch his plate it sounded like the clamor of cymbals. The bell has rung, round two. The champion is angry. Nothing is turning out as she had rehearsed in her mind. She slowly rises, all the while biting into her bottom lip. She tastes the bitter blood and delights in it, just as a vampire would.

Hell announces its presence. She grabs the edge of the table, rage enters on to the scene. Justification is the one that gave her the courage to rise and now he has empowered her to turn the table over on to Sean. Sean jumps up screaming "are you crazy"!?

While steak, onions, mushroom gravy and red wine and the rest of the dinner portrays her anger unto what was once a wonderful cream of Apricot colored wall with white molding. Now it has just become a canvas for her anger. She hears nothing she sees nothing but fog she wants to die. Her coach is thinking that payday is coming very soon.

After all these years the roots of rejection are choking the life out of her. She did not see a dinner table, she saw the judge's table from the contest. Abigail did what she wanted to do that night. The spirit of rejection and his cousins had come to claim her mind. Suicide is in waiting to assist her. She runs out of the room, Sean chases her into the bedroom he grabs her arm and firmly says. "For God's sake what is going on with you?!" She looks past him. Her eyes catch the flame from the scented candles that surround their garden tub. The same tub which she had hoped their evening would have ended in. "Look at me Abigail, ok we've been through this before. You think I am having an affair don't you?" She just stares into space as her head rests on the wall. This is her favorite room, she surrounds herself with soft pink and mint green English Roses that complement the bear claw oriental canopy bedroom furniture. No answer can come out, the lump has control and it has barricaded her voice. Sean releases her and raises his arms above his head. He watches helplessly as she slides down the wall. Abigail lies down with her face half on the mahogany hardwood floor and the other half on the floral Oriental rug that matches her roses. He walks away, he has just been knocked down. She tries to stop him but something worst has hold of her. This enemy was deadly the spirit of pride had stuck its ugly head into the picture. Sean returned and blurts out "this is not supposed to happen in our home Abby! isn't it bad enough that I am battling who I really am? I should not have to figure out who this person is in front of me! not in our home Abby! Especially not when a doctor lives here too, damn it! why won't you talk to me?! We need God's help right now" she said nothing so he walked out again. She crawls to the bed and pulls down the silk raspberry comforter and wraps herself in it. She says to herself what she wishes she could say to him that "she feels like such a failure, it just didn't matter anymore because it was not God's attention she was trying to obtain, but his". An exhausted Abigail fell asleep on the floor where Sean left her.

The next morning, Abigail got up and dressed. She was putting the last touches to the bed when Sean walked in and announced. "OK Abigail there is no devil in hell having my marriage" (The Monarch of Hell) says "sorry already taken" (Satan and his demons laughed)

"I have called the bishop, I have alerted the prayer warriors, the battle is on". [Round three] Abigail just looked at him and replied "for what dear?" Sean taken aback, replied "for what? Remember the table thing?! you know one minute I am eating my dinner next thing I know am wearing it, because my wife decided I needed to! and you're asking me for what!!". Abigail responded to him "oh that... I am so sorry dear, I am probably having P.M.S. attacks". The spirit of dishonesty has now announced itself, and not only that, but it has also announced that it is taking over this whole situation to help Abigail out.

# REFLECTIONS

Abigail leaves in her smoke grey Bentley. She was not alone, the spirit Rejection and all his cousins jumped in. She travels along a curvy country lane which is filled with weeping willow trees. They are stunning during the day but can be spooky at night especially when the southern moss clings around the branches. This day the lilac and honey suckle bushes are in full bloom. It is a spectacular sight with an extraordinary aroma, but she misses her English country side and her forget me not flowers.

She slows down as she approaches a sight that was so inviting to the eye, she embraced the sight until her tears validated the beauty of it all. There it is, Caviar Pond. Its ripples truly resemble millions of glistening Caviar. The lilac trees were reflecting on a part of the pond that was still. The green from the willow tree has caused the water to resemble a bouquet of spring foliage. White wash stone benches were aligned around the pond, volcanic looking white rocks dressed the out skirt of the pond. It sits off peacock lane which is also known as lover's lane. She pulls over and absorbs every square feet of the pond. Abigail sits on one of the stone benches under a grand old oak tree. It stands majestic along with the weeping willow trees. The reflection of the trees is magnificent on the surface of the pond. 'Nature's mirror" thought Abigail. The wind gently blows causing the images to dance on the pond.

She inhales and then exhales. Abigail whispers "even nature anticipates a wow moment, and truly pond you are a WOW". She puts her hands into the pond and speaks to the pond, [while her coach is trying to persuade her to jump in and die so he can finally be paid). God breathes his spirit on the pond.

"Hello pond we are a lot alike. Nature reflects its wonderful colors upon your face. The seasons come and bring with it the summer greens, the brilliant crystal of winter wonder land, spring multi color blossoms and the grandest of them all, autumn red and gold. Every season commands a" wow" from you nevertheless, it is just surface stuff. Beneath you, there is probably so much rubbish and slimy rocks entwined with other people's heartaches. When the night comes and the moon is not illuminating there is no "WOW" is there? You are then just a cold dark lonely pond. I also depend on my makeup. I am painted up with different colors for different seasons, I deck myself with only one intention, and that is to get the "WOWS." When the night comes, my dear friend pond, I too am just a cold lonely person who houses a lot of rubbish in the depth of my heart. Do you like the fog, pond? At least when the fog comes we can hide. When winter arrives and the beauty of the snow commands its wows from you but once the snow has vanished from the trees the reflection of their bareness is reflected and you are then blamed for the mirror image of the grayish brown twisted branches. The branches just do not realize that you can only reflect what you see. Until the next season, the next thrill, they have to be content with the state of their image. Oh pond, I feel like the bare trees. All the time needing "wows" even out of season, to survive. I must create my own season's pond so I can reflect whatever is needed to survive at that moment. Pond, you will not believe what I just did at home.

I wanted it to be so special. I thought maybe by me preparing the dinner and not the cook that he would at least appreciate me, but he does not. The mystery woman is always on his mind. She comes and visits with him in our bed. Right now pond, I hate him so much but the dreadful truth is I love him more. I feel like I am losing my mind after what I did today I think that I may have totally lost it. Pond I cannot stop thinking about my father's words to me after one of his friends were exposed in the local news paper for cheating on his wife. Worst still, he was leaving the wife for this mistress. It was my one and only relationship talk between father and daughter. "Abby" he would say "it's easier for a man to kick a woman out of his bed than it is for him to get a woman out of his head so make sure you are the one in his head and not his bed". Pond, right now I am not the one in his head".

After three hours of crying, Abigail contributed many of her salty tears to the body of water. It's as if the pond understood Abigail's troubled heart.

The pond sent millions of caviar ripples over to embrace Abigail's tears and carry them to the heart of the pond where her secrets would be safe. When the ripples had stopped, the pond was mirrored again. Abigail stretched her swan like neck over to look into the reflection of the pond. At that very moment a strong wind came, and as the ripples returned, the mirrored pond became Caviar again. Abigail smiled and said "wow its all right pond I know you can only reflect the truth, and my tears must have spoken to your heart. I understand your refusal to reflect such ache. I thank you my friend. Keep my tears safe as they converse to you of the excruciating pain which has saddled my heart, riding me close to destruction".

If Abigail had seen the truth of her pain, wallowing in it, and drowning her self in self pity, she would have jumped in and died. ("Ok what just happened, why she didn't jump in?!", growled Satan?)

Abigail arose to leave. She was extremely weak from all the crying. She was so intense with her own pain, she did not notice the grand mansion that stood on top of the hill and neither did she notice the ancient eyes that were observing her.

She drove back to that foreign land called her home, where she knows trouble awaits her. As she enters the house, Sean announces. "We have to talk". Wrong response, Abigail wanted to hear "are you okay dear"? Followed with a much-needed hug upon the strong chest of her husband hoping he would press closely unto her heart so close that he could feel that she has an irregular heartbeat. His awareness of her pain would have been a great wow, for Abby just awareness sometimes creates a wow.

"Tell me what you want from me Abby" Said Sean, again wrong response. In Abby's mind if she has to tell Sean what it is she craves from him, then it is not the same as him being in tune with her needs.

Instead it becomes a directive. She thinks to herself. "This is not the University of Broken Hearts".

Abigail wants to be able to say. "Wow, he knew what I needed" but to dictate a need does not command a wow". She looks into his eyes with such disappointment and wishes they were the pond.

Abigail blows out the many candles which had surrounded her raspberry marble tub which had been burning all-night and part of the day. The aroma of *Oscar de la Renta* perfume has been replaced with burnt wax. She enters the dry tub and sits in it feeling so sorry for herself and her marriage. She hears Sean call the housekeeper for help to clean up. He then made another call. "I need to stay home. I think she knows something, yes me too".

Abigail gets out of the dry tub and slips in to her bed. Sean followed her soon after. She went through the horrible ordeal of love making with Sean. That's his answer to everything "give women sex and everything will be ok", thought Abigail. But that is when her nightmares become reality. That is when her husband performs his "duty" but that is all it is a duty. She feels his body pressing next to hers she wants so much to respond with all her being but that would mean bringing her wall down and that is all she has left to keep her from totally losing her own head. She knows his mind is thinking of someone else anyway, the one who has his heart, who at this moment is sharing their bed.

Abigail stared at the ceiling until it was over. Her cheeks this night would not feel the frequent visit of her hot tears. She had already given them all to the pond. Sean falls asleep. His sleep was not the only thing that would fall into their bedroom a strange spirit that waits for the sun to go down so she may rise with the night. Together they would travel to a place where Abigail could never enter. His sensual moans that filled their bedroom broadcast to Abigail that she was not invited. A powerless Abigail watches as her husband is having what seems to be cyber intercourse in his dreams. She senses this spirit is one who has come to seduce his body and soul and to inform Abigail she was not satisfying to her husband and she has come to satisfy him.

The moonlight peeks through her window, the glow of the moon brought a smile to Abigail's heart with pleasant thoughts of how the pond must be glistening in the late summer moonlight with her secrets resting in the heart of the pond. Abigail does not know how long she can go on existing like this in a "pharaoh palace." A place of bitterness where her spirit cries out, "free me". The hard task she feels is that she will never get the strength to escape. She will not betray her husband's position in the church. If she does then it would be such a blow to the church. Abigail was concerned about the turning the table over thing, she did seek medical help and was told she was suffering from an acute case of depression. Abigail took her medicine but she knew in her heart that this was deeper than any so called depression. These meetings at the pond continued for many years.

Today Abigail and Sean are still struggling with their relationship. Abigail is determined her marriage is not going to be a failure. Whatever it takes to keep the head of her household intact, she will do. Abigail tries to turn to the bible daily for answers. She questions God's plans for her even though the word says *He will not put any more on us than we can bear.* 1st Corinthian 10-13

Abigail wonders just how much she can endure in this fight. Her faith has been tested daily but it is all for those who will come to her for refuge in the future. Abigail loves the stories in the book of Exodus the great coming out of Egypt. She feels like she had become very much like the people who had forsaken the true God for the idle gods of the Egyptians. Sean was her idol and her god she trusted only in him. If love was like a cool drink to a thirsty heart then Abigail is now starting to realize this relationship is dehydrating to her. She is the only one pouring into the relationship. She holds on to some precious words giving to her by her mother. "God will only satisfy that which belongs to Him".

Abigail thoughts down memory lane were suddenly interrupted. She took her feet out of the pond to answer the phone. It was too late, a message had been left. "Sorry Abby, I will not be able to meet with you for dinner. Something came across my desk and I need to attend to it. I have finalized everything concerning Jordan's wedding. See you later", Click. "Oh well pond, enough reminiscing. We have been together many years. You're still caviar pond and I am still a functioning

27

miserable Abigail. He has done it again, what he does best. He has disappointed me. Well here goes my romantic dinner plans. So much for confronting my demons with him, do not worry pond, I will not be turning any dinner tables over. I guess the surprise is on me".

Sean has been taking more and more speaking engagements, but never has he called home. He would always say "I thought it would be too late to call" or "I knew you have to be at the hospital early"so this time when he called, Abigail knew his pattern had changed which was a red flag.

# GABRIELLA

Abigail was restless, tossing and turning wondering who it was that came across her husband's desk and just how exactly is he attending to her.

Sean was not the only one moving up in the ranks. Abigail was to be promoted, and rightfully so which would make her chief of staff. She had not given an answer because she needed to speak to the head of her household first, but he never came home. She finally fell asleep.

Something strange was again happening in her bed but this time it was with Abigail. She was not sure, was it a dream or a vision that took her from her bed to the pond? She was not alone, an elderly woman was there. She informs Abigail. "I have been watching you my dear for many years; you love the pond don't you? I am the owner. This is my property, come let's walk". The woman reached for Abigail's arm.

They walked a little in silence "My name is Gabriella". Abigail started to introduce herself "I am". The woman interrupted her "I know who you are Abigail the only child of Montgomery and Mona Charles born in Yorkshire, England, who trusts no one but your beloved cousin Montana Emanuel. You love the blue bell flowers and the for-get me not. You were cheated of a crown that rightfully belonged to you. From that day on you lost yourself. The for-get me not your mother gave you is pressed in your bible. Have you forgotten Abigail? I have never ever put a do not trespass sign up. I see how much pleasure people get from the pond. That is why you have come all these years is it not my dear? Abigail smiled and nodded. I have to tell you something, you must not be alarmed my dear, but you, yourself, are dealing with a trespasser.

29

The Monarch of Hell Lucifer, he has sent someone to trespass in your life." Abigail gasped, she was in shock. Gabriella embraced her until she was calm again. "Time is drawing near for me in this world dear." Gabriella went on to say, "my estate is going to be on the market for sale tomorrow I want you to purchase it". Abigail felt compelled to say "yes" she looked into Gabriella's crystal dark eyes. She felt as if she was looking into the pond. Her eyes sparkled like Caviar. Gabriella said to her "you said yes without asking the price". Abigail said, "I do not care what it is, one thing I do know, it is priceless". Gabriella smiled and motioned her head in agreement.

"Hell is after your head my dear. You have been elected to be "executed." the monarch of Hell has chosen to collect on your father's collateral, which happens to be you, Abigail. From that day long ago when you stood up to your father even though you lost the beauty contest, you won the rights to your integrity. The Monarch has been waiting for the right time to get back at your mother for disarming one of his demons that night. He owns the soul of your father, Abigail and you his only offspring are collateral in return for the wealth he has acquired". Abigail was speechless, "why? why me?" she asked, as the tears again found her cheeks. "This is not about flesh and blood Abigail. This is bigger than you and Montgomery. Your father might have used you for collateral, but what he and the Monarch fail to realize is your mother has an amazing relationship with the God of Abraham, Isaac, and Jacob. You will be in the protective custody of the spirit realm. Your enemies will form their weapons against you, but none will penetrate deep enough to kill you. Knowing this wisdom will clothe you. The "wows" you have been chasing will come, but it will not be what you expect. Words of Wisdom (wow) are for the right time. The words of God will take you through this battle. Now look into the pond." Abigail bent down to look into the pond, the ripples did not come this time to hide the image that had surfaced on the face of the pond; Gabriella had hold of Abigail. Abigail was petrified at what she was seeing. The pond had reflected her headless. Her neck was streaming with blood. Abigail reached for her neck while screaming. Gabriella calmed her. "You have just looked into the spirit world my dear" said a tranquil Gabriella, "that is what Lucifer is attempting to do to you. The recruiters of the dark world are direct descendants of Herodias daughter Salome. Step daughter of King Herod Antipas, Who performed the deadly dance for the head of our beloved John the Baptist. One of the same spirits has trapped your husband, she now has the blade ready to claim his head, the head of your household Abigail Monroe. If Sean is the rightful lover of your heart then you can demand his head back to you, but you must know he too is collateral for his father's wealth, but he has chosen to reap from his father's powers. Your love for God will be your compass. He is your lover and the cover of your soul and you are in protective custody. Stay grounded in your faith it will always point you in the right direction. When Sean took you as his wife, he obtained favor that came with a promise from God. Once he breaks those vows the favor slowly starts to diminish". Abigail asked "What if he is not the lover of my heart?" "Only you can answer that my dear," Gabriella replied, "remember when the storms come, recognize them and learn to read the clouds." If the storms are too blinding and the needle is scrambling making it impossible to read the compass, do nothing but stand and pray God will find you. Remember keep your integrity, even in a headless situation. God is the head of all but we all have the free will of the turning of our necks, so always turn to the path of compassion and help others. It is your destiny." "Help them?" Abigail snapped, "are you joking?! Apparently I am not doing a good job keeping my own head! How am I to encourage or help others in their pain?!" she then paused as she remembered something, "Wait a minute, I already help a small group of women, is that not enough to keep this from happening to me?" Gabriella answered, "I know your secrets Abigail. I know about those women and the help you have given to them. The results are astounding, you have accomplished so much. Your days in the medical field are numbered, your service will soon be needed somewhere else. There are countless numbers of women that are waiting for you."

Gabriella reached out into the atmosphere, an extraordinary bottle that resembled a precious stone not of this world manifested into her hand. She opened the bottle and poured what seemed to be an oil of some sort on the head of Abigail and blessed her. A massive multi pastel colored whirlwind with many growling evil faces appeared. They tried to remove Gabriella so they could reach Abigail to harm her. Gabriella stretched her hand, and with a voice like thunder, she commanded the spirits back to Hell.

# THE AWAKENING

A perplexed Abigail awoke in a sweat, her silk mint green pajamas were soaking wet. She called out for Sean, he didn't reply. Lately when he is late coming home he will sleep in one of the guest bedrooms but he had already left for his office. He left a note "we have to talk".

She ran to the mirror to see if she was back in one piece. She was, so it would appear. The shower was a welcome contact, but not enough to relieve her overly tightened muscles. She really did not feel too relaxed while the shower was beating on her neck. It was too close for comfort after that horrific dream. She got out of the shower slipped, into the Jacuzzi; she put the jets on and let them work on her body, but not the area of her neck. Abigail tried immensely to figure out her dream, or was it a dream? "It was so real" she kept whispering to herself, "so real. Who are these women I am to give refuge too? And this Gabriella what a dream, I must call mother and see if she can interpret this dream."

Abigail is glad that Sean has already left for the day, and that her daughters were not here, they had spent the night at Jordan's. Abigail secretly wondered if there really is going to be an auction of the estate. "Oh get hold of yourself Abby". The doorbell rang, a messenger handed the maid a registered letter, she placed the important letter on Abigail's dresser.

Abigail got dressed, her mind is still occupied with her dream. While opening the envelope, something she read caused her to drop the letter. She backed away from the letter as if a scorpion was crawling out of the envelope. She reached for her neck while gasping for air. She allowed her knees to bring her to the floor. "Get it together Abby," she commands herself.

After she regains her composure, Abigail reaches for the letter as she sits at her dresser. The letter came from an attorney named Madison Brown, Informing Abigail she was named sole inheritor to Gabriella's estate.

A still shaken Abigail immediately rang the office of Madison Brown to see if they had made a mistake. "No we have not made a mistake, Dr. Monroe. Gabriella died a few days ago and was buried yesterday at the property. However did you see the clause in the will? You must be willing to have her body stay on the property overlooking the pond". Abigail never replied. She hung the phone up still in a daze. Abigail screams at God. "What is going on God? I don't know whether to go see a lawyer or a priest to perform an exorcism on me!" After regaining her composure, Abigail decides to go to see the only person she fully trusts, her cousin Montana.

# MONTANA P. EMANUEL

Montana has now become a cold, high profile criminal lawyer, a very serious woman, regarding herself as one with no time for games, and no time for searching for or entertaining a mate. She is like dry ice. The only time "mate" is used in the same sentence concerning her is when dry ice sublimates: where it goes from solid to gas. It skips the middle phase, never even getting to liquid. She will never pour into any man, and no one will ever tame her. It is easier to tame a mustang. A smoke screen is eternally in her presence, you can never make her out. If you get too close to her you will be infused to her; she will slowly rip into you like frozen lips being ripped off a block of ice.

It is rumored her bedroom comes equipped with all the comfort of a law office and adult entertainment. It is a dark secret that has left Montana as a wild mustang no one can tame. She shall never marry, only "borrow" husbands for a while. A man can get into her bed, but her head is off limits. Montana still calls herself a "free agent" she belongs to neither Satan nor God she thinks Satan's price is always too high, and God comes with too much guilt. She considers herself the captain of her own destiny. When asked what does her middle initial (P) stand for she slyly always replies, "oh I'm glad you asked, it stands for Perilous".

Montana rationalizes, "Abby I guess it is yours as much time as you spent at that stupid pond all these years I always thought that was kind of barmy (crazy) you and that pond…. Well anyway, I guess she felt like you have earned it. Doesn't this woman have any living relatives"? "I do not know, Montana" "Abby," Montana sighed "this entire 'head being chopped off dream' stuff is crazy. Come on Abby, I need facts here; you know I do not believe in all this other worlds mess. The world I am in is screwed up enough. I do not need to add to it and I surely do not need to try to go and float into another one because Abby that is what you are doing, floating. Now get back to earth and talk to me in the language of facts! are you sure you really called this law firm and they do exist? Are you sure in all the years you have been going to the pond you have not met this woman and maybe forgot or you did a good deed for her in the hospital? Oh, just let me call". Montana rolled her eyes in frustration as she dialed the number.

"Hello, this is Montana Emanuel of Emanuel Law I need to speak to whoever is in charge of a Gabriella estate. This may sound ridiculous, because I do not have a Sir name to give you and this is probably a great error on my client's part". The woman responded "Oh no Ms. Emanuel you are correct, and might I say I am an admirer of your work. Gabriella, for a reason not known to us has named Dr. Monroe, your cousin I believe, her sole beneficiary. She has no other living relative, trust me. You will find everything in order just a signature is required. Attorney Madison Brown personally took care of this herself".

"Madison Brown? I have never heard of her. Is she new in town"? Inquired Montana, "Actually, she has been here a short time. She came in from England a few months ago" said the woman. "Then how did she acquire this estate from this woman'? They knew each other in Europe that is all that has been revealed to me"... "Thank you dear" said Montana..." Well I guess you are not crazy maybe this Gabriella person was on drugs, who knows. Abigail do you realize there is a mansion on this property?! my goodness this property is worth at least seven million dollars! let us go see what you have inherited".

The grand estate was Tudor style, old English brick with mahogany wood trimming, Twenty thousand square foot, ten bedrooms fourteen bathrooms all done in Italian style marble. Each faucet was in the shape of a black crystal swan. The black crystal resembled the pond. It has a well-equipped theater, Olympic size indoor swimming pool spa style with six saunas. Five great rooms, each are decorated to represent five different countries: Japan, France, England, Swiss, and Africa. The majestic foyer displayed a crystal chandelier that made both Montana and Abigail stop in their tracks. The chandelier was extravagant, but that is not what caused them to gasp. It resembled the one in the grand ballroom the night of the beauty contest.

Montana said "I guess we can have Jordan's wedding here Abby. Oh, by the way let me go look into the pond and see if I am headless! Abigail frowned at her mockery of her. "Oh and I almost forgot speaking of headless, a client of mine gave me tickets to go and hear a motivational speaker. Her name is… are you ready for this? Contessa Emanuel! There is a 3pm session. they thought I might have been related to this person, and I can't believe the topic it is the dignity of the headless woman". Montana, we have to go! This has to all be connected! It has be a sign" …"Very well Abby" Montana sighed, "as long as there is no religious stuff involved. Here sign this deed and let my office deal with the rest".

Montana Smirked. "So how is your low life husband lately? Wait until he hears about this! I will make sure the deed is solely yours not his or his little church. … Abby… do you ever wonder what would have become of us if we had stayed in England? Does Wellington ever come across your mind? we hardly speak of him anymore. Abigail replied "I do miss home, Montana. I still believe we did the right thing though, coming to America to study. I love the freedom of America but it comes with a price. As for Wellington, his love for England would not have him live anywhere else. Even down to the native flowers. I remember he loved the English rose so much, so every now and then when the fragrance of a rose drifts past me it will bring his sweet memory to me. If you are asking me what I think life would have been with him, I have no doubt he would have made sure I was the happiest of women, but that was long ago, and this is life now". Montana whispered "Well said, Abby well said".

# DIGNITY OF THE HEADLESS WOMAN

Montana and Abigail arrived at the Hilton. the conference is being held in one of the ballrooms. They had just made it to their seats on time. Contessa had just started to speak. Abigail looked intently at Contessa, wondering what magical afternoon awaits Montana and herself.

Contessa was five foot two inches, 128lbs, yet despite her small frame, her presence commanded your attention.

Contessa started by saying "In the beginning God created man and from man God created woman. If it were God's plan for man to have more than one wife, he would have created more women at the time of creation for Adam. After all Adam had more ribs to spare." The crowed chuckled. She continued, "If Eve had only kept her mouth shut and not taken that bite but worst still Adam had to take a bite too."

Genesis 3-18 *the lord God said to the woman. I will greatly increase your pain when you give birth, you will long for your husband, and he will have RULE over you.*

So here it is! God said it not me "man will be head of the woman". For those who doubt the word of God, go into a delivery room and ask that woman while she is ready to give birth just how painful it really is. Most of the time it seems like men are more interested in finding a good woman rather than asking themselves "are they deserving of a good woman" and surly this is also true of women. When a man takes a wife, she takes his name. She will trust him enough to give up part of her identity, her surname her father's name given to her at birth and now she is to become MRS. Unfortunately some see the word (M.R.S) as My Rightful Servant. When I was a child I remember my mother interpreting dreams for friends and families and I know I am blessed to do the same. If you dreamed of a wedding many of instance, its meaning was death.

I have this theory. When a woman picks out her wedding dress, she is also picking out her burial dress. I know that sounds crazy, but think about this. Her identity before putting the wedding dress on dies as soon as she say's "I do". The woman who puts the dress on is not the same woman that will take the dress off. You are now one with this man and you have accepted his name. He is now your husband, your lover, your cover. He is your head. Some women are strong enough to keep their own identity, but the majority loses her identity in her husband, part of her dies. He is the head of her household. I often wonder how many men really understand the involvement in giving up our birth name... seeing that they do not have too. Montana clapped encouraging some other women too as well. There are too many, EX Mrs. in this world who are trying to grasp onto some sort of identity. They are always inquiring "how do I survive as an EX? Is there a manual?" The truth is you are still attached to a name that is now meaningless and has gained you the dreaded title of EX. The first wife has bragging rights. She can always say 'I was the first.' Why is the letter X used? What, exactly, does the "X" represent?

1. 24th letter of English alphabet: representing a consonant sound.
2. "X" indicating something: an x-shaped mark used for indicating a vote.
3. Or showing that something is INCORRECT. Encarta ® World English Dictionary

So there you have it. I will address the third description of the "X". So we can say the 'X' is used to vote us out of the marriage that something is INCORRECT about us.

This X, rightly should be, AD. After Divorce The majority of the time it is because of an affair with another woman or man why we become divorced. In some areas of England, dessert is known as "after's," the ending of the meal. Just as divorce is the ending of the marriage. AD, worst still, you could still be the wife living in his house but just a meager after thought. His mistress is always the first course.

Montana crossed her long Tina Turner legs and folded her arms and whispered ('I will never have to worry about the letter X, I suppose I might be the reason? Nope I just borrow even though I like the AD part its only validates my theory about men. I could never be any man's after's")

"So now that we have established the headship, let's expose how the head hunter comes into play. Generation after generation, Satan has empowered Perilous women with the spirits of being Headhunters. Some deadlier than others these women abide with Satan, even though he is a self-confessed Misogynist. This inevitably also makes him a Misogynist one who hates marriage.

# HEADHUNTERS

The most remembered of the headhunters in history... You might recall that deadly dance that was performed by Salome, daughter of Herodias, the wife of Herod Antipas, brother of Philip for the head of John the Baptist. Her mother needed a favor from her daughter the beautiful dancer. Herod was intoxicated with Salome and her dancing. He offered her half of his kingdom if she would only dance for his delight. I heard the dance is called the dance of the seven veils. I imagine before she removed the last veil, she stopped and asked for her pay. With an intoxicated Herod, what else could his weak flesh do but give in to her wish? After all, he had given his word in public. The head of the cousin of our Lord Jesus, John the Baptist was granted. He was beheaded to silence him from accusing her mother of being an adulterer, a "Headhunter!" Her spirit has not stopped. It is still present in women today, hunting heads.

Contessa paused to take a sip of water.

Let us not forget Delilah, Judges: chapter16. She exposed the secret of Samson. She persuaded him to tell the secret of his strength. Like a secret agent she transferred the information to his enemy the secret of his strength which was the vow he took to be obedient to the law of the Nazarene and never let the razor touch his hair. Samson's head was shaven then he lost all of his mighty power. This tragedy manifested because a woman persuaded him to be disobedient to his God and himself.

Some women Behead and others Weaken, the Salome's are most dangerous than the Delilah's, they have no mercy on their victims. Salome will want your head, your house, your cat and dog. She does not care if he is a family man or not he will be dismembered. She is extremely dangerous. She travels with her chainsaw attached to her hips. Ultimately you are left with a name that you cannot identify with any more because she takes that too. Which will make you the dreaded EX. (The has been)

Delilah on the other hand just wants to weaken him, so she can play her little games with him. No permanent attachment, but sometimes her games can cause death (of a marriage.) Just like the proverb 7 woman.

("That's what I do," joked Montana, I need to read about this Delilah person that woman is deep; she has given me greater respect for Eve. She knew what she wanted and found away to get it". Abigail ignored Montana).

You will find many of these women in the strip clubs, escort service, nightclubs, health clubs, super markets, and of course churches. They are made up from all lifestyles. She is usually single. Her married sisters can be just as deadly if not more because they end up destroying two homes.

Your man could easily be targeted to become a sugar daddy. He is first marked for target practice before you are beheaded... All because his strong ego blinds him, he cannot see how weak and pathetic he really is. Therefore, he thinks he is the player when all the time he is being toiled with. Toil comes from the Latin word (toiler) meaning to be dragged around. If you think gambling is addicting or Russian roulette is dangerous those two games are nothing compared to the deadly addiction that comes with these women. These women have mastered in the area of delighting your husband in their secret gardens. The secret garden is the place where men are persuaded to tell all the little secrets of your household. Perhaps one of the secrets is that he has not been delighted with you in a long while. Then like a cunning snake my dear she shows him the way to her secret garden to delight him by serving him juicy ripe passion that is saturated with poison. Maybe before it is too late he will be the one to say, 'what have I done". Ask yourself this question "is there enough love in your marriage to make a man remember you before he allows his shirt to be ripped of him. Is his collar a ring of love or bondage"?

Misogamy's (haters of marriage) are at work every day in the form of principalities and powers to destroy the holy institute of marriage. God himself has ordained marriage to be Holy.

Genesis2-18 *it is not good for man to be alone.* God gives a wife to her husband to be treated as his queen. Satan has women chosen and ready to dethrone the wife.

If the headhunter (the adulterer) comes and is successful in taking your head (your husband) then in theory my dear you have just been beheaded! Ouch' again your identity is murdered.

'(Oh my, is she deep or what"? Again whispered Montana)

There is another one that is not as visible but can be just as deadly that is the mother in law. The mother that is attached to her baby boy and no women will ever be good enough for him. She has enabled him since birth and expects you to do the same. If you don't, she will do whatever it takes to behead his family.

Salome and Delilah are being well equipped and dispatched from hell everyday do not let your marriage be Hell's executioner's next victim.

Now on the other hand there are marriages where women are screaming to be beheaded. The monster she has attached herself to who has no other desire but to destroy her dignity by brutally abusing her. Then there is the colorless bruise, mental cruelty.

One of the best examples of a be-header I can think of is Monica Lewinsky. Not only did she behead Hillary Clinton, but also the United States of America, blinding it's chief in lustful passion.

Through it all, Hillary Clinton in my view walked and talked with such dignity while the axe was being sharpened, her husband's head resting on the chopping block. Her love for her man and her country put her faith in action and stopped the execution.

"Can I ask you ladies a question, "how many of you have ever had to call for a TOW truck"? (Half of the room raised their hands up) "What was the reason"? (Some said "car broke down" then someone said "we got towed for parking in the wrong place" everyone laughed). "So how many of you have ever driven in the tow truck"? (No one raised their hand) "Usually you are watching your vehicle be towed away right"?

"Now if it was towed for a parking violation most of the time you have no idea where it is towed too and that is a horrible feeling. That was not part of your plan when you started your day. We could say this tow person interrupted your life. Well my dears hold on to your seats I have news for you. T.O.W. tow it stands for "The Other Women". (The women gasp then laughed) "T.O.W Trucks only come when something is broken, violated or being repossessed".

(Contessa's voice is now elevated).

"Is your marriage broken?! is the tow ready to pick up your husband? Then there are those who simply don't know what happened you woke up in the morning married, went along your day as usual, but he does not come home that evening. Has he violated your vows and been towed away? There is a possibility he was hijacked by lust, that would be Delilah she will drop him off after she has had her full of him it's all a power game with her. I personally do not have much respect for tow-companies; it is always about getting easy money. If you don't have the means to get your car out it can cause such interruption for some families. You can't get to work so you may lose your job etc, domino effect comes into play. You get the picture. The same interruption happens when the other woman arrives. Women learn to be able to survive during any interruption, have a plan in place that includes a saving account". (The women all cheered).

"The word of God tells us about strength being in two. "God says in Deuteronomy 32:30 *that one of us "...have chased a thousand, and two put ten thousand to flight"*

So together we are stronger I need everyone to write down the word together on the note book that was given to you. Now concentrate on the word. When I was a child my spelling teacher would say this word is easy to remember just think of your sister who is in trouble and you need To-go-get-her. (Together) If we stay together we will be strong and dedicated like the marines they never leave a man behind. We should never leave a sister behind. (The women again were standing and clapping and hugging each other, (Montana said wow "now that was neat".)

44

"So guess who does not like that. Satan the Misogyny (hatred of women) has proven to us in many ways he has come to steal, kill and destroy but first he has to be able divide us. There are still women who resist his demonic power of influence. When the untimely autumn intrudes into our life, we must defy its power of change and elimination! The leaves change, then the branch eliminates the leaf.

By holding fast to our faith, God, and our identity, a preseason of autumn has no power over our will. We cannot be changed or eliminated.

Even if we have been made an EX, We must be true to the God that is within us and of course very importantly ourselves. We must not conform our ways to the ways of our enemy. Do not let the enemy toil with you don't let him drag you around. Learn to be steadfast and unmovable always abiding in the word of God. Let the husband change if he so desires to. Sooner or later she will eliminate him and look for another, either that or nothing but turmoil will befall the both of them for defiling holy matrimony, God is not mocked. These lust thirsty women are never satisfied just as Hell is never satisfied". ("Ok, now she is getting too religious" whispers Montana. Abby nudges Montana to hush).

### The carrier's of Gods Favor

"We married women need to remember who and what we are, our husbands Good Thing. Too many so-called Godly women are the cause, why is it so easy for their husbands to be hunted by the headhunters? Have you ever wondered what triggers your husband to want to go to the strip club or turn to the porn channel? Well while you are studying the home work you have brought to the bedroom someone is studying the frustration on your husband's face. The bedroom should not be the bored-room. The bedroom is not to study in, especially when your husband is in there waiting for you.

Women learn how to fight back! Be your husband's private dancer. Learn how to give him a lap dance or something of the sort. Help his passion to crave for you. I guarantee you will stay on his mind, causing him to be mindful of you. Then it will be more difficult for the headhunter to persuade him to cheat on you. The T.O.W will also drive by.

"Find out what turns your man on. Probably the same thing you did to get him. Cause your man to go to work with a smile on his face. Here is a secret for you. You may need to visit Victoria's secret before Victoria shows your husband her secret. Be a lady in public with your husband but in secret come out of the closet every now and then as Victoria or whoever you wish at that playful moment. Don't ask him what you can do for him? JUST DO WHAT YOU KNOW HE NEEDS!

Unfortunately there are those women who were "Good Things" to their husbands. They did all the right things even when they did not feel like it; they were true to being his Good thing. Nevertheless he still was tempted to go astray. I say to you that his unfaithful action does not make you less of a Good Thing. His unfaithful action does not make you unauthentic. His unfaithfulness may cause the painful severing of his headship, for a while your passion will feel paralyzed you cannot think straight, loss of appetite or gain. Anger and rage has befriended you, you will be tired of hearing "you are better off without him". To you at that moment that's like saying "you will be better off without your lungs to breathe with". Your body is dehydrated from so many fallen tears, trust took the first plane out of town and hatred and rejection landed on your drive way. You want answers to the great old question. "Why me"?

You may lose blood platelets (platelets allows your blood to clot so you don't bleed to death) and bleed mentally for a while, keep praying keep believing eventually your platelets will increase your blood will thicken and the inner bleeding will stop. Remember "this too shall pass". It will be like bypass surgery nothing else left but RECOVERY. If you don't feel better yet, well the answer to that old question again "why me", because you were "CHOSEN TO SURVIVE" that's why, God saw your strength, your determination, and He let Satan know "that's my property" and he better watch out because when you get back up in the morning, knowing your midnight is almost over you will then realize you are more than a failed marriage. You are a "GOOD THING"!!

The hall exploded with cheers women were jumping all over the hall.

Contessa got louder. "Remember the word of God! HE said "you are a Good Thing!"; it does not get any more authenticated then that!".

"When a man allows his wife to be beheaded, he is also removing himself from the favor of God... Can you say give me "RESPECT" or lose the FAVOR! I AM the carrier of your "FAVOR" sir!

If a man would only realize the gift and the abundance of favor that comes with his wife, he would treasure her... I am telling you now, go to your war chest which is your makeup bag, fix yourself up, get your hair done. The French soldiers had the right idea they never went to battle without being well dressed. Baby girl, you dress yourself for the fight of your life, fight for your integrity and look good doing it"

Once more the hall erupted, women were jumping and shouting all over the place, even Abigail was on her feet. Montana had an amused smirk on her face.

"Please Montana stop being so catty" said an agitated Abigail as she tried to consume as much as she could from Contessa.

# SUCCUBUS AND INCUBUS

When the women calmed down, Contessa continued in a more sober tone.

"We know that the Kingdom of darkness is governed by it's own rules and regulations. They frequently cross the line and come to interrupt. We have dealt with the headhunter's women that you see every day in the flesh. Now I need to take you into the Current Affair of the underworld

Let me read to you what the book of Jude say about this. Jude 1-4. *Men have crept in unnoticed, who long ago were marked out for condemnation, ungodly men, who turn the grace of our God into lewdness and deny the only Lord Jesus Christ. 7: as Sodom and Gomorrah and the cities around them in a similar manner to these, having giving themselves over to sexual immorality and gone after strange flesh. 8: Likewise also, these dreamers defile the flesh, reject authority, and speak evil of dignitaries.*

"Likewise also these dreamers defile the flesh…The kingdom of darkness has its own pleasure club where the Incubus and succubus reign. Webster describes them as. Succubus *a woman demon, having sex with men: a woman demon that was believed in medieval times to have sexual intercourse with men while they were asleep*

Incubus *Male demon having sex with women: in medieval times, a male demon that was believed to have sexual intercourse with women while they were asleep.*

"This world is where men and women ascend from Hell to seduce your husband or you during sleep, dreamers that defile the flesh.

(Abigail grabbed Montana's hand; and whispered "that's it! Oh my God, that's what I am dealing with almost every night!")

This creature that is called a Succubus and her male counterpart the incubus is equally deadly. How do you combat the atrocity of a

48

woman who visits him in his sleep and steals your husband away to Hell's pleasure garden in your presence? Giving him pleasure you have not or never will be able too, the taboo of it all causes him to want her more. Sexual encounters will happen that your mortal mind cannot even begin to visualize never mind trying to process it. When it is over your husband will resemble a corpse he will not be able to feel your touch. Actually she has paralyzed him as a spider does her prey. His heart is frozen from all guilt and shame. He is now a subject of that Kingdom and will be governed and live by the laws of Hell.

She will remain a spirit for a while then eventually she will manifest into a human body. By then it is usually too late. The spider has moved in for the kill beheading you is never enough for her; she will flaunt her power in your face. He will protect her by denying her existence until she is ready to be known. She will cause him to disgrace you in countless ways. These creatures do not come to play they come to steal and kill.

Contessa stopped for a while and stared at Montana as she shocks the room by announcing. "I have experienced the male counterpart for fourteen years, I was seduced by them. The truth is I enjoyed the pleasure".

The crowd gasped. "Yes ladies I understand the pleasure your husbands are fighting. It is also Hell's dirty little secret they have on us mortals. The one who came to me was extremely effective; without him my joints ached as if one with a severe case of arthritis. Nothing absolutely nothing or no one could ease the pain until the night visitation from Edward. That is what he called himself. When he touched me I would be intoxicated with sweet poisoned passion which could last for hours sometimes days. He was my cocaine and Satan was my drug dealer. Edward started to manifest during the day. I was his slave and I performed whenever he wanted me too.

Some of you are in such judgment of me right now. But tell me ladies how do you go to your pastor and tell him you are engaging in an erotic love affair which takes place in a demonic spirit world; worst of all you are having so much pleasure that your husband is unable to satisfy you anymore?. On the other hand how do you explain being raped by spirits? Ladies being raped by the spirits is not the secret. Enjoying the pleasure which intoxicates all your senses is the secret. If you know of such a pastor then I commend him don't you ever leave his church or place of worship".

(There was not a sound in the room not even the sound of breathing). "I promised if I ever was delivered from them I would expose Hell's dirty little secret at any cost. Including the shame I go through every time I share this dark side of my past. If one person gets help from my disgrace then it is worth the shame".

Contessa composed herself as she wiped the tears that visited her high cheekbones and continued. "So how are you delivered? I first fasted to condition myself for the spiritual warfare I was to enter into. Like any other addiction, I had to acknowledge I was addicted to Edward, and other spirits who came to give me pleasure. I asked God to give me wisdom, daily strength and understanding to fight the addiction. I also asked for God to expose the void in my life that is causing me to be satisfied with the counterfeit.

I went to the bible 2nd Corinthians 10:13… I studied the scripture and then I lived it day and night, let me read it.

*"For thou we walk in the flesh, we do not war according to the flesh. For the weapons of our warfare are not carnal but mighty for pulling down strong -holds. Casting down arguments and every high thing that exalted itself against God, bringing every thought into captivity to the obedience of Christ, and being ready to punish all disobedience when your obedience is fulfilled"*

"One of the first things I had to understand and admit to myself. Everything we do is a choice. No being raped is not a choice. The choice was I subjected myself to demonic atmospheres.

Yet, if demons are real then so must be the angels who are assigned to guard over me. I had to believe that with all my heart. I had to remember and get the true understanding of the sacrifice of Jesus. My blood bought rights which Jesus Christ died and raised for me from the dead.

"Somewhere down my bloodline I was probably collateral for one of my ancestor's sins. I had to remember Jesus paid the price for my sins. My debt was paid in full. Unless you can really believe this you might as well forget it you have already lost the battle. But if you do believe, then every dirty stinking bloodline in your generation that has sold out their future generations to satanic powers has to be subject to the power of the blood of Jesus. For even today, the Blood speaks and the power is prevailing! I recognized I was a case that had been misrepresented. Satan is a daily accuser of the people of God. I collaborated with believers that understood and had knowledge of my struggle who were there for me day and night oh especially in the night hours. For a while, I was not sleeping, scared of the darkness of night but all that changed when I understood I had not been given a spirit of fear but of sound mind 2nd timothy 1:7 *"For God hath not given us the spirit of fear; but of power, and of love, and of a sound mind.* I studied the word of God, and found my blood bought rights as a legal citizen of heaven. *"Submit yourselves therefore to God. Resist the devil, and he will flee from you". James 4:7.* [When Satan would try to threaten me I would remember the words in Colossians 2:15... *And having disarmed the powers and authorities, he made a public spectacle of them, triumphing over them by the cross.* Colossians 2:15

He is disarmed. he is only a good Poker player. He likes you to think he has the winning hand over you, well he doesn't. He is disarmed - an empty gun is harmless but when loaded it is dangerous. I was the only one that could give Satan ammunition against me, in other words I held the bullets. Across the world I tell women do not give Satan the bullets to use against you. Bullets are many things: unforgivness, hatred being two- faced, and much more, and disobedience to God is like giving him a rocket. He can only get victory over you when you are not in the will of God. Do not give him any bullets! keep him disarmed. We triumph over him by the cross. Glory!!!!!

I researched every scripture I could to help me with the battle. It was not easy, but the formula works...there is a list of scriptures in your package.

"When the spirits would enter into my bedroom, I knew to wake up and start fighting and command those spirits to go they were not welcomed here and I would usher in the Holy Spirit... I then entered into Hell's territory. I told Satan I was divorcing his hold on me. The marriage was over. That was one EX I was proud to be.

There would be no more dealing on this corner of my life any more his drugs was no longer needed. Hell had been served papers. DO NOT

TRESSPASS AGAINST HER! The blood spoke loud and clear. I am here as a living witness, His power lives… Glory!

(Again the Hall exploded this time Abigail was one of the one's jumping up and down). "Run it out if you have too" said Contessa as she herself was jumping up and down praising her God, Jehovah.

Abigail's church acts like this but this was more powerful than she was used too. Something touched her, she said to Montana "move Montana move out of my way, there is something burning all over me it's like fire I need to run this out". Montana didn't know what on earth Abigail was talking about, or what to do, but to comply with Abigail's demand.

Abigail took off running around that great hall. She came back to her seat to a shaken Montana which had a tight grasp of her seat. Montana felt helpless, she thought Abigail had lost her mind totally. "Oh, Montana I am so alive! I feel so…so… free! and empowered!" "Oh! …uh… good..!" mustered a confused Montana, a smile spreading awkwardly across her face.

Contessa motioned the crowd to sit back down, those who could, and she continued.

"There are pamphlets in your package under your seat that will go into more detail about the Incubus and Succubus". Everyone began shuffling under their seats for the pamphlets like anxious school children, thirsty for more out of the lesson.

"For you single women and maybe a couple of married ones, a word of caution. Ladies, if you are having intercourse with the wrong person then you are on the wrong course of life to begin with, you could develop a soul tie (a toxic addiction like feeling, extremely harmful and dangerous, not to mention deceptive to your being) with a person who is poisonous to your soul, wreaking nothing but havoc in you. There is nothing but pain and misery on that course so Jump off of it now".

Montana just stared off and thought of the entire wrong course that she found herself on just this year alone. Then in Montana style, she thought, "Well, I was behind the wheel, I drew the route"

Abigail could not see Contessa anymore; the cascade of tears had blurred her vision. She was not alone, others were still crying.

"Wipe your tears," she heard Contessa saying, and look around, some of you are not here by mistake, this is the beginning of your destiny, a divine connection has brought you here."

She looked right into Abigail's tear filled eyes. Abigail quickly dried her eyes. She could not believe what she was seeing, Contessa for a second… resembled Gabriella. Contessa went on to say. "Someone in here will be on the chopping block soon; it will not be a swift cut. Unfortunately, the axe that has been chosen for you is a blunt one. The execution will be slow and painful. It has to be so. It will validate your empowerment to survive. Then you will remember when the other wounded ones come your way. You will be compelled to aid them".

Once more Abigail was in a ballroom crying but this time it is different. The first ballroom Abigail was like a beautiful bouquet of cut flowers. Now she is a rooted plant. Cut flowers are beautiful, but they have no roots. They are heading for death. God had planted Abigail as a blooming cactus in the desert, where only the strong survives and become empowered.

Contessa opened the session for questions. Not too many hands went up, some were still trying to process all they had heard today and others were simply still basking in the glory of God.

A woman stood up and said in a soft timid voice. "I believe everything I have heard tonight, I thank God for you sister, Contessa. I have but one question how do I stop loving a man that is poisonous to me? is it taught? I am one of those that you spoke of that is being mentally abused; I believe you said "colorless bruise?" but I love him still so much. Can you teach me how to stop loving him?"

Contessa replied. "Before it got to that stage, my love, if we are to be honest with ourselves, we should have seen the RED flags right? I am not talking about the stars and stripes kind of flag. I am talking about "Rejection" the RED flag you cannot avoid... Take a moment and think about when your heart first responded to his rejection. I want you to go as far back as pre-married days. Were there moments he rejected you? If you are one of the millions that does not handle rejection well you need to know that love is often confused with rejection. However, let me say in the defense of rejection, too often rejection has been given a bad rap. We love to challenge it, always wanting what we cannot have. Then this emotion of loss makes us feel empty and desperate and confusing our state of desperateness with love because somehow we rationalize this pain with love. What's happening to you, my dear, is instead of accepting there might be a chance that you are entangled in an unequally yoked situation, a spirit of pride emerges and convinces you to recite. "I am not good enough!" Our inner voice can sometimes be more dangerous than what is being said to us from our enemy. Deadly venom can be spewed out of us, entering into our minds causing us to be eliminated from being successful in many areas of our lives.

Some of you look lost, I will explain what I mean later. In reality, in times like this, rejection has come to befriend us. Just as a heart transplant that has gone wrong, his heart is rejecting yours, you have made excuse after excuse for him. You have blamed everything and everyone else… but him. You became his enabler, he has never had to take responsibility for his actions; you were always there to cover up for him. For instance, excuses are manifested why he cannot find a job, so you work two jobs to keep the family together. I call these men legal pimps but they are not to blame. Women created the opportunity for them to be so. You are in so much denial about his heart rejecting you that you are trying to be the antibiotic for the problem. You are trying to force his heart to accept the transplant, all the while he is telling you it is not working. Instead of love, which would make for a healthy relationship, you are causing illness, but trying to force something. Would you not be grateful if rejection came to reject a deadly virus from your body? Of course you would. Then let us learn to give rejection the same respect when it is trying to spare us from a counterfeit love".

"Many of you are here today just as she is because you are tired of being rejected. you want to stop the madness and the excuses. If any of you were as I use to be then you will understand this. I was so sensitive to rejection that if a flea bitten three legged dog rejected me, I would still be greatly affected by it. I had to learn to consider the source I was looking towards for validation.

The writing is on the flag waving at you everywhere you go. "He is cheating" "he simply does not want or love you." Denial will wave around again, and again you make up more excuses. 'He is just going through some issues" "he will love me eventually." "He wants to be with me, of course he does, he just doesn't realize it yet." Then Rejection has so come fierce and slashed your heart out. You are now on the waiting list for a heart transplant. It hurts like heck but I need you not to give up on being loved. It will come. By the way love, what is your name?" Contessa asked the timid girl, "Sarah." She replied. Contessa continued, "When you are ready Sarah, the teacher will come in the form of truth to direct and teach you how to be redirected from the path of destruction. I will tell you this you must love Sarah more than the chokehold he has on your emotion." He is nothing more than a terrorist in your mind. He has come into your STATE of mind terrorizing your will and declaring martial law on your subconscious mind commanding bravery not to show its face in your presence."

God has elected you back into power over of the state of your mind. You have been elected president of this house where your mind abides. When you accept the presidency the former president that had rule over your state has to depart. You have to make it clear to him he has been voted out of office. Now when you are fully back in control you have to decide who stays and who leaves. I need you to repeat this.

*"Through spiritual recognition and identification I am inspired and renewed, I rejoice, knowing this is a day filled with the attributes of the Holy Spirit. I claim joy, peace, love and beauty, for within all this I am. Any old patterns or appearances of stress, struggle, depression, failure or strain are removed, eliminated, and dissolved. There is only clarity and joy in my experience. As I recognize, appreciate and accept the gifts of joy wholeness, my heart opens and my life is filled with boundless blessings from God. My heart opens fully to reveal the presence of the true living God… Today and every day I will listen with gratitude, and in the stillness, my voice gives form-empowered blessings in the name of Jesus Christ of Nazareth."*

Contessa grabbed Sarah by her arms and looked into her teary eyes and asked her "are you ready to be paroled out of your prison"? The parole board has granted you your pardon. It is up to you to accept it. This day you can be free and you shall live. "Yes, yes!" screamed Sarah. "Hold on" said Contessa, as she motioned one of her staff to bring a gift bag to her. Contessa reached in and gave Sarah a t-shirt. It read "I am Empowered to survive IT".

Sarah read it and took off running around the room screaming "no more, no more! I tell you no more! I am now free to love me! Thank you Jesus" everyone once again was in tears and rejoicing. Some of the women were on the floor praying.

Then suddenly, something strange happened. In the midst of all the rejoicing a confused woman with a gun in her handbag walks up to

Contessa and pulls out the gun. Everyone who noticed the gun started to scream. Montana jumped up and thought, "Finally, at least some action I can grasp on too". She hurried to get behind the woman to wrestle the gun from her hand. Montana has a permit to carry a gun, she has not pulled it out yet but she does have her finger on the trigger in her purse. Contessa raised her hand and motioned everyone to be quiet while her eyes were fixed on the woman with the gun. Contessa saw Montana and stretched her hands to her motioning her to wait. By now Montana had her gun drawn and resting down on her side. Abigail lifted her head and saw what was going on, she arose and went to Montana's side. The room was quiet, the woman started to scream, "I hate him! I hate me! I can't do this anymore!" then rested the gun to her temple. Contessa reached in towards her, she could see in the woman's eyes that she was not a psychopath, not a murderer, but one whose identity had been murdered. Montana grabbed Contessa, but Contessa said "I will be ok, but if you want you can stand next to me but please put your gun away". Of course Montana did not listen until Abigail got to her.

Contessa said to the woman "your name dear, is? The woman replied, sobbing, "Susan." "Ok, Susan" Contessa continued softly, "what is it dear, that has you wanting to end your life?" Susan stared at Contessa and looked around the room as if searching for someone she could connect too. But she was disarranged for a moment glancing at some of the women that were still screaming, gaping at her in disbelief and horror. Contessa motioned for the ladies to be quiet. Susan said "I have a room upstairs I was going to leave out of here and go and kill myself." I was sitting at the bar across the hall way, and it was like I could not get drunk no matter how much I drank. I even accused the bartender of watering down my drinks. I heard voices over here so I came to see what was going on before I went upstairs to end my life..." she lowered her voice, embarrassed at how crazy she must sound to everyone. "I do not know why I came in here... it was as if I was... lead here. I sat at the back and listened to you talk about women being beheaded, and for the first time, I felt like I was not alone. (She gave Contessa the gun sobbing). After hearing your words, I wanted to live for my children.

They need their mother. I wanted to kill my husband, like the heartless dog he is. He hurt me so much, and he had his woman come to our home his "personal trainer" he had said in the past. I found them naked, wrapped around each other having sex. I pulled the gun out as I was walking towards them. I wanted him to know before he died who his executioner was. When he noticed me he jumped up and came towards me and said I was a weak and pathetic woman who doesn't have the courage to pull the trigger. He also said he was going to lie and tell the judge I was an unfit mother. "I'll make sure I get full custody of the children, and that you get put in a mental home." he said. Then he barked, "bitch get out of my damn house! Then with an evil smirk said "my woman and I have unfinished business." He reentered her right in front of me, and they continued on like dogs. I decided right then to kill myself. the pain and humiliation was too much. It was like someone pouring acid all over my heart, there is no emergency room to go to for this kind of burn, the vision of them is like a porn movie that is glued to my eyes and I cannot turn it off. He will not let me have my children He and his whore want to raise them! Please help, me he will not give me my chil-..." she trailed off again, having another sudden realization of how foolish she must sound. "What am I doing? What can a group of churchwomen do against a crooked cop? What was I thinking? It is best if I just die I will forever be ruined anyway. I'd rather die than have to relive this incident everyday"

Contessa and every woman in that place including Montana were tearing up. Contessa motioned for her staff to come and get the woman. Abigail and Montana rushed to her side then asked Contessa where she will take her. Before Contessa could answer, Montana said to the woman, "Well I am not a churchwoman, hell I don't even believe in God. I do not even know why I am here. But I am telling you this right here and right now that low life and his whore will not get your children I promise he won't. I will take your case Pro Bo-no. In other words love, no fee".

Abigail interjected "do not worry dear a phone call has been placed you will be picked up in an hour or so, I am a doctor here in the city; you and your children will be flown out somewhere safe".

Contessa got the crowd silent, and she shared what happened. The women started to come out of their seats placing hands on Susan, some even placed money at her feet. Susan was so over whelmed with this act of love she could not stop crying. Twenty thousand dollars had rested at her feet; Contessa gave every penny to her. Contessa thanked Abigail and Montana. Montana, who seemed to be acting strangely ever since Susan told her story, asked Susan for her address. "I'll need it for your case," she explained as she wrote it down and shoved it in her purse. She then left the hall and said to Abigail "I shall return".

Susan was escorted to her room to get whatever belongings she brought with her. Her children's pictures were all she had.

Contessa closed the session and assured every woman that Susan will be in good hands. The crowd left empowered. The women including Abigail came and shook Contessa's hand as they were leaving the great hall. The anointing fell on Abigail. She whispered to Contessa as she hugged her. "For your shame you shall receive double, may the spirit of retaliation stay away from you. May God pour back double back into your life for what you have poured into others" When Abigail finished praying Contessa embraced her tightly and said "be ready for the fight of your life" and thanked her.

Montana had returned in a matter of 30 minutes with Susan's children. The staff took the two girls and a boy upstairs to their mother.

Contessa was astonished at how fast Montana had returned. Abigail quickly said to Contessa "please don't ask her how", but she did, and Montana being Montana replied, "Let's just say I gave that low life and his whore a bloody offer they could not walk away from". Montana was fuming. "I do not have time to hear all the religious fluff you're probably wanting to throw at me, so if you're going to pray forgiveness for me, do it now. I told that dog "you want a bitch, here I am we can do this right now". I knew who that low life boss is. That dog was at least 6ft and what is Susan? 5ft?! if that".

Abigail calmed Montana down and apologized to Contessa. Contessa replied "Montana's reputation precedes her, its ok; I only wish we had her in God's army, but in a way we do. She's just not aware of it yet, God moves on her with compassion. Montana is as good of a friend as she is an enemy to women. After tonight, Montana will see hurting women, instead of "a bunch of dumb wives that can't please their husbands." Montana replied to Abigail's surprise, "Oh right, I can see that maybe happening, good night Contessa, I was entertained by your talk today" she then walked away, but not before turning around and saying to Contessa "I guess you did not get a chance to explain what you meant about us being our worst inner enemy, is that what you meant"?

Contessa smiled, "I guess you were listening Montana. Well, One day my husband and I were on our way to dinner. It was a crucial time of my life I was trying to hear God's voice for my future. I was trying to decide should I go back to work. I was on sick leave. I felt the calling to come into the ministry full time. On the way to dinner my husband was complaining about there was not any gas in the car and he was tired of having to do everything and that I was not respecting the up keep of the car and if anything went wrong he was not going to fix it. Oh my pride jumped into me. We had a "town hall meeting," pride, self-righteousness and the one and only self-pity were all present. I told myself I was going back to work. No man is going to have a financial hold on me. I will have my own money. And he could not tell me what to do with my own car or anything else not me the mighty Contessa. If he can complain about gas what next and I started a list in my mind. I hated him at that moment. Then God came to my madness uninvited if I may say so. He told me 'I was sowing more damaging words into my spirit than my husband had into my ears and I knew better". Montana if I had listened to myself and gone back to work I would never had got the courage to walk off my job and do the ministry full time. I don't want to even think what if this meeting did not happen today? What if Susan was in this hotel by herself? So yes, you are right. We are our own worst enemy, fully equipped for self destruction".

Montana would not let Contessa know that her story touched her, and got her thinking about how many of her self destructive words had cultivated and are fully grown and are now slowly destroying her. But that battle will keep for another day. She just simply said. "I will be in the car Abigail" and walked away with that famous Montana runway walk. Contessa just smiled and kissed Abigail good night assuring her they will meet again.

Montana had made a call to her resources who owed her a favor or two. They were waiting for her by the time she arrived at Susan's home. The husband knew who Montana was; he was not going to challenge her, after all she had her gun placed on his groin.

The chauffeur dropped Abigail home first then Montana.

Montana poured herself a brandy, by the third large glass, she had a humorous thought. How she would have liked to serve Susan's husbands balls on a silver platter, "headless... ball less, all the same to me. To think I have competition in another world, succubus huh well darling appear if you dare. I love a good challenge. Please" she slurred, practically delusional at this point, "I wish I would allow some demon or whatever you call yourself, to be more satisfying with my lover than I am. What! The only problem I see here is Hell would first have to be real, but it's not, they are all crazy".

# HELLS EXECUTIVE BOARD MEETING

Abigail fell on her knees by her bed and cried to God "why me? I do not have the strength for this; but if this is the battle you have chosen for me Lord, then I trust you will equip me. You art strong while I am week".

*Judge me, O Lord; for I have walked in my Integrity; I trusted also in the LORD; therefore, I shall not slide. Examine me, O Lord, and prove me; try my reins and my heart. Gather not my soul with sinners or my life with bloody men .But as for me, I will walk in mine integrity; redeem me and be merciful unto me .psalms 26: 1, 2,9,11.*

Abigail prayed for hours until she fell into a deep sleep. Her dreams did not take her to the pond this time, but down to Hell. This night she was witnessing a meeting. she was the topic of discussion. Hells board room looked like any other upscale office board room except the table was in a half circle. Satan was sitting on a golden throne in the center of the room. He was wearing a well tailored black suit.

Satan started the meeting "I cannot stand that woman Abigail. Every morning before her feet touch the ground, she starts trouble. Why can't she just die? After all she is my collateral. I love the little cousin though, even though she was acting kind of crazy tonight. Here is our focus demons, Abigail's family. I want them destroyed. I already own the husband, the honorable Bishop. Persuasion I want you on this one personally not your wimpy low ranking demons but you!" Satan yells, she was not supposed to meet that traitor Contessa; after all what I've done for Contessa that is how she repays me. She is a bloody mutinous. Under no circumstances was Abigail supposed to attend one of her meetings! Where do we find Abigail? In the meeting of the mutinous high Treason! that's what this is!" yelled Satan. Persuasion took it personal, he did not like Satan yelling at him. Satan' noticed the displeasure on his face, "what! Do you have a problem" asked Satan? "Yes," said persuasion," Wait a minute before your answer goes any further persuasion I need to show you something". Satan draws the walls back, a certain wounded demon in chains is being tortured. "That, my friend, is your failed suicidal demon that could not kill her or Sarah! who was there tonight! at the bloody meeting!; Abigail was supposed to be persuaded to throw herself into death! Many of years went into planning this. Now soon I will be exposed to her and she will... well I am not even declaring that yet".

Persuasion stood up with all his power some of his generals that were with him appeared on the scene to let their presence be known.

Satan just shook his head and stood up slowly and said. "What is this? Is this supposed to intimidate me"? Persuasion answered. "Satan, Let me invite you into MY anger! When we decided to try to overthrow heaven with you, we knew there would be no turning back either any forgiveness. Because of that we don't want anyone else to be forgiven. So we make their hearts hard, we were given power over the air, we get great pleasure creating destruction and pain every damn day. We believed in you and you of course being the master of all persuasion. After all you were successful in persuading a third of us to act with you. We were kicked out of heaven and you organized us and we have become a powerful force to reckon with for humans and angels. You have to remember the faith believing ones are powerful, and you know even in the kingdom of Hell there are certain rules that we have to abide by, certain boundaries that we cannot cross. Satan you know it is written," If they resist us", you know how it ends so don't you start on me. Damn you Satan! You know we have to flee from their presence. Any way I am not the one who could not hold". Satan interrupted persuasion... "You had better not mention His name here. I want her destroyed". Persuasion asked... "Why her any way, what is so special about her"? A subdued Satan answered... "Because I know she is only one but that strength and integrity of hers empowers her daily. You saw how she empowered those six women I sent turmoil unto. She is living that secret life of hers. The other traitor is also with her not even the cousin knows the whole truth about the six women. If she survives, she will empower thousands more if not millions. I cannot have that. Now Montana on the other hand is a woman after my own heart, I trained her well through circumstances but she loves that cousin of hers that could become a problem, this love stuff is so overrated", growled Satan. Persuasion nodded his head and said, "I know Satan, love drains you and hate motivates you, I have persuaded many to engage in those thoughts. I will send the dancer of hate to Abigail she will Tango with anger she will do such a dance with hatred she will embrace them. Abigail's mind will be yours Satan." The demons all smirked, nodding in agreement.

# HOLY SPIRIT VISITATION

A petrified Abigail woke up and reached for her bible and hugged it like a security blanket. The corner of her bedroom had illuminated. Abigail was about to have a nervous breakdown, but Gabriella appeared and said "it's ok are you ready Abigail? the time is at hand. God has greater need of your service". A shaken Abigail said "oh there you are Gabriela! I am going crazy I just had a horrible dream and I don't understand about the mansion." Gabriela explained… "It belonged to a dear saint who went back home to England. She passed away soon after and left the Estate to let's say, friends of the Kingdom, they knew Madison. She took care of everything after I told her I wanted you to have it, she was in agreement. Now Abigail, get ready" (Gabriela blessed her and left)… Abigail stretches her arms towards heaven and said "here I am Lord, your humble servant to do with as you wish". (The anointing of the Holy Spirit fell on her as she accepted the next assignment of her life). "Order my steps father. Equip me with your words, dress me with knowledge and anoint me with faith. Make me as fearless as David was with Goliath. Give me the wisdom of Job, the faith of Abraham, the integrity of my sisters Esther, Leah, Ruth, and Deborah. Esther in her dilemma said "*if I perish then let me perish*". I Abigail said this day; I shall not perish with God as my head. Not only order my steps father but also order my heart to stay turned towards righteousness".

The bedroom was still illuminated, for a moment Abigail stood up. Nothing about her looked different, but she knew she was not the same. Empowerment had clothed her mind. Satan as usual was looking in as he does any time Gabriella appears. He was not pleased. "So she has powers to look into us" asked persuasion. "No persuasion she does

not, a meddling angel opened the gulf and directed her dream to us"
growled Satan.

Sean had stayed out again another late night, however Abigail was
grateful this time, so she could have the time she so needed with the
Lord.

"Knowledge is powerful" so the succubus must be in human form
by now. Not only is she not in my bed, neither is my husband. Help me
to sleep my Lord I am so exhausted".

# THE GREAT INTERRUPTION

The next morning Abigail got dressed and journeyed to Montana's office even though she had just had an amazing spiritual experience. Persuasion was now in action. Abigail was now on a warpath about Sean not coming home last night and is certain that the spirit who visits her bed has now manifested in human form. Abigail for now has forgotten her vow to the Lord and that the visitation was more than a dream. "OK Montana!" stormed Abigail into her office. "Shhh, stop shouting Abigail" whispered a hung over Montana. "Montana I know my husband is having an affair I just cannot prove what it is; is she real or is she the succubus".. Montana screamed "Then leave him!" while holding her pounding head. "If he is with the Hell woman, Abigail I am not equipped for this today, I did not sleep at all last night". Abigail Asked "What hell woman"? Montana slurred, "You know the Succubus… whatever she is called, if you want me to intervene where do I go, Abby?" Ok I will represent you, ah but wait where do I send the subpoena to Abigail? And by the way do you happen to have a zip code for HELL? Sean is who he is today only because of our money. I said nothing Abigail when you wanted to use part of my inheritance to support that dog; but there was only you and I in this country cousin, and it was only money and we have lots of it. When he moved up the ranks and became bishop over millions of dollars you may see souls but I see dollars Abigail. By the way did you not recognize yourself in any of what that woman said last night? What is it about him that makes you feel like a failure Abby"? Abigail Blurted out "she does, you would not understand Montana. You have never allowed yourself to love or be loved you have never had the pleasure of a pain that slowly consumes your being it's like being gradually dipped into boiling oil; but at the same time you remember when the oil was used to give you the most marvelous massage. That same oil would rub all your troubles away. I could have asked the same question that lady asked last night. "How do you stop loving him?" Montana interrupted her. "Give me a break Abigail this love stuff is so overrated. So what you watch every one else breakdown last night and now what, today is your turn?! You are more than that Abigail". (Abigail was becoming unglued) "That's ok Montana it is like Contessa said 'this is not a flesh and blood battle this is an attack from principalities and powers of darkness". I have proof oh my God what am I doing? I was anointed last night and that quickly I forgot who I am, Oh no" Montana asked "now what?" Abigail went on to tell Montana about her visions of Hell and Gabriella's visit.

Mean while Hell is preparing her next move. Satan is not taking any chances just in case persuasion fails again. The great interruption is ready to python its way into Abigail's life; it will threaten to crush the life out of her and her family. "Abigail I cannot take much more" said an angry Montana. "Ok maybe, just maybe, I can grab hold of this Gabriella thing; but now you want me to believe you went to Hell and sat in a meeting?! With a "demon" named Persuasion? Just what did "persuasion" look like Abigail? or did he "persuade" you to forget, hmm? And this holy language thing… you have lost your mind, Abby. Please listen to yourself." Abigail sobbed "Montana I don't care what you think, it's getting ready to start. I do not know when or how. I just know she is ready to make her move to behead me. Her powers are becoming stronger and she is closing in." Montana screamed at her, "Abigail, what on earth?! Stop it! Stop this madness! I don't believe any of this. You cannot come in here and turn my whole concept of life upside down. Maybe I am a married woman's worst nightmare. Hunt or be hunted that's my motto. Hell Abby at least I do send them back home. I am not a home wrecker; they come to my bed, not my head. I am Delilah remember? I just play with them but I am a real flesh and blood human being. You and that Contessa woman who by the way, I think is a psycho that likes to get her freak on with a few toys but she would rather blame it on the other world of succubus and incubus. Give me a bloody break Abby! She then snapped sarcastically, " If there really is an incubus, don't you not think he would have visited me a long time ago?" Abigail yelled "Ok Montana! I see you are going to have to be persuaded some more". Montana yelled back "Oh no not the persuasion thing again!" "Montana God has angels to persuade us the right way also!" yelled Abigail. Both women were coming apart.

Mean while the phone rings, Montana's secretary interrupts the women.

"You have a visitor," Montana replies, in a collective voice as she stares at Abigail, with a, hold that argument look. "I am not accepting any visits today Gloria". Oh, it is not for you Ms Emanuel; it is the Bishop, for Dr. Monroe. Both women stared at each other. Montana put's Gloria on hold. "It is starting," said Abby, Montana rolled her eyes at Abigail. "The only thing that is starting is that deranged man of yours is tracking you down; maybe his bank account is in the red". Montana released the hold button, but before Abigail could reply Montana said. "Show him in Gloria".

Sean walks into the office his suit resembled Satan's well tailored suit. There was a shift in the atmosphere. It altered Montana back to her true nature. 20c dried ice, followed by a smoke screen. Montana stood up "I will leave you two alone". Montana and Sean's eyes clashed against each other as she was walking out. If one weren't mistaken, you could almost see the shaving of ice fall from the two unto the hard wood floor.

Abigail braced herself for the purpose of his visit."Is it one of the girls?" she asked "No it is not" said Sean. Abigail said "You did not come home last night; but I see you are fine, this must be very important for you to track me down Sean." "It is" he replied, then as he went on to explain why he was there, she felt like someone had kicked her in the stomach. Her husband, head of her household is announcing to her he wants and annulment after many years of marriage... (The dance begins)

"You want what?!" blurted out Abigail. "It is not working Abigail. It never has. Look into my eyes Abigail, and tell me you are happy with the way things are." Feeling out of breath, Abigail quietly responds, "Yes I am Sean, I love you. Sean our daughter is getting ready to be married in a few weeks. Does that not matter? What is wrong with you? So you get rid of me, what about your children?! You also plan to annul them as well? As if they never happened and make them bastards?! this cannot be happening". Abigail caught herself, she realizes the storm is here. "So she has finally made her move" thought Abigail. She remembered Gabriella words "when the storm is blinding and the needle of the compass seems broken, don't move. God will find you." Sean coldly responded, "No Abigail, the divorce isn't about our children, I want to go on as if you never happened, not them." That statement was a little too much for Abigail to bear. It felt like the oxygen had suddenly been vacuumed out of Montana's office. Abigail slowly slid her hand up from her heart to her neck. The slow painful cut was beginning, the beheading process; she started to see visions of bloody heads floating in a circle around her. It was all too much for Abigail; she fainted and dropped to the floor. Sean stepped over Abigail as he walked out of the office. "Montana, I think you're needed in there" he coldly said." "What have you done now Sean?" demanded Montana "I informed her, just as I am informing you also I am getting an annulment" Montana stared at him in disbelief, fuming. "You dirty low down bastard! Like hell you are!" Sean warned her. "You stay out of this, Montana".

Their words had become like two sharpened daggers stabbing at one another. They went at each others' head like two vicious pit bulls, Montana felt as though she were in the court room again, defending her cousin's heart against a mad man. "Like Hell I will sit back and watch you destroy my cousin! There is nothing for me to stay out of! She has always been too good for you! And this is the thanks she ge_" Montana stopped, as she watched Sean move towards her, fists balled, but that just enraged her further, all she could think of was how much hurt she had seen her cousin endure because of him. She lost it. "You know what! If that's how you want to do this, then come on! Just bring it on Sean! Bring it to daddy." Sean smirked "Should you not be saying "bring it to mama" you deranged bitch?" Montana yelled at him "Nope, I am growing balls as we speak you bastard. Get the hell out of my office… On second thought, leave Hell right here, I am going to ride her right back into your cold murdering heart. Montana's voice suddenly became calm, "Believe this Sean Monroe, I am going to be like a pit bull on crack. I am bringing you down "Bishop," you and your whore from Hell. You are messing with the wrong cousin. You know what BISHOP, Here is my confession. The pleasure of your death awaits me. Sean swallowed and replied, "You do not have a clue what you are coming up against, not a clue, Montana." She laughed at that response. "Oh, you don't think so? Sean my anger is usually by invitation only; you want to crash this party? Welcome to the world of Perilous. You're right I am a bitch, correction I'm THAT bitch, the bloodthirsty she- dog that will gut your wicked ass and watch you bleed".

Sean does not realize Montana will be the perfect one to weaken the muscle of this python which has slithered its way out of Hell to perform this illegal act. She has mastered the art of war of the minds. Those were his last words as he slammed the door. Abigail was coming too as he was leaving. Montana was still going off in her head "he's not going to win this battle, trying to destroy Abigail, not while I'm around. At that moment she glanced at Abigail curled up on the floor, already looking defeated. "Get up Abigail Monroe, from that damn floor! Get up now. This is not any spirit stuff this is real flesh and blood stuff. The low life wants to make a fool out of you! A total fool, Abby! Where is the integrity in that? Ask Gabriella that! I told you, you are all a bunch of idiots, and while you are floating on your little halleluiah clouds, your husband is planning for your crash landing!" Screamed Montana... "Then God will send me a parachute Montana!" yelled Abigail as she is getting up from the floor, irritated by Montana's rampage on her. "Right and you will land with nothing Abby," Montana said in a now much calmer tone. She gave her a hand up and they both wrapped their arms around each other. The two ladies calmed down. "Montana... can he do this? Oh I hate him so much right now." (*Satan was looking in "oh no not the H bomb, ha, ha,"*)

"There is only one way, Abby" Montana responded, "he must have consulted with the network of the "good old boys", the tribunal of protestant bishops which belongs to their denomination. They will try to change the existing laws to make it happen on the behalf of the so called Bishop, so he can still be in good standing with the Holy Scriptures.

A Bishop can only have been the husband of one wife right?" Abigail nodded slowly, "right."

"Knowing Sean, he has started the wheel turning on this. He is going to move quickly, as to give no one time for preparation. I need to move quickly on this and find out just how far he has gone with this. I need to collect some debts." Abigail interrupted, "Montana we do not need any money"... "No Abby I am not talking about money. Some of his preachers owe me big. I have represented them in the past. I will get to know what I need too"... Abigail sat quietly for a minute, then said "There is no dignity to what he is doing to me Montana but I will walk through this shadow clothed with integrity. I will not let him put me into an "early autumn" nor allow him to affect me in this way. I can only be eliminated from myself if I change who I am". Montana snapped at her... "Whatever Abigail, you just said you hate him, and rightfully so. I don't understand all that "season" crap you keep rambling off about 'oh the autumn leaves are blowing to the West in my heart, and what have you.' Montana mocked, I just want to hurt him. Actually I want to replace his eyes with his balls." (Satan was observing as usual, beaming. "I love that girl").

"Montana if this happens to my children, they will become bastards, and I will be the Bishops idiot. I can deal with this for me, but he cannot do this to our children. So he is trying to make me his fool, so she can become his wife, Hell truly has spoken this day."

Montana looked at Abby and closed her eyes and did a quick shake of her head, putting her hand up as if to silence Abigail and said... "Hell has spoken?" There you go sounding ridiculous, yet again. Hell has not "spoken," It has just sent us an invitation to battle, but don't worry about anything, Abigail you know I always choose my battles. If Hell is indeed inviting us, I will RSVP. The Perilous one will attend. Remember all those ball room dance lessons you, I and Wellington attended as children? How we became good enough to compete in all the competitions, but we only chose the ones we knew we could beat, do you remember what your dad would say? "don't just go to compete, go to win. Beat out the competition."

"Yes and you became an accomplished Tango dancer" replied a confused Abby, she was not sure where Montana was going with this.

"'I don't win cases Abby. I beat the hell out of cases. This is just another dance I have been invited to compete in. the dance of Perilous they are about to be exposed to just how dangerous I can be. You go home, love, no better still... Gloria!" Montana called out to her assistant, " arrange Abigail a suite at the Four seasons hotel; then call her house keeper to put a overnight bag together for her, I will be by to get it." Abigail had other plans "Montana, no. I want to go to the pond but yes, I will go to suite later but now I need the pond..." Montana just nodded, she was too preoccupied in thought. "Ok Abby I will see you later; I have some business to attend too." I wonder who he has representing him thought Montana. Montana felt alive. This was her arena. No spiritual stuff, she thought; just good old getting dirty in the courtroom. She lavished the thought of bringing Sean down.

# P.O.K.E.R

A subdued Abigail once more was contributing her tears to the pond. Today, the pond is clear as a mirror. Abigail just stared, but the pond sensed her presence and responded to her pain, the ripples came and took her tears to the heart of the pond; when they reached the heart of the pond the face of Gabriella appeared on the surface. "Abigail." She heard a wind-like voice call to her ... Abigail looked and saw the reflection of Gabriella's face on the pond. "It is only a reflection, my dear. I am above you, but do not look up. I want you to always look into the pond and see what she is saying to you. The Monarch of Hell is the prince of the air. That right was given to him. Look dear, look very hard. The clouds are reflecting on to the pond, what do you see?" Abigail was horrified with what she saw... "Compose yourself my dear. Whatever you do, don't let him see your hand; put your best poker face on now." Abigail could not be composed. She screamed... "Gabriella, I see my daughter Jordan... oh my God! she is being beheaded! The enemy is coming after my child!"

"Abigail, remember in poker, "what it seems like is not always, what it is." Just watch. Be still and pray, have faith and know that you have the winning hand. It is the job of his demons to persuade you that you have a losing hand so you can fold in defeat. You must get total Power over Knowing Evil's Realism. (P.o.k.e.r) Pray Abigail. Pray in the spirit, there is no other way. God will give you strength and wisdom to stay in the game. God will WOW you. Abigail he will give you His wows His Words of Wisdom when you need them. The thing that Sean has approached you with this day is only the beginning; Hell might have spoken but God has to be in agreement or else Hell will be rejected". Then Gabriella disappeared.

74

Abigail prayed in the spirit for two hours until she heard someone say "There you are." It was Montana .Abigail told Montana what she had seen on the pond and what Gabriela said to her. Montana said, "Ok Abby I am not going to say I believe you, but this time I won't say I doubt you. Now that poker thing was somewhat neat, I can't see you coming up with that. Just take care of the things of this spirit world that you are consumed with; and I will take care of the Bishop and his boys. If this God of yours does really exist, I cannot see him being in agreement with this action. If he's such a "God of justice" as you say, then he will be glad of what I am about to do to his unholy man. I still can't wait to hear who is representing him. I am ready for battle".

Montana did not feel the presence of the band of angels that descended from heaven to protect and strengthen Abigail for battle by keeping the battlefield level. Abigail got on her cell phone while she and Montana were walking back to the car... "Sean dear, so ok you don't want me that's fine then divorce me; remove your headship or should I say behead me like a man and divorce me; my shoulders can take it. While you're thinking about that, Sean ask yourself is she really worth what you are doing to your family. And by family I also mean the church. Listen to me very carefully Sean Monroe. An annulment will not take place. I am not a purchase that you have changed your mind about and now you want to void the sale I do not think so. You took a vow to be the head of this woman; to be my lover and my cover and now I guess you are saying the umbrella is closing and I am being christened your mistake" Sean interrupted her... "I do not have the time for this little rant of yours, Abigail and by the way, didn't I leave you on the floor?"... Abigail continued in an oddly giddy tone "Oh my dear Sean I am so sorry to have kept you in the dark. That person you left on Montana's floor, she has remained on the floor. I arose out of her. I cannot wait for you to be better acquainted with me, let's just put it that way, love. From now on you will consult my attorney. She will be dealing with you. Hope you have an antidote for a British bull dog on crack because that's what I am letting loose on you." She said, throwing a sly smile at Montana. "Don't forget Sean, I lost my head today. What you need to be concerned about is who is covering me know. I suggest you pray that it's not Satan." Click.

"Abigail I am so proud of you, It's about time some good ole British fearlessness entered into you, Love the Poker thing, "Power over Knowing Evils Realism" not bad at all, even though I am not a believer, it's still clever." laughed Montana... "That's alright, my God is about to show you just how real he is, Montana" said Abigail... "Whatever! but you are going to be just fine D. H. W, you're not the only one with catchy little phrases," the Dignified, headless women" smiled Montana.

Both women laughed as they walked towards their new challenge that will change their lives forever... Abigail held Montana's hand and said. "Come on we have a wedding to prepare for. He will not do anything until Monday. He has a special service tomorrow." "On a Saturday?" asked Montana "yes, it is a special program. I am supposed to sing." replied Abigail. "Are you going?" Montana asked... "I would not miss it for two reasons, Montana. One, because I am singing and the last I checked, my God Jehovah and I were still in love" ... Abigail glows up like the Eiffel tower when she talks about the lover of her soul, Jehovah... "Then second, when all of this comes out to the public, the women are going to remember through all of that she still kept her head up and sang glory to her God. The woman last night, Montana! what if we were not there? And, you my dear cousin I am so proud of you. I know how it was hard for you not to call some of your clients to take care of her husband for good. I know that man would never be heard of again"... "Yes but the wife would have been blamed" replied Montana... "Exactly, thank you for thinking of that. So having said that, please do not do anything to Sean. Let's do this the way of the law, promise me no matter how ugly this gets. I know when you are involved my dear cousin things can get extremely dangerous. Promise you will stay focused and give the law a chance"... "Ok Abigail I will try" smiled Montana.... Abigail bellowed. "Lift up your heads all yea gates and the king of glory shall come in" that is for every head the enemy is trying to behead, Montana!" beamed Abigail, her hands raised in the air emphatically. "Yea, yea Abby whatever" said Montana, rolling her eyes and turning irritably in the opposite direction.

(Satan looked in and said) "We will see just how far your joy will last. I am about to rock your world, lady. FEAR come here, I'm letting you lose, it's your turn. Don't let me have to turn on you FEAR, now do me proud and create so much turmoil in her life she will regret the day she was ever born. Hell I know I regret it" Spewed Satan, grinding his teeth.

# JORDAN

Abigail and Montana had forgotten they had to meet with Jordan. They were to go and make the final walk through with her at the hotel ballroom for the wedding reception.

"Mother, I knew you would be here it was bad enough that you stood me up, but not you as well Aunt Montana!" said Jordan... Abigail put her hands to her face with shame... "I am so sorry dear, it has been a very straining day." Montana said "we were just about to call you; we wanted to show you another choice for the wedding." they walked up the hill and looked down into the valley, "see that Mansion?" Jordan shook her head in disbelief. Montana asked. "Would you like to be married there?" "Of course I would! ... This is not a joke is it? So you really did not forget me? Now I feel awful, you both were looking for another option. But... who does this belong too?" It's like something from Disney land, Mother, it's close to your pond. Did you get permission to use the property?" "Something like that" answered Montana. (This was not the time to tell anyone about Gabriella's will). "I can't wait to show Patrick!" said an ecstatic Jordan.

Abigail knew her daughter like a book. She also knows Patrick will be wonderful for her. Jordan was ready for her new life with Patrick who has been in love with her since the day he set eyes on her. Her inner and outer beauty caused him to whisper to himself, "I have found my good- thing".

Patrick is a very successful preacher. He comes from as Montana would put it "a good stock of money." He also comes with a secret that could be deadly to their future, but he chooses to keep it to himself. He is sure he can overcome this weakness. All his life that is all he has ever wanted is to serve God and marry a virgin. When he marries Jordan, he

78

will also be starting a new life, not only as her cover but also as pastor to five thousand members. Sean has secured that position for him. He has groomed Patrick for years for this great responsibility. However, in the midst of all the happiness, Jordan has a blank stare on her face. Just as a blank page of paper waiting for knowledge or adventure to be written on to it. Her new life with Patrick surely is going to be a new chapter in her life. They all decided to sit under one of the six lavender covered gazebos. The aroma of lavender was wonderful. Jordan shocked Abigail with this announcement...

"Mother, I am scared what if I don't satisfy Patrick sexually. I do not even know what to do on our honeymoon. Montana almost choked on her diet Pepsi she could not wait to hear how Abigail would answers this one... Abigail stuttered "Well dear... just... well, what do you want to know?" Jordan continued, in an almost embarrassed tone, "I want to know how to keep my man from wandering to other women just like you have with dad. Abigail forced a smile onto her face and nodded. I am aware of the divorce rate mother, just as I am aware that there are women who look the other way from their husband's infidelity because they are scared of being alone. I do not want any of that to happen to me. I want to be a Rebecca. "A ...Rebecca?" asked Abigail. "Yes, mother, in the bible Sarah shared Abraham with Hagar. Rachel and Lea shared Jacob; but Rebecca never shared Isaac with another woman. He was the promise, it was just him and Rebecca and he loved her so much. I am not naive I over hear my sisters when they come home for school break talking to cousin Montana about their sexual experiences. Abigail shoots Montana an "I will kill you later" look.

Mother you have given us the talk about the secret pleasure garden that we women have. A place where our husbands may enter to on our honeymoon, you have also told us that some women treat the garden like the carnival, multitude of rides to be ridden by whomever".

Abigail interrupts Jordan. "When Patrick holds you in his arms nature will take over and you will do what comes naturally to you" said Abigail.

Jordan became suddenly irritated by her mother's prudence. "You are not getting it mother! this is not the animal kingdom channel! How do

I keep my husband from getting bored? From straying? I see the women in the underwear commercials. Even a commercial model has the power to threaten me. Maybe I should be talking to cousin Montana. I hear people say she borrows other people's husband. I do not want that to happen to me. I do not want to be lying on my bed looking up at my ceiling wondering who else has been looking up at my ceiling. Aunt Montana must know why she can get men from their wives. I want what she has that makes a man want her so much that they do not consider the consequences. I want my husband to want me that way and still be a holy woman of God. Is that possible"?

Montana interrupted "Abby let me take it from here. First, of all, Miss Jordan I don't go after other women's men, they come to me. I surely do not enter their bedrooms. I will never be looking up at another woman's ceiling. Most of the time any ways it is too late for me to care. By the time I find out they are married, they're already hooked on me. I do send them home. I just thought I would get that straight. Now about your concern, hmm, let's see… you love the ballet yes? What is it about those dancers that bring you to tears? "The way they are one with the music and the passion of the story" replied Jordan. Montana continued, "You have taken ballet for years Jordan. Just imagine your bedroom is the stage and that you and Patrick are the only two in the ballet and you are to seduce him with a special potion that is laced in the grapes, or whatever fruit you choose. You must get him to eat the grapes or else you will not be able to seduce him, because he loves another or his work more than you. Instead of a ballerina you are a mysterious belly dancer., Get about 12 silk scarves take one and wrap around your hips and loop the other eleven on to the scarf around your hips it will appear as a seductive skirt. Oh make sure you have very little on underneath, motion for him to lay with you on the floor. Now as you get up on your knees swaying to the music take one of the scarves off and wrap it around his neck. Put the scarf in your mouth and bring him up on his knees, dance with him a while. Your props are a bowl of fruits you have previously place at the foot of your bed. Take a small bunch of grapes by the stem in your mouth. Have him eat off the grapes that are clinging from your mouth. He will eat his way to your sweet lips. Then grab a ripe mango from the bowl while he is kissing you. Pull away gently and have him open his mouth squeeze the juice of the mango in his mouth make sure you are staring into his eyes, miss his mouth purposely a few times, then you drink of the juice from his chest. By this time, the look of desire would have dressed your face with its presence and your body will react. Trust me, by then he will gently take it from there. All you do is follow his lead, dance the dance of love, be one with him. Be your man's private dancer, Jordan, any time someone will come and try to dance with him he will let them know his dance card is full. Get creative baby, when the two of you go shopping you will never look at the fruit section the same again. Let your passion be everywhere love".

When Montana finished speaking, everyone was staring at her in shock, "why, Montana," said Abigail, startled, "I wasn't aware you had such …passionate advice… lying inside of you" Montana chuckled and responded matter-of- fact, "I have many sides, like everyone, that just happens to be one of them shoved in there somewhere." Jordan threw an arm around Montana, "Well, I feel like that was some pretty good advice, wherever on earth it came from. Now I feel a little better, thank you. Aunty I am glad you are my aunt and not my competition." Montana said, "Right, cheeky (sassy) this one is, eh, Abigail?"

Abigail was uncomfortable with the conversation but delighted with a much welcome distraction to her day. "So where are your sisters?" asked Abigail, changing the subject. "Shopping and trying to get hold of dad to have lunch with him." "Mm" replied Abigail, gazing off.

Abigail canceled the suite at the four seasons. She feels empowered enough to go home. She has a gown fitting for Jordan and her bridesmaids in the morning.

# HELL'S ASSAULT

The next day was a warm, June morning. The sunrise has left behind crimson colored rays which have swirled into a bouquet of rainbow colored clouds that seemed to canopy beneath the bright torquoise sky.

Jordan's sisters Olivia, Savanna and the seven bridesmaids have all arrived to be fitted into their gowns. There is so much white and rose puff netting everywhere, you have to walk side ways to get to the adjoining room where Jordan, her mother and Montana are going over everything. For a moment it seems like yesterday was so far away. Abigail has put Sean's threat on hold. she has to get through this fitting with her daughter and sing at the church this evening. She is wearing a confident poker face; no one will ever know the hell she has been through with Sean. She will sacrifice the pleasure of self-pity by not letting anyone know she had been terribly hurt.

Jordan is glowing like a Chinese lantern. She is so grateful for the talk she had with her cousin Montana. Even though her sisters and Montana had teased her about being a virgin for many years, they were proud of her. The love and warmth of her sisters, family and friends filled her bedroom, everyone laughing as Jordan prepares to be fitted for her gown for the last time before the big day. Jordan stretches forth her hands towards the sky as her mother and Montana raise the dress over her head. The lavish white taffeta beaded Victorian dress her sisters had spent long hours shopping for in Milan, Italy is spectacular. An exact replica of Princess Grace Kelly of Monaco's wedding dress. It took every ones' breath away. Her mother said "truly this is a 'wow' moment, my dear." Even her hard core sisters and Montana had tears visiting their eyes. Olivia said "I guess I will never know the true pure moment that comes with the white dress, but sis, you deserve this moment and more.

You truly are a beautiful gift to your husband. Olivia leaned towards Jordan's ear and whispered "I wish I had saved myself" and kissed her.

Abigail was in the middle of fastening Jordan's dress, which had delicate pearl buttons. A hurricane sounding wind was coming through the bedroom window the shutters started to rattle almost off their hinges. Abigail tried to continue fastening the dress but the wind took her and slammed her on the hard wood floor. The rose colored taffeta bridesmaid dresses and white netting was flying everywhere. The bridesmaids were screaming for help while being thrown around like rag dolls. Abigail's daughters and Montana tried to shut the windows, but they too were all being blown to the other side of the room. A powerful force was holding every one down, Montana's firm Tina Turner legs, for the first time felt like wet noodles. Meanwhile, a disoriented Abigail tried to get up to help. The blustery wind got stronger and this time it started to growl with sounds like that of angry dogs. Abigail had left Jordan sitting on the bed grasping to one of the four mahogany posts of her bed. Abigail was half way to help her other daughters when Savannah was able to get a scream out: "mother look at Jordan." Jordan's veil was wrapped around one of the four posts of the bed, the atrocious wind had blown life into the veil and wrapped it around Jordan's neck. Everyone was screaming and trying to stop from falling over one another while the veil was attempting to strangle Jordan. Abigail new from the distance she was from her daughter she could not get to her in time. Her daughter was taking her last breath the strength of the veil was too much for her. Something caught Abigail's attention outside of the window not a leaf was moving on the trees. Poker she thought," What it is, is not always, what it is", in a poker moment. When she looked at her dying daughter the whirlwind had manifested images of growling disfigured faces. They had the forehead of a Gorilla, eyes of man nose and mouth of a wolf, and beard of a Billie goat. At least six of them where in the whirl wind circling Jordan and watching her die. The same faces that appeared right before Gabriella anointed her. With everything in her Abigail screamed, "In the name of Jesus Christ of Nazareth let my daughter loose!!!" as she made her way to her dying daughter. Abigail supernaturally ran and grabbed the veil from her daughter's neck. As soon as Abigail touched the veil, the wind ended as sudden as it arrived. You could hear the demons screaming as they were leaving. Abigail gently removed the tangled veil from a dying Jordan's face and neck. She could not help but think of the vision she saw in the pond about her daughter being beheaded. She leaned over and opened Jordan's mouth to resuscitate her, but Jordan coughed and opened her eyes. She held her mother crying hysterically. Abigail got everyone to settle down, they all thought it was the weather, an accidental slip of the window, letting in a fierce wind, but Abigail knew different, she knew a new battle was forming in the Atmosphere.

"Lord, keep the devil away from my child" Abigail said while rocking Jordan.

The phone rang. It was a strange sound compared to all of the war zone sounds that had just left. Heather brought the phone to Abigail. She was shocked to see the state of the room because the rest of the house was calm. Heather had no idea what went on in there. A strange voice on the other end had only this message. "The one you were inquiring about, we still do not have her where abouts, but we have found out she is armed and dangerous." Abigail hung the phone up.

Abigail sat down. Sadness had dressed her face, but she had just had a daughter with a veil that was trying to kill her, she cannot deal with anything else right now.

Abigail acknowledged that Hell has announced its deadly presence again. Master fear has been chosen to dance against her. The spirits have a battle ahead of them. Abigail knows she cannot afford to lose this battle. If the spirit of fear conquers he will command legions to come and occupy her.

"So my season of peace has temporarily been interrupted again. Nevertheless, this too shall pass. She takes a deep breath and exhales.

*"I let go of any fear that is trying to overtake my mind, I release it from my mental atmosphere and emotional acceptance. I embrace the divine strength that is flowing through my being now. There are no dead end streets, in Jehovah. He will always make a way of escape. I give thanks that my words are planted and rooted in the rich soil of my mind. I release it to the law, knowing it is done. And so it is and let it be so".*

Half an hour had passed. Jordan and her wedding party were settling down. Abigail announced this would be "all the fitting for today ladies" as she hugged each one. The limousines were waiting to take the traumatized wedding party home, including Jordan and her sisters.

# Combat Zone

Montana grabbed Abigail "you talk to me now Abby!!" "Why, Montana?! So you can keep mocking me and justifying to yourself that this is not a battle of the spirit world?" That my daughter was not almost strangled by that veil? and I know you heard those animal noises that came from that demonic attack!

Something has Hell shook up! And, now it is trying to shift my course. First Sean, now this and what else is Satan planning?! Before Montana could reply, there was a strained look on Montana's face as if she had seen a ghost. "I think you can ask the devil himself" said Montana. Abigail turned to look and see what was causing her fearless cousin to look so shocked. Abigail was not ready to look upon what had just entered into her house. After seeing those demons, what could have Montana looking so devastated? Abigail slowly turned her face to the direction that Montana's face had frozen to. It was not demons that had Abigail gasping as she rubbed her eyes. She thought, "Is this a trick of Hell or what"?

Standing at the doorway was a figure of a man and a woman that her eyes had not set on for many years. It was Montgomery and Mona. Abigail's parents, they had aged and the path of bitterness had left its marking on her father's face. Abigail ran to her mother and hugged her, Mona whispered in Abigail's ear. "He is dying Abby." Abigail released herself from Mona and ran into the bathroom. Montana went to follow her, but Mona stopped her "leave her alone right now dear". Montana took her aunt and uncle to the guest quarters so they can rest from the eight-hour plus flight that it took from England.

Abigail ran up the four steps leading to her tub. She hugged one of six roman pillars that are on the edge of her tub. The last time she saw her father she was telling him she chooses life after he asks her to choose between her future and his rules. A breeze entered into the bathroom with Abigail. She heard a familiar voice. "Abigail it's I, Gabriella. I know what you're thinking, but you have to forgive him or else you will be powerless to protect your daughter and the others from what awaits them. He does not have long in this world. Whatever he does or says remember he is your father, your mother's husband who has forgiven him. Abigail demanded "Why is my father even here?!" And where were you earlier?! Gabriella's voice remained calm and even, despite Abigail's distressed screams at her, "Your father is here to make it right with you. And, where was I?! Who do you think stopped the veil and chased the demons out? asked Gabriella, "Abigail please take my hand" Abigail gave Gabriella her hand. they were no longer in Abigail's bathroom; they were standing at the edge of the pond. Gabriella said "look into the pond." Abigail gazed at the pond, it had become a chilling pond of blood. Abigail was horrified. "What does this mean Gabriella?" "It means my dear, if you do not forgive your father for being consumed by the generational curses that have haunted him; this pond will run over with the blood of thousands of good women who happen to be headless. They are waiting for you to come and empower their minds and reinstate their status back to a GOOD THING and save them from bleeding to death. Their cries reach the throne day and night. "When will the bleeding stop? please stop the bleeding…" Those who cut their wrist to cause their own death we call them bleeders. When a woman's mind has been mentally or physically abused her spirit starts an inner bleeding process, she is en route to become a bleeder, but when she becomes empowered to choose life she will hear from the throne of God saying. "I said live, Good Thing, I said live!" the bleeding will then stop."

Jesus's last act on this earth was to forgive the thief on the cross and accept him into paradise. He asked his father to forgive those who had wronged him because they knew not what they were doing. Jesus knew the secrets to kingdom power living would be one of the hardest things for humans to do. Exercising love and forgiving each other is part of the power. The world has confused the strength of forgiving with weakness. To forgive is the same as being released from self-destruction. The thief that was forgiven on the cross, Jesus said *"this day he will be in paradise"*.

When you forgive, your mind is released from the death sentence of the cross you have nailed yourself too. Your mind is then released to a state of paradise where love flows freely. This is where you need to allow change; this is where change and elimination is required. Like the autumn tree, the leaves change and the branch eliminate the leaves so the new can come through next season. Change your will to stay angry with your father and eliminate the anger, Abigail. Satan is toiling with you. The spirit of fear he sent earlier which you have conquered for now was a distraction, and now we know why God allowed it, so you could confront the un-forgiveness you thought you had dealt with. You were chosen to bare this Abigail, whether you like it or not you have been empowered to enlighten and empower women. However, this cannot be done unless you walk with a forgiving heart. Please do not hand over a bullet to Satan, keep him disarmed.".... Abigail released her hand from Gabriella and walked into the pond. Her summer white linen dress had turned crimson red. She closed her eyes and lifted her hands towards the heavens and said "*lord do not let this blood that has stained my dress stain my heart; eliminate from me the bitterness I have towards my father and Sean. Help me forgive them as you have forgiven me. I do not want to be an instrument being used by Satan. I ask that your blood cleanse my thoughts and remove pride far away from me, remove me from the throne of self-destruction*".

When Abigail opened her eyes, Gabriel was gone and she was back in her bathroom her dress once again summer white. Abigail opened the bathroom door and Montana was waiting for her. "Are you alright Abby?" asked Montana, Abigail smiled "of course I am dear, why wouldn't I be?" Montana looked at her cousin strangely and said, "Yea right, there you go again Abigail" "Where are my parents, are they ok? Montana where are they?" Before Montana could answer, Abigail's parents walked in the room, her father wearing an exasperated look on his face. "Father, you must be tired. Come and rest" said Abigail as she walked towards her father with open arms. Montana gasped, Abigail said to her "breathe Montana, you are starting to turn purple" as she walked pass her. Abigail embraced her father. Montgomery collapsed into Abigail's arms while saying "forgive me Abigail". Abigail felt her father's pulse, it was weak. "Please forgive me Abigail" his voice groaned out of him. While gazing into Abigail's eyes, his breathing had become worst. Each breath was taking between 15 and thirty seconds to surface from his lungs.

Just then, Hell stepped in, unseen. As far as they were concerned, today was payday. Satan has put everything on hold for a moment to observe "Come on home to pa, pa", said Satan as he watch Montgomery take in some of his last breath on earth. "Watch the mother. Create something so that they will not have time to administer his last bloody rites to him." Pull his last breath out of him now do it now Death do it take him out of his misery". Death replied "I cannot Satan, something is stopping me." Satan growled "It is the mother! What are you waiting for?! Bring him to me! I own his soul... Never mind! Out of my way, Death, do I have to do everything?!"

Mean while, another demonic whirlwind appeared again, the atmosphere once again is chaotic. Abigail looks at her mother. Mona locks her eyes with her daughter.

Montana is screaming she has just been hit with a flying curling iron; "lie down on the floor everyone!" screamed Abigail. Abigail noticed that on the lower level where she and her father were sitting, nothing was moving. "Father," she said, "I am not the only one that wishes to forgive you. Ask God too as well."

Montgomery held tightly on to Abigail's shoulder and rose up from her lap. Mona stretched out her hands and spoke with authority "enough Satan! Enough! I come against this spirit right now. You must be still in the name of Jesus!" It was done the spirits were still.

Satan screams "I hate her! I hate her! She is gaining strength!"

Montgomery said to Abigail "it is too late for me. You chose life in spite of my threats Abigail. I chose death for my wealth. I have a debt to pay, I failed, I was not able to give you to him. Yet knowing you have forgiven me, I can accept Hell. Where is Montana?" "I am here uncle," Answered Montana quietly. "Do not meet me in Hell Montana. I wronged you too. It is ok if you do not forgive me just do not join me. I owe your mother that."

A sobering Montana asked Abigail "can't you give his last rite or something?! I forgive you uncle, just do not die I have questions I need answers for."

# DEBT CANCELED

Satan is enraged. "Oh no, is he going to except his last rite? Death get ready, If he does I want every one wiped out in that room! Starting with his wife, then his daughter even Montana! I want everything in this room to-"Satan was interrupted.

"YOU do NOT own the sting of Death! God does and you only get what He allows you to have! I am still on the scene Satan" said Gabriella, smirking. There were a host of demons standing with Satan, he looked behind Gabriella and grinned, "So what if you're 'on the scene,'" he mocked, "you are alone!" Gabriella's wings appeared for the first time, during her assignment with Abigail. There was a mighty rush of wind as she opened and closed her wings. Behind her appeared a host of fierce angels, ready to wage war. "We too, are waiting Satan we are here to make sure his free will is not interrupted with. He was loyal to you in life; let us see what he chooses during his last moment" said Gabriella.

"Do not worry about me father. He cannot touch me. You can give your last breath to God and he will accept your soul." Abigail stroked her father's head, "I will be with you, father, as you labor in death I will pray that your labor won't be long suffering." Tears rolled down Montgomery's cheeks, "his love really exists Abigail? I mean... even for me?" "Yes, father," she whispered. Montgomery's eyes rolled to the back of his head, as gasped for air. He was just barely releasing his breath, this time they were coming least forty seconds apart. Then with his eyes fixed on Abigail, he coughed up a trickle of blood. The death rattle came with this breath. "Lord, forgive me a sinner that I am," rattled out of him, each word he labored greatly with. Then Montgomery took his last breath and died in his daughter's arms. Gabriella watched as the heavenly hosts took his soul. Mona exhaled and said "it is finished."

An infuriated Satan exploded "why did he grant him mercy?! This is not fair!" Mercy has never been "fair" now has it Satan? After all, you and your third are still around. His debt and his daughter's have been canceled Satan, live with it and move on." Said Gabriella while ascending back into heaven

"Oh no you don't, let's see how clever you are with this one," Growled, an infuriated Satan.

While Abigail was closing her father's eyes, a maggot came out of his left eye socket. Montana screamed. Mona cried out "push him off your lap right now Abigail and come here!" It was too late; maggots were consuming her father. His body went into a rapid form of decomposition. She rolled his discomposed body off her lap. Some of the maggots were clinging to her dress. Mona shouted "take the dress off!" Abigail removed the dress and threw it over her father, who by now was all but completely eaten up by maggots. It was a most horrific sight, so horrific that it caused the mighty Montana to fall into a faint.

An angry Mona said "you might destroy the flesh Satan but not his soul. I have seen worst in the realm of your world. Your theatrical stunt doesn't phase me, far as I'm concerned all you've done is make a mess." Abigail got one of the empty gown bags and a tablecloth, she and Mona rolled what was left of Montgomery into the bag. None of the maggots were clinging to Mona so she handled the body while Abigail held the bag open.

This time it was Abigail's turn to command Montana up from the floor, just as Montana had done her in her office when she fainted around Sean yesterday, which now seemed like a lifetime ago. "Get up Montana, now." Montana was shaking "I need a drink and I need it now!" Montana not saying another word went to her bag, pulled out her cell phone, and instructed her chauffer to bring her a drink immediately from her Bentley. "Will a piccolo (small bottle of champagne) do madam? "Yes, but bring the brandy with it" an aggravated Montana replied. He was in the room in what seemed like seconds, out of breath, and handed the chilled bottle of piccolo to her. She declined the glass. Montana turned the bottle up in a most un- lady like fashion. "What the Hell is going on? I am going to be paying for therapy for the rest of my freaking life!!!" Montana glanced at the bag with a slight hump. "What... is... that? She asked slowly, pointing to the white garment bag, almost afraid to hear the answer. 'My father" replied Abigail. "No, no... stuttered Montana, unable to wrap her mind around what she had just heard. "Where is the rest of him? Oh bloody heck why does all this freaking Harry Potter madness keep happening?!" Therapy I tell you, for the rest of my stinking life!" One of the maggots got loose out of the bag and crawled on to Montana's feet she screamed. "Get it off me! Oh, I can't deal with this anymore! What is this, the Twilight Zone?! Why is this happening?!" Montana was becoming hysterical. Mona walked over and slapped her. "Get your self-together, child we all become maggots at the end." "Yes Auntie, I do believe your right but feel free to correct me! Am I not still alive?!" screamed Montana? "Montana, you have no fear in your little world of justice, I do not entertain fear in the spirit world. Satan has released fear from Hell... I will find out why later. You have shown more gruesome pictures to jury's, while battling a case with no fear. I might add this is no different. Do you still call yourself perilous"? Just from hearing that word, Montana lifted her head up and said "I do, auntie. I do". "Then act like it child. I am a defendant for Jehovah. I will not buckle under from demonic theatrics." After Mona said that, she walked over to the bag and said, "He had better be whole In the name of Jesus. My daughter will not have to deal with this nonsense". Mona unzipped the bag and Montgomery was fully fleshed again. Montana took another drink and wept as she said. "Oh bloody heck, my therapist is going to need therapy when she hears about this, maggots eating my uncle and bloody flying curling irons!" A concerned Abigail said, "Montana, you have to keep it together. It will soon be your turn and you have to handle Sean in the court arena" "Oh, Abigail with everything going on I totally forgot what that low life is doing to you." "That's my girl." said Abigail, "keep that thought."

Montana's phone rang. "Yes, yes thank you. Yes, I need you now, it is an emergency." Montana summoned her driver again, but this time to drive her to her therapist who has agreed to have an emergency session with her. Mona stopped her and asked her where she was going, "to my therapist auntie," Mona said "Montana, you are not going to that woman to rape your mind." Montana furrowed her eyebrows "What are you saying auntie?" "Montana, have you ever wondered why the word rapist is in therapist? Actually that word really says THE RAPIST, they "rape" your mind, injecting nonsense, forcing things they want you to think is helping you into your mind, and then rape your wallet in the process." "Oh, oh, no, there you go with that weird wordplay, metaphoric thing, between you and Abigail, my ears want to jump off my bloody head! Abigail come and get your mother!" hollered Montana, while running to her car.

She made a few phone calls from her car and came back in to the house. "See, thanks a lot, now I cannot get the rapist part out of my head, I need drugs I just can't believe this is happening to me!" Abigail and Mona both yelled "shut up Montana this is not about you right now!" Like HELL it's not! All this witchcraft nonsense I've been exposed to! I am coming apart!" "No, Montana my husband is what came apart! Like you said, you are still in the land of the living!" shouted Mona. "That God you always speak of... can't you pray to him now to stop this or... or something!" said an unnerved Montana. "So do you believe in God right now, Montana?" "No," Montana replied, her eyes darting around the room, "but something has peeked my interest and I'm going to keep an eye on it. What uncle said before he died does have me concerned. If this God of yours is real and cares about me, then he will know how to get to me, not scare me, but touch me. I await him Abigail". After that Montana, took another drink. "Abigail, we need to call the ambulance to take your father away said Mona. "Yes, mother I will call my hospital; they will take care of everything. I need to call Jordan and the girls to see if they are ok." "I have already called them, Abby, when I was in my car. They are fine actually Savanna insisted that they go out and get some lunch said Montana." Abigail said "I cannot believe this day. In a matter of three hours my daughter is almost getting strangled by a veil, my parents are in the country, I did not know anything about them coming to visit, and my father is dead and it's only lunch time."

"Mother I need to fill you in, Montana will you be staying or are you going home? I'm taking mother to the pond." Montana replied, "I don't feel like being alone, and anyways I need to be reminded how much I hate Sean and how I am going to nail him."

93

Abigail filled Mona in with everything that Sean is trying to do. Mona turned to Montana and said, "It's your turn perilous one. Battle well, but I am concerned Montana, that you are not strong enough, for this will be a two-fold battle, spirit and flesh. Let me bring our solicitors (lawyers) in from England. Your uncle owns some of the city's most corrupted lawyers, but they get the job done for him". "No! I am the one auntie, please. I am not equipped for your world as you said. But, I was born to argue the law of this land. My mind is well furnished for this. I know where each piece belongs. I had a temporary moment of… well I don't have a name for it, but I am back auntie, trust me." An offended Montana replied. Mona nodded, "Then let it be so. When it is time, God will take over." "Auntie, quick question, not to be offensive, but, why are you not a bit more… shaken up? Your husband just died. Mona replied "Montana, your Uncle Montgomery has been dying for a long time. That man was so cruel to me in life; his power over me shall not follow him in his death. I am free. He cannot come to me but in time I can go to him. Montana what you have witnessed today was not for anyone's sake but for Abigail's. Montgomery kind of benefits from it, but it was for Abigail. God had to make sure Abigail did right by her father so she could be released from her prison of bitterness and anger. I knew he was dying and there was a chance he may not make the trip, but I felt the Lord encouraging me to get him to Abigail. Mona turned to Abigail that is why I didn't let you know we were coming. I knew you would probably have left the country. Abigail, don't be troubled my dear. As long as you are true to your God then it is his responsibility to protect you and the children."

"I know one thing, you are not the girl who left my house you are a mighty woman of God with an awesome responsibility to fulfill. When I was younger an Angel appeared to me. Gabriela was her name. When you were born, I saw her again. She told me that you had been chosen to serve the God of Abraham, Isaac and Jacob but it would not be easy for you because of what your father had done, but when the time came she would appear to you.

Now is there anything else you need to share with me because with all this Hell going on I would have thought she would have appeared."

Abigail began to sob "mother yes, yes, she has visited me but I did not want you to think I was crazy. Montana does not believe me".

The two hugged. Montana said "I am so tired of this I had better not see this woman... Angel... whatever she is, I cannot do this. Heck, it is bad enough waking up this morning thinking I was going to have a normal day, then I get thrown into a horror film, tell all your little spirits whatever they are to stay the heck away from me!" Mona said "Montana your day is coming love it is coming and the first thing I pray God to do is wash that mouth of yours", they all laughed. "So are we going to church this evening in spite of everything" asked Montana. Abigail said I would not miss it. The morgue has daddy they will prepare for him to be flown back to England. Mother, will you be flying back with him? Abigail, there is not a soul that will come to your father's funeral. His last wishes in his will are that he be cremated. I have called Morgan funeral home, they will pick up his body and do the cremation. Abigail just stared at her mother and said "whatever you say mother. Well anyways, There will be a great preacher there tonight. I am so tired but I am going on". "One of his good ole boys I presume?" asked Montana. "Yes but he is a great preacher Montana." Montana rolled her eyes, "I bet he knows how to pimp that money as well, what's the going percentage these day for the one who raises his own offering? Abigail don't you give me that righteous look. I know what goes on behind those church doors. Well, fine let's change the subject. Abigail why are you not curious about this Madison Brown? Do you think she will represent Sean? Abigail sighed "I do not know but Montana you must promise me at church my girls will know nothing about what Sean is trying to do. Mother the girls know nothing of this." Mona nodded her head and held her peace.

Abigail continued "Montana you know what, Satan is sure not chasing you love, he already owns you." Montana shook her head slowly grinning, "As much as it may seem like, no he does not. I have told you already I am a free agent. He is not even real to me and neither are these succubus, demon people you always bring up." Montana looked at them sympathetically as far she was concerned they were all a helpless case. "You are all crazy," she continued, "but I love you both my darlings." The women hugged each other and chuckled, though Mona did not really find any of it amusing. Abigail's heart was heavy for Montana's soul, she feared for her. "There must be a way for me to prove to her that God is real" she thought as she hugged her beloved cousin.

*Meanwhile Satan is fuming in Hell. He has called an emergency meeting.*

# HELL'S ASSASSIN

Abigail kept her word and sang for her mother at church. She sang her mother's favorite song *amazing grace*. Montana came to church, but only because she wanted to protect Abigail from Sean and make the deacons and the wives feel uncomfortable.

Sean sat in the pulpit as if nothing had gone on yesterday between him and Abigail. Patrick was also in the pulpit as well as other guest preachers. This service really was an annual fundraiser for the bishop. There was at least seven thousand in attendance. They all loved Bishop Sean Monroe. Everyone stood and applauded as Sean made his way to the podium to announce the speaker. "The most holy Bishop J.W.! Bishop the floor is yours there is no more to say you are well loved and welcomed here, what else is there to say to you but feed my sheep."

The giant looking handsome preacher stood up. He wore a double breasted black suit. Even though he was at least 6ft 2in, the Armani suit draped his frame well. He had a flamboyant personality, a smile that would make women say. "That man is just too handsome to be preaching the word; he has come to bed eyes."

"My sermon topic will be different than what you are expecting to hear. I know this is a fundraiser and we like to be shouting and holy dancing all night long, but God visited with me last night. He informed me that some of the women in attendance tonight were in trouble and I need to warn them. I wrestled all night with God on this, of course he won.

The Bishop looked at Mona and said "welcome to America Miss Mona sorry to hear about your husband". He then paused and looked out to the congregation and said "I am going to preach on the "integrity of A Headless Woman". Abigail looked at Montana and said "out of the

97

mouth of two witnesses'. Montana said "What the hell... oops sorry... what does that mean Abby?" "I will explain later," she said, her eyes fixed on Sean, "let's just listen to what the spirits are saying." "What spirits Abby?" inquired Montana.

The preacher looked at Montana and continued his sermon. "The word of God tells us in Ephesians the 5th chapter... states to us that man is head of the woman and God is head of the man. Even the law asks on the tax return form. "Are you filing as head of household? So the law recognizes someone has to have headship of the household, God has ordained the husband to be over the wife.

Therefore a man without his wife is just a head without a body and a woman without her husband is a body without a head. So the saying it's not only biblical it's also part of our society. In a perfect world, a woman's head would be her father until her husband takes his place. (*Olivia nudged savanna]* Nevertheless, this is not a perfect world and principalities and darkness rules with one intension to kill the family. Many times, a woman's first taste of being beheaded comes from their father.

Abigail's eyes reflected the memory from her father beheading her, and now he is in a body bag.

"Hell has women planted in churches to aid in the destruction of the family. We will call them the headhunters. The Salome and the Delilah and of course we all know Jezebel are the main three recruiters in the bible. Salome comes with a chainsaw attached to her hips. She does not only take over your bed, but your husband's head. She is always ready to have you beheaded. She is not alone, her power is assisted by the incubus, an evil spirit who comes at night to seduce the man in his sleep; she rapes him over and over again. Now Jezebel does not have time for childish lust games, like the other two, Jezebel goes after power. She does not go after a house. She hunts countries and leaders."

The church is silent, everyone is one edge waiting to hear him explain further. The spirit of Salome keeps seducing his mind until the man himself starts to believe she is real. Then one day unexpected her look alike enters into his life, he then becomes helpless because until now he believed he was not harming anyone else. And now here she is manifested into flesh and blood traveling with her axe, ready to have you executed. Now like King Herod your husband will offer her anything she wants if she will only dance into his life. Trust me she will. Her price is always deadly.

I have seen bodies of great men that have committed suicide under her spell. SLAM! He makes noise as one being beheaded with an axe. He then leans over the podium and gazes at the congregation and says in a chilling voice. You might be wondering right know who in here is safe, or are you? [*Women are now slowly rubbing their neck*]

Savanna says, "Damn I wish I was that bad". Olivia replies, "He seems and sounds like he has tasted her his dang self." And with an irritated side glance added " and, you Savanna, you're getting there just ask the French men. ( *They giggled*]."

"Is she here to behead you? How will you handle being beheaded? That is my point today. Can you walk in dignity while you are in the battle of your life to regain you're head of your household? *Sean is stone faced, he did not expect this.*" When a man is sent to war, he leaves his wife behind to keep the family together. She never knows if her man will come back home or not and if he does, will he be whole or will parts of him be left on the battlefield. Worst still, he may become a prisoner of war. The first act the enemy does to prisoners of war is to have them blindfolded. So they become disoriented in their surroundings. To avoid being captured in battle a soldier depends heavily on his partner to keep him covered at all times. Someone has to keep a watchful eye on the enemy day and night. If Salome comes there are three stages your husband will be subject too.

1st He will be under fire with temptation.

2nd He will be wounded causing him to be weak eventually shattering his vows.

3rd Then he will become a blinded prisoner of her war.

Totally disoriented he will be, even in the familiar surroundings of his home. He will not notice the axe he has resting on his wife's neck. If this happens all you can do is pray for it to be a swift blow. The blunt axe is the worst, your neck is being ripped apart slowly as the world watches. There will be the ones that came home but parts of him stayed on the battle field. It's not always an arm or a limb but his sound mind. Does the headhunter have your husband's mind? For some of you there is good news, You have the blood bought right to demand his release from the other woman! Screamed the preacher, however, just then his sermon was interrupted. Satan was still waging war. (*Satan*) *Oh they have a right do they? I am tired of you too preacher. Its payday for you today, Satan looked around and did not see Gabriella. Hmm, he is free and clear for the taking I guess. Hey, death do you see her around?* "*No, I do not Satan*". *Then get ready to do your thing after my girl does hers.*

The doors of the church opened and a stranger walked in. A beautiful woman dressed to kill one might say. Her tailored navy and white silk suit was accented with a wide brim navy hat with a white Swiss dot veil which covered her face. The veil was not able to hide her wide voluptuous wine colored full lips. The fragrance of Cartier perfume lingered at vestibule in the church. A mysterious breeze seemed to have entwined itself with her scent, but for now it too will linger in the vestibule. She stares at the preacher and glides seductively down the middle of the church her hips are in rhythm with her thoughts as if she were walking the runway competing for a Miss Seductress pageant. She has been seated behind Jordan, who was not going to be rude like her sisters and turn around to see who she is.

The preacher tried his best to finish his sermon. Beads of his sweat started to roll one into the other forming what looks like miniature springs which flowed from a reservoir on the top of his head. He held on to his throat as one choking while turning purple. He tried walking towards Sean for help but he collapsed, his tongue was protruding out of his mouth, and his eyes were wide open with fear staring at Sean. Abigail ran up to the pulpit to help. She loosened his tie, he grabbed her and said "don't let them take me" and died. Abigail returned to her seat where Montana was, she did not want her panicking.

Montana said "Damn what the hell is going on?!" "For the first time Montana you are right" replied Abigail, her voice strained, "Hell has returned."

Mona was quiet, but her spirit was preparing for battle. She was not sure if Abigail was to be targeted. The church was in a panic.

Sean dismissed the church. He has always been a master in stressful situations. He masters in how to show a firm face, but now the stone is slowly being chiseled from his face. It took a while to get seven thousand people out of the church, but the staff took care of everything in a timely fashion.

Abigail had called an ambulance. She could not revive the preacher. The paramedics pronounced him dead on the scene and took him away. Sean glanced at Abigail then at Montana, who gave him the finger. The church was now totally emptied except for the personal family. Nobody felt the mysterious deadly breeze that made its way to the pulpit. It passed by Patrick and Sean but rested on the preacher right before he collapsed. It then evaporated just as mysterious as it appeared, clear and dangerous.

Jordan noticed the woman is still seated, not even her veil had been ruffled. Jordan turns to walk towards her to apologize. She pauses and realizes she does not even know what just happened. Hoping it was not to be a repeat of yesterday. Jordan puts her hand towards the woman "I am so sorry that you had to witness this".

*Satan laughed. "Witness this? Baby, my girl delivered that sting."*

Abigail hurried to seize Jordan hands before she could touch the woman. "Jordan love, your fiancée needs you". Patrick had not moved, he looked like he had literally been frozen in time. Montana walked up to Patrick and stared at him, moving her head slowly from side to side and said, "oh my, therapy, therapy, off to the rapist you will be going".

'Well, anyways I can at least give you a proper greeting, after you coming here for the first time and having to experience this. I am Jordan, and you are?" As she is walking towards Patrick, the woman replies, her voice was as chilling as Betty Davis when she announced "fasten your seat belts it's going to be a bumpy night"

*Satan announces "here we go demons every one lets fasten up. Let's see what happens to your precious integrity now Miss Abigail. Keep the mother away spirits. Ok here she goes let's observe".*

The woman finally spoke. "Shall I introduce myself, Patrick? Or do you want to'? Patrick was frozen. "Why don't I?" she continued, smirking, "you seem to be preoccupied." Patrick tried to stand up, slowly he rises, but back down he went. He seemed to have aged twenty years in that short moment.

The woman turned to Jordan and says "your husband to be, my dear, has been my lover for the last year." Savanna went crazy and screamed "Hell no! What did you say whore? Stop lying, you're probably just some jealous old flame come to stir up trouble! Well this is the wrong place and the wrong family!" and launches herself toward the woman like a demented pit bull. Montana, Abigail and Olivia restrain Savanna. Abigail rebukes her daughter."What about the bishop, your son in law to be, mother? Who is supposed to be the watcher of the souls, but apparently he took time off from watching the herd to go wolfing in her pasture, why does he not get rebuked?" Montana whispers to Abigail "she has a point... "Another time another place bitch, I won't let my sister dirty her hands but watch yourself, I'm coming, and Hell is coming with me. That day, let's see who Hell honors".

*Satan is delighted so far. "Where has this excitement been? Oh my, I am in love". Justification reminded him. "Just remember who her mother and grandmother are". Satan growled at him and shoved him out of his view.*

Montana jokingly tells Abigail "Savanna is not going back to Europe; I need her and her fire in my office. Olivia grabs savanna." "What kind of talk is that savanna"? "I am sorry mother, I will take care of her" said Olivia and pushes Savanna towards the wall.

Jordan's knees give way. It's all too much for her. Abigail catches her before she hits the floor. Abigail blows gently into her daughter first, and prays over her. She lays her gently on the floor. Mona takes over the prayer

Jordan's eyes opens, she looked into her mother's eyes, Abigail recognized that look. It was the same look Abigail had worn herself many times, an expression of hurt, the sting of betrayal. Abigail helps her up.

Jordan stood like an ivory pillar. Her appearance had changed, the mild kitten had a lion look about her. She walked past the woman to Patrick. In a stern voice she asked Patrick "am I getting ready to go into battle with Delilah or Salome?" Before a stunned Patrick could answer, Abigail raised her voice "she is not Salome, my daughter she is

Delilah, but she is a Salome in waiting. Her mother was a Salome." She said, a wave of anger and disgust washing over her face at the memory. Montana screamed "what the heck?" Sean asked, "you... know this woman Abigail? Or is all of this part of your sick cousin's plans to destroy me?" Montana replied, "I don't need anyone to help me destroy you, the pleasure is going to be all mine, trust me. My goodness all you ever think about is your damn self". Sean remarked 'We are in the house of God, Montana can you not respect that". Look Sean, if your God have a problem with my mouth let him appear and tell me so. Oh that's right he is not in the house is he Sean, you know what he knew you would be here so he went on a vacation did you not get the memo you hypocrite?! Abigail interrupts, "You know what Sean, they say when you sleep with dogs you wake up with fleas, and fleas are annoying flesh biters. This one my love, has come home to bite you Sean. This is what you produced in the bed of Hell when you allowed that door to be opened in your spirit and slept in it with her mother! This Sean, is your daughter. Her name is Manuela. Her Aunt Ramona in Vienna raised her and she was educated in both France and Italy. She did and internship in Japan, she is fluent in seven languages and is fascinated with Satanism. I lost track of her a year ago but I see she has been busy. The last report I got about her was she is armed and dangerous. Montana and everyone else was speechless, and staring at Abigail in disbelief, wondering how on earth she had found out all of this. "I warned you Sean, I rose out of the corpse you left me on at Montana's office floor, Are you sure you are ready to tangle with me? Abigail glanced at Montana and said "trust me Montana, I can take it from here". Mona smiled and watched her daughter take on HELL.

Abigail sensed Gabriella was with her, as she walked towards the woman she spoke in a powerful whisper into her ear. "My fight is not with you, dear but with your master, the strong hold who sent you. Now I bind every evil thing that has come here to destroy us in the name of Jesus Christ of Nazareth." The woman hissed like an Indian cobra and turned away from Abigail. She walked towards Savanna and grabbed her by her throat and in a male voice she said; "I will be in Hell personally to greet you Savanna". Again Montana was shook up, not scared just shook up it's to the point where she is getting use to all these supernatural problems. Montana replied. "No bitch, come greet this!" Montana pulled out her gun and pointed it to the woman's head. "Release her or I will blow you and your Kentucky derby hat straight to your Hell." She released Savanna. Satan gave the order. Abigail screamed. "No Montana! No don't shoot her!" Abigail ran to savanna, she had turned completely pale. Abigail glanced at Montana to see if she had lowered her gun, and she had, she knows Montana is trying to bring this fight into her arena.

Abigail grabbed her daughter and gave her to Mona, all the while keeping eye contact with the woman and Montana. In a fearless voice, Abigail confronted Satan "your fight is with me Monarch. Now loose this child. You want me then here I am. Leave my children out of this." *Back in Hell's arena The Monarch grins in amusement and says "so the lion has risen. Do not let that girl, go demons hold on to her. Let's see how long this little courage surge will last"* It was too late Abigail had entered into Hells arena. "Who are you"? Commanded Abigail, "Loose her" demanded Abigail again, she rested her hand on the woman's stomach; again she commanded Hell "loose this child!" Then Manuela screamed like a tormented woman in labor and fainted as the evil spirit departed from her. Her hat landed by Sean's feet. He picked her up and laid her on the red cushioned oak pew.

Abigail turned around to a petrified Patrick and in a stern powerful voice she asked "Where have you been meeting with her? Answer me now!" Patrick threw himself to the ground and grabbed Jordan's ankle. His voice sounded like a radio out of wave range. He was trying to speak, but his crying and sobbing was breaking his speech away he was practically hysterical. Jordan bent down to him and looked into his eyes, slapped him and said "please Patrick, mother needs the truth." Finally his voice found a frequency and he blurted out "in my dreams! I promise she looks like the woman who visits my dreams and seduces me, I have not been unfaithful to you or the church Jordan, I promise". The woman got up from the bench and ran out of the church. She knew she was no match for Abigail. Hell and all its power now knows it has underestimated the strength and power of Abigail Monroe.

(Mean while in Hell*)* *Satan demanded "Where is she going?" Then he noticed the spirit which he used to possess the woman had reentered Hell. "And why are you here?!" A petrified spirit replied "I could not hold her down Satan, Abigail had more power than I did, and that mother of hers was silent but she gave the last blow." Satan growled while grabbing his head 'Why won't this family just die?! Don't worry, she will return and there will be seven more demons to help her out. Put it into the mind of that sugar daddy of hers to go and search for her"*... Satan is not having a 100% victory day and Montana has just witnessed the reality of the succubus in the flesh. A confused Sean asked "what has come over you Abigail? What are you talking about?" Abigail turned to face him "This, dear husband, is yours and Madison's daughter." Sean was shocked, Montana screamed "oh blooming heck! Heck no! Abigail you knew all the time who that woman was and said nothing?!" "Yes Montana, I did and I do not want you killing her." Sean for the first time in years is petrified; the stone face is now reduced to mud. He gets on his cell to ask his attorney to come over to the church, he needs a witness but there is no answer. He looks at Montana, then Abigail and says "this trick you both have put together. I am the one to pull it a part". Abigail instructs everyone to stay out of the war which is brewing between her and Sean. Abigail turned to a confused looking Patrick and said to him. "Patrick you will stay away from my daughter tonight. She must go home to seek God for answers, then she and only she will decide are you worth the battle that is ahead of the both of you" Sean yells, "hold on, I am the head of this family and I give the orders not you. Abigail don't you think I would know if I had a child out there?" Abigail replies. "Sean, do you want this negative exposed here or do we need to go to the house?" Montana interrupts "I am not missing this for anything, as she motions Abigail's daughter to get into her Bentley. Savanna asked "auntie why do you always have a driver?" "because, I do not drink and drive love, now get into the car."

# EXPOSURE

B ack at the house an explosive Abigail is ready to confront Sean for the first time in all the years she has been married to him. "It is about time everything is exposed Sean" our secrets are like old rolls of films that are put away after vacation in drawers never getting to the place to be developed just undeveloped negatives laying around. Sean fires back before Abigail could say anything else. "Girls, I have something to tell you about your bitter mother and her deranged cousin! I asked your mother for a divorce! (The girls were in shock) So they have hired this girl to do all of what you have witnessed here today! A fuming Montana replied

"You lying son of a bitch! Why don't you tell them the truth? It was not a divorce you wanted but an annulment and that would make Abigail your whore and the girls your illegitimate children! Oh, I guess we planned the preacher to die too". Savanna got into her father's face "is this true daddy?!" "Do not get into things you don't understand savanna." He replied "Why don't you help me to understand then daddy?!" (Her nose is almost touching his) "Get out of my face like that savanna." Montana grabbed Savanna away and embraced her. Jordan interjects. Let me get this straight, father you are getting ready to disown us and remove your headship from the family? Is this what I am hearing? I have idolized you; I have done everything the right way because I believed in you and God. Now if this is true not only am I not getting married I am going out to get drunk tonight. You know what daddy, in a single moment you have just destroyed every ounce of faith I had in God and all the teachings of the church. To hell with all this! You and Patrick can go to HELL! Sean screamed at Jordan "Who are you talking to? I will deal with you later!"

Sean I was hoping we could do this with dignity tonight but I see we will not be able too, we can meet another time to if you wish. "Abigail no that's ok tonight is just fine". Jordan I am sorry love I love you and admire your strength but I have just seen a good friend of mine dropped dead at my church. A young lady or a demon whatever that was, I am being told by your mother this is my daughter. Sean turns to Abigail "She has to at least be Jordan's age it is impossible Abigail, this cannot be so. Abigail replied "I do know for a fact, Sean you were not aware of this child being in the world I don't think she even knows you are her father. I knew about you and her mother being best friends for years, you attended Eaton and she went to T.A.S.I.S (a branch of the American school in Switzerland in the U.K.). You both studied law at Oxford University. The two of you were supposed to take the world by storm. She loved you and only you. Of course you loved her after all that was your first love. You walked away from the law and her to serve the church, that decision did not sit well with her. None of it made any sense to her according to her for a while you were both living life like you owned the world then one day you announced to her you are taking a trip alone. She knew why I guess, but she could not understand why she was not going with you. Then the plane crash brought you to me. One might say you "crashed" my life. Yes, you had amnesia for a while, then you regained what we thought was all of your memory.

You left the hospital and started your new journey. I went on with my life, I never thought of you again except wondering how you were doing; you did after all spend three months in the hospital with us. Your journey brought you back to the hospital. That is when we ran into each other again. New Years Eve you brought a young man into the hospital; I was the doctor on duty when I saw you again, I knew I was in trouble. I do not know who the worst case was that night, the boy or I. Even though I was a doctor I was an emotionally unwoven basket case, which you thought you could weave back together with compassion. You could have had any woman you desired but you chose me, why I didn't know, but I see now I was nothing but a scape goat with money. I was at the right place at the wrong time. How could I say no to the man whom I thought gave me life? With all my money and knowledge I was still empty. You came to me and I received you like a bowl of pasta to a carbohydrate deprived dieter. I could not get enough of you. We were married and I came with many physiological problems from my past. I spent hours by the pond. I do not know if I started the beheaded procedure or not. She found you again, it seemed every time you were in trouble she showed up. She heard about the bishop that tried to accuse you of having an affair with a prostitute so you could not be appointed Bishop. Even then I was not concerned about our marriage; I knew if not for me, you would never disgrace your God so I thought. That Sunday we went to visit his church. I knew she had sent those seven call- girls to his church while we were visiting and the seven sat on the second row. Everyone was excited, thinking those girls had come to be saved. She sent them, she had learned from one of her clients, who happened to own the escort agency that the bishop l j. was a regular client she paid them to be there and he dropped the charges that next day. That is when she decided to bring her axe out to be sharpened for my head; after all she had you first. I guess she thought you needed her to protect you. When I think about it, who better than her with all her connections? Sean you said "I do" to me but you gave yourself to her! I guess we could say you were in my bed but she was in your head and that is why we are here today.

I spent hours in the book of Genesis studying about Leah and Rachel. The bible states that Leah was not loved by her husband Jacob, who worshiped Rachel. These two women shared one man. I often wonder was I Leah or Rachel? That was so stupid of me to think I could even be Rachel, the love of Jacob. In reality I knew I was Leah; I was not your first pick .As a doctor people came to me broken all the time and I would fix them. I ended up being stuck with a broken heart I could not fix. My insecurities came back and I started searching to be wowed by you. I needed to be wowed by you just as Leah needed to be wowed by Jacob. She gave him all those children, but it was never enough for him to wow her. He loved only Rachel. I even knew when you and she became lovers again [*this time a tear came out of hiding from Abigail's eyes*] I know you fought it Sean I know you did. I put everything into my work I even made time to have our children. It still was not enough for me; you the children or the hospital could not fill this void that had been with me for many years. Then I found out who the real wow giver was and that was God. The same God that noticed Leah was unloved by her husband. (Genesis 29-31. *When the LORD saw that Leah was unloved, He opened her womb, Rachel was barren.* When it was time for Leah to give birth to her 4th child she named him Judah his name means Praise. She thought Jacob would have to love her now for giving him all these sons, but it would not happen. The day came when she stopped trying to please Jacob and started praising her God who gave her grace to go on in an unloved situation she had no control of. The bible says Rachel was barren. Sean I know too well this feeling of barrenness, to be empty and almost dead, nothing can grow in or around you. For years Sean I felt nothing from you, I stand corrected, I felt loveless. We could have labeled our marriage barren. With prayer and fasting the spirit of Praise came back to me. I remembered I was a "Good Thing". Sean, in the midst of it all I raised our three daughters, did not miss a day at the hospital, I ran our household which included paying the help their salary. Whenever you desired me no matter what time of day or night I never said no, then your desire for me stopped but I kept faithful. We could have labeled our love barren. Then you heard she was dying of cancer. She had power wealth and beauty but still she was bitter with God. I knew her better then she thought. I am after all a cousin to her sort. Montana and her they are from the same cloth and I love Montana dearly. (*Satan said "there goes that overrated love thing again*). I once heard one of her employees opened their paycheck, She overheard the girl saying "thank you Jesus". She summoned the girl into her office and asked the girl "whose signature is on her paycheck", "well, yours" the girl had replied confused. She told that poor girl "Then you had better never ever let me hear you thanking him for what I gave you. That name Jesus isn't anywhere on your check, now get the hell out of my office". (Montana muttered that's absolutely right).A different kind of cancer was always eating at her for years and then the real one came for payday. I know she went to the Seychelles hoping to be healed by their witch doctor, she called him an herbalist. When that was not working she called for you to come and pray for her on the other side of the world and you went, probably hoping to save her soul. Sean was shocked; he put his head down into his opened hands." Abigail let me explain". "No Sean, let me finish. You went but you did not pray hard enough for yourself because out of pity I am guessing, you honored her last wish and made love to her. You and she made more than love you both made a child. What a mixture. The seed of a man of God rested in the womb of an Antichrist. Somehow she survived and the baby grew. In her seventh month she came back to America to have her baby and to receive the best medical attention money could buy. Being the legal powerhouse she is, she had everything documented and sent to me to make sure if the child lives and she dies to get the child to her sister in Vienna. She also stated there was no other woman for you and she admired how I fought for you with integrity. I could not believe that she signed herself into my hospital and requested me to be her doctor. I went and visited with her and we spoke for hours. I shared with her how much Jesus loved her and I convinced her to make her peace with God. God came and visited her. She said if this is how Sean felt no wonder he chose God over me. She wanted to make it right so I led her to Christ. And now here we are Sean, with a demonic child of yours and your lover. I don't mind divorcing you Sean, I cannot make you love me, but I will not let you do this to our children.

A couple of nights ago Sean I heard a woman ask a question. "How do I stop loving him?" I am asking right now how I stop loving a lie." Sean's heart instantly returned to its usually coldness as he said "well I see you did your homework so it is all in the open. How did you put it, 'the negatives have been exposed?' I do not care about your feelings Abigail. I love my daughters but I love her as well. I am sorry girls, I have to be with this woman. She is whom I want to spend the rest of my life with. You girls are adults, you do not need me anymore, but if that girl tonight is my daughter she really needs me."

Before anyone could respond to Sean, an angry Abigail encounters him. "How dare you stand here and say these things to your children! What do you think you can do for that possessed girl?! Sean, spiritually you are as dry as the dust. Even your sermons are dry. I would only say Amen because it was my duty as your wife. It's only because of my favor that God has kept you going all these years, you are powerless, you are a like the rotten wine holder that Jesus talks about. He cannot pour any new wine into you. You cannot hold the true anointing of Jehovah. Well, this as good a time as any Sean. Get your things and get out of my House. You have one week to make arrangement to get them all out. Whatever is left, I will cremate and have the ashes delivered to you." Sean looks at Abigail and spits on her. Montana quickly pulls her gun out; the girls are screaming, Abigail grabs her daughters. The gun is resting on Sean's temple when Montana coldheartedly says. "Pull your shirt out and wipe her face otherwise I will be wiping both your brains and spit off her face." Sean looked into Montana's eyes, her pupils were gone, only a black hole stared at him. He knew she wanted him dead more than anything and would use anything as an excuse to kill him. He complied with Montana, not saying a word he used the bottom of his shirt to wipe Abigail's face his hands trembling the whole time. Montana removed the gun from his temple. Sean ran out of the house. Abigail had hold of her petrified daughters and said. "Thank you Montana", Montana wept "I wanted to kill him, Abby how dare he cause all of this turmoil in your life, yet be so arrogant about it, then have the nerve to spit on you!" "I know love," said Abigail, "but Jehovah kept your hands clean to battle another day." Abigail turned and looked at Mona and said "Mother I understand your wish with father's will, but it is not happening. We are all going home to England and giving father a proper burial. Montana, when you get yourself together, please call Gloria to book our flights first thing in the morning. We leave early next week. I am so exhausted. Are you girls ok? Everyone responded yes. They all spent the night with Abigail including Jordan, who still has to pray to God about hers and Patrick's future.

The Journey

It was a grey, cool summer day in Bradford Yorkshire England where Abigail buried her father at the family plot, on the parish church grounds where Abigail attended church as a child. There were only ten people at the funeral, including Mona, Abigail, her daughters and Montana. After the funeral, Montana flew back home to America to prepare for the hearing. Abigail walks the grounds of her father's estate with her mother. Mona squeezes Abigail's hand, as they walk the grounds Mona says "Every business tycoon has wanted to purchase this property to build English country side estate homes or hotels, but your father always said no, he would say, "maybe my Abby will come back home." Mona stopped and looked at Abby and said "please use the property for your ministry. The cottage is surrounded with forget-me-not flowers. Oh, Abby let's call it the 'Forget me not' retreat! "Mother, that is a brilliant idea!" Abigail beamed, "women will come here to remember who and whose they really are, and some will be reintroduced to themselves." "Oh yes Abby let's do it!" her mother replied, "Oh and I almost forgot, Abby, Wellington phoned. He is sorry about daddy, but he is on safari in Kenya otherwise, he would be here." Abigail's heart fluttered a little at the sound of her good friend's name. "Oh that was nice of him, I am sure he and his family are having a lovely time. Mother, walking these grounds of forget me not's, is causing me to hear the cries Gabriella had informed me of. I hear the voices of the women, it's only a whisper, as fragile as the flower is. I hear 'do not forget us.'"

Mona replied, "Abigail as a child you would sit by the brook with the flowers, the blue bells and the forget-me-nots. You were always fascinated of how each of the forget-me -nots had five blue petals with a sun in the center. You had theorized that the yellow center represented that God is in the center of all their troubles." Mona sat thinking for a minute then said "I will make the necessary arrangements this will be a retreat by this time next year. Here we will also have a memorial for those who have lost their lives from crimes of passion and our sisters which were battered and murdered. The world will know their cries were real."

After assisting her mother with the legal matters of her father's estate, Abigail flew back to America to face Sean and the Bishops. Montana met Abigail at the airport. The two women hugged. "We have three days left to prepare Abby, are you ready for all of this? He has gone public with this amnesia crap; it is a circus." Abigail sighed and said , "I Am ready Montana. Let's get this mess over with." Just as soon as Abigail said that, in came the media throwing questions at her. "Mrs. Monroe is it true that you married a man who was delirious and did not know who he was? Montana's bodyguards took care of the press and safely got Abigail into the car.

The next morning, there was a meeting with the board of the hospital. Abigail was informed that it is best if she takes a leave of absence while the hearing is going on. The hospital does not need the negative publicity. Abigail was not surprised someone on the board had shared this info with Montana, but it still penetrated into her heart. She had given so much of herself to the hospital, and now at her time of need, they will not stand with her. She graciously agreed and walked out smiling as she thought of the forget me not flowers. The hospital has chosen to forget her. Abigail went to the pond. Gabriella was waiting on her.

"Abigail do not be hurt. This is all a part of God's plan for you. Your time at the hospital is over. Your appointment book has been cleared, but God has reappointed you to a new chapter of your life. Sean's plans will not go any further than God will allow. You are not alone on this earth. In due season, you will reap what you have sown. Tomorrow has already been prepared for you. Fear no one, and tell the truth. The lover of your soul has not forgotten you. Abigail there is a German folk legend that while God was naming all the plants, a tiny plant fell out and cried 'forget-me-not O Lord"! God replied "that shall be your name." God will not forget you, Abigail. Gabriela disappeared. "Ok, pond", said an encouraged Abigail, let's see what this new chapter will be in my life."

# Montana's Arrival

The black limo slowly pulled up to the Great halls of Bishops. This is the place where pastors, elders and ministers meet to bring a charge against the illegal actions taking place in this particular denomination. The chauffer gets out and opens the door. As soon as the media sees Montana, they swarm the limo. The police remove the press so Montana can get out of the limo. The door opens, a set of navy leather pumps with five-inch heels hit the concrete, her slate gray silky sheer stocking leg appears, and then the other leg. Her knees bend as the rest of her six foot slender runway body appears. It is draped in a navy and salmon pinstripe linen suit with a salmon silk shell. There were more legs than any other part of her body. Her Chanel briefcase matches the purse hanging off her shoulders. She looks stunning. "Montana!" the crowd calls "will you be representing the bishop's wife, Abigail?" Then another voice "you give it to those stinking bishops Montana! make them hurt!" "is she in the car with you?" someone asked. ... "Yes, I will hurt them and no she is not in the car" She replied bluntly, as to not lose focus on the task at hand. She prepares to walk up the many steps to the arena of bishops that await her. Montana was hoping the Bishops of twelve districts plus their leader would have given Abigail a closed hearing before this went public, but it was too late. Someone in that group of twelve she hopes will have the nerve to shut Sean up and sit him down if he starts to disgrace Abigail. She is hoping he remembers the gun on his temple. Like a gladiator, Montana takes each step while contemplating the joy of her victory. Arrangements were made so Abigail could escape the circus of media and well-wishers.

# MONTANA OPENING

There is such silence and anticipation mixed with the stench of mothballs and stale cigars in the atmosphere of the great halls of bishops. Abigail gracefully walks in to the room. She is wearing a navy and white polka dot two-piece suit accented with a wide brim red hat and navy shoes. She slowly removes her white gloves as she makes her way to Montana's table where a chair awaits her. Montana had Abigail brought to the back of the great hall in a secret car to avoid the press. Mona, Abigail's mother always dressed her in polka dots when she was a little girl. She would say to her. "If you ever get bored or nervous my dear count the dots." Montana starts by saying.

"Good morning Bishops, my name is Montana P Emanuel. I will be representing Dr. Abigail Monroe. We are here today because my client's husband decides he does not want to be married to her anymore, he wants an annulment. The man is head of the household, right? After all your good book does say so in Ephesians 5th chapter 22:23… *Wives submit your selves unto your own husband as unto the Lord. For the husband is the head of the wife.* Bam! There it is gentlemen. I cannot help but feel Dr. Monroe is being treated like Joan of Arc, who was burned to the stake. Correct me if am wrong in your bible 1st Corinthians 7th chapter 9thvrs does it not say. *For it is better to marry than to burn.* Is that not correct? Or is she to be treated like Ann Boleyn the wife of HenryV111. And be executed in the way of being beheaded from her husband's headship? We are here today because her husband, the Bishop wants to pursuit his pleasure in the arms of another. Are you going to let your bible be made a mockery of? It says, I quote, in 1st Timothy 3:2. *"The bishop is to be the husband of one wife, holy and blameless."* I also peeked into" *2nd Timothy 3rd 1-5 it quotes. This know also, that in the last days perilous times shall come. For men shall be lovers of their own selves, covetous boasters, proud, blasphemers, disobedient to parents, unthankful, unholy. Without natural affection trucebreakers, false accusers, incontinent, fierce, despisers of those that are good.*

Timothy must be talking about the Bishop Sean Monroe, the truce breaker and me by the way my middle initial "P" it stands for Perilous and I have arrived like your good book says. Let us take the words blameless, innocent, untarnished, scrupulous etc. If you grant this annulment to the bishop, not only will the blame of this great injustice rest on your shoulders, but you will strip his daughters of their birthrights, a name that is rightfully theirs. The children were conceived after the marriage . You will all be at blame if you give him the power to ordain his children bastards. None of you will be blameless. Montana's opening was interrupted.

Four beautiful women walked in all in tailored multicolored suits and all with veiled hats. Montana's first thought was "oh my goodness, not again" the last time she saw a veiled hat, it was on Manuela. She was at ease when she saw Abigail stood up to greet them. Abigail had a Look of shock and joy upon her face. Montana continued." Bishop Monroe has told the public as we heard on CNN all week, that he is recovering from amnesia. When he first met his wife he was really engaged to the love of his life, who he wishes to finish his life with, and would want you, the holy court of bishops to believe that the last twenty odd years never happened. He is requesting that you too use your power, like some cheap sorcerer to make it all go away. Therefore, he can still be in good standing with the church. Dr. Abigail married this man for better or for worst. Again I believe it was Paul that said in your bible "*it was better to marry than it was to burn*" so either way it seems like my client got married but yet you are ready to burn her. "Blow torches anyone?"

The bishops are numb. They have never encountered anyone like Montana before. They don't realize she has just got started. Montana removed the black cotton scarf that was covering a block of wood with an axe resting on it, she lifted the axe up and slammed it into the wood and said. "Gentlemen here it is, the axe so you can behead the family. I do not understand why we are even here. Personally I wonder if Bishop Monroe was not as wealthy and powerful as he is, would we even be here? However I was invited into this arena and I accepted the invitation and here I am, and gentlemen trust me I will not leave defeated. I myself am not governed by your bible, but please gentlemen do not get confused. I am a very learned scholar of the 66 books of your bible. In the days of your lord and savior, Abigail would have been giving a letter of divorcement. Listen to me carefully, Montana pointed to Sean "your good old boy Monroe had intercourse with my client, a virgin wife she was." The bishops all stared at each other and shook their heads. "I have only this to ask (And then more drama.)

Montana's butler came in with a glass filled with ice and a pot of hot tea. Montana picked up an ice cube and said. "This is an ice cube it knows it is an ice cube it delights in being that, now when hot tea is poured over the ice, it dissolves into the tea. It is no longer an ice cube. It has no more form or shape, one could say it has lost its identity. It has become one with the tea". Montana holds up the glass of tea she reaches into the other glass and picks up an ice cube slowly she walks around the circle of Bishops looking each one in the eye like a lioness ready to hunt. Every one anticipating what is she going to say next... "Gentlemen if you can tell me how to go into this tea and get the ice cube back out of the tea and get it back to its original shape and identity, if you can perform this miracle, then your Bishop can have his annulment. You see gentlemen, my client became one with him and gave up her identity, and now she is to be told it never happened. Oh hell, excuse me. No gentlemen, Abigail Monroe was his cup of tea and I will not allow him to throw her out as a useless tea bag. "Bishops we all know your good book states "none is without sin" I do not know what the bishop has threatened you with. But I promise you if I have to, gentlemen I will go back and research into each of your lives from the time you were conceived. I will know who likes girls and who likes boys who like toys and drugs. I will even locate your birth marks. Your bank accounts in this country and abroad will be looked into. Can you say IRS? I am reading your faces now, you are thinking 'can she do this"? Gentleman trust me, have nothing to lose. Not only can I do it but the perilous one will do it. The one you can blame for bringing me into your lives is Bishop Monroe.

Dr Abigail is also my cousin if her life is to be wrecked I swear to you right here and now I will (Montana paused)…Montana again holds up an ice cube She could not resist. Being Montana, she put the ice cube toward her mouth but let it accidentally drop on her chest as she walked around the circle of bishops. She did not blink an eye as she reached down her blouse to remove the ice and put the ice in her mouth and continues. "I will bring every one of you down with her as said I do not have a God conscience. If I have too I will turn over every one of your churches from here to Europe until I find what I need to destroy every one of you. There is not too much good in my life but my cousin Abigail is dripping with integrity. She is what I refer to as a Good woman. Over my dead body gentlemen, will anyone stain her reputation by trying to render her the bishop's whore" Montana reached for a penny at the desk. "This penny says in "God we trust". You had better trust that He gets to you first, to do the right thing before I do. Give her the dignity she deserves and grant this annulment a mistrial. If she is to be beheaded then grant her a public execution of divorce. Gentlemen I do believe we have here a Judah and Tamar situation. Here you can find that in Gneisses 38th chapter. Good day gentleman I wait to hear from you.

Montana walked out of the arena. She strutted like a gladiator who has just been declared victorious in battle. The invited guests were all on their feet clapping. Madison looked at Montana with great admiration.

Montana had exhausted the bishops. The youngest one on the panel was 60 years old. They were not prepared for what they had heard and they surely were not ready for the ugly press the church was getting from all of this. They all loved Abigail, but they also had been handpicked by Sean. Every one of them were in great debt to him and he wanted to collect if they did not comply with his wishes, but knows the question they are now left with is do they fear Montana and her threat more than Sean. They realize Montana is smart. It was like they were the ones on trial and not Sean.

Not even Sean was expecting this kind of response from the press around the world. The hearing was adjourned for three days. Madison walked up to Montana and said "I have heard about you, now I know the rumors are true. I would hate to have wasted my talent on a wimp." Montana replied, "So you're the mighty whore who hunts other women's head's. I do not know why my cousin would not let me expose you. I do not care because if they keep this up I am bringing you down too." Madison glanced at Abigail and nodded her head; she still had that sympathetic look in her eyes. Madison then turned back towards Montana and said "about that whore thing; I guess it takes the original to recognize the copy."

Montana did not want to entertain Madison anymore. She was distracted by the way Madison looked at a couple of the four women that came in and Madison bowed her head to the women in a monk style greeting. Madison whispered something to Sean and left the meeting.

Montana turned around to Abigail, "what is going? On who are these women how come Madison knows a couple of them"? Abigail kissed Montana and said "you did well Montana. Let us go home and let the Lord do the rest." What rest? I have already done the work." Abigail laughed and shook her head at her nutty cousin, "Come on Montana, I have guests to attend too."

# THE OVER COMERS

The women entered Abigail's house ecstatic with what they had seen and heard from Montana. When Montana arrived, the women cheered her on "bravo! Bravo!" said one of the women, another said "so this is the mighty Montana Abigail has spoken so much of?" "Yes." said Abigail as she walked over to Montana and hugged her. Abigail has helped all these women in one- way or another. They were some of the 'bleeding' women that were scattered on the roads which were leading to Abigail's destiny. The women's group in Abigail's church is called Broken Wings International. This chapter from Abigail's church is linked to other battered women shelters around the world. Every now and then a case which Abigail could not ignore would come across her desk. She would financially support the International cases so her local center would not suffer the chance of being bankrupt. Flying families around the world can be very expensive, some cases are life threatening. They and their children must leave the country. These four women live in different parts of the world and come from different lifestyles, but they all have one thing in common, they survived life after being 'beheaded.' Some also escaped the beatings that could have led to death.

*Autumn*

Was first to arrive she is true to her name. She is a welcome change to any group. Her strong presence comes with a lot of warmth, just like the beautiful glow from an autumn sunset

*Penelope*

As stunning as any run way model, always having great confidence in who she is. She often rubs people the wrong way, especially when she allows her mind to be vocal. She knows what she wants and goes after

120

it unapologetically. The word fail has been erased from her vocabulary. Opportunity is her word of choice.

*Frances*

Is the one mothers would probably accuse of, "still waters running deep". She is very quiet, but when she speaks everyone listens. She doesn't get worked up about too much but if you were to rub her wrong, you would wish it was poison ivy that had stung you instead of her.

*Grace*

The day she was born, her father heard these words from the Lord. "She is the beginning of your strength." She is a milder Montana but one who loves the Lord

*Jane (has not arrived yet)*

God's true wonder, L.O.M.S. is what she calls the Lord "The lover of my soul" she went from having no trust in anyone or anything, to the one everyone trusts and depends on.

Abigail greeted each of the women. "I know some of you are shocked to have learned of Sean and my problems, especially having to find out this way. Autumn said, "only one thing matters Abby, we are here to be with you." "Thank you." said Abby. True friendship is not something I take lightly. Friendship is like a marriage it takes a lot of work, more so if the fit is not just right at first. I thank each one of you for being that section of my life that would have been an empty space if you were not part of it. I should have shared earlier of what was going on with Sean and I, but I did not have time to. I was spending so much time with denial for many years.

Autumn said "We are here now and we have something for you"; the ladies gave Abigail a beautiful box wrapped in blue satin-like paper with a thin silk yellow bow. Abigail slowly opened the present; her heart melts as tears travel falls from her eyes. She gently removes the fragile crystal gift; it is a crystal bunch of for-get-me-not flowers, every detail was given to make them resemble fresh cut flowers. She caressed each of the ladies with love and thanked them, even Montana was moved. After the women settled, Abigail shared with the group all what she had learned at the conference with Miss Emanuel. She shared about the headhunters and the pain of being beheaded, and the succubus, incubus and disarming Satan. The women were fascinated by it all and wanted to know how to get to hear the woman who seems to put their pain and trial into perspective.

"As the years went on, I realized something worst was happening. I was losing me. I was 'missing' me; I guess I can say I forgot me. Abigail picked up her glass of chilled mint tea to sip from, then, on second thought, she held up the glass to the women and said "This tea reminds me of one of my many bad days in the midst of this hell I resided in. I was sitting with my husband at a restaurant sipping iced tea. I placed my glass down, I could not help but notice the ice was melting away into the tea. Strangely it was drawing me to its tragedy, the once beautiful crystal ice cube was slowly melting away. No longer was it in existence, there was no shape or form to the ice any more. The ice cube had conformed into this brown liquid called tea. The ice had no voice, how could the ice prove it ever existed? The tears started to explode I, for a moment, felt like I was one of the melting ice cubes. I was melting away and losing my identity. I had no shape or form to my life, no meaning at all, just liquid and I was leaking away. I freely gave up my name, my heart no longer knew a regular beat. It would now beat to the drums of rejection and betrayal. My surname has been melted away. I had become one with this man whose name I am trying so hard to hold on to he never once noticed what I was going through, he was too busy eating.

When we get married we should refer to our status as being born again. Think about it, of course we are. We are given another name, sealed with it is the "until death do we part" quote. So divorce, I thought, must be one of the many faces of death. I was going crazy that day and by the look on some of your faces you still think I am. Oh and yes, I told Montana the story that is where she got the ice idea from, but I did not have anything to do with the end part (everyone laughed)

A man has to learn to listen to his wife. I said a lot to Sean, but he did not see to hear. [*Everyone looked at her strange again*] put it this way when a hearing-impaired person comes to our place of worship, we have those that do sign language to communicate to them. They have to see the signs to hear them. That's how it is with women who scream out for help in so many ways, too many times our signs are not read, our cries fall on blinded eyes. Maybe if some men had learned to see what their wives were saying to them, maybe they would still be alive today instead of being a self inflicted victim of a crime of passion. Society always says. "She just lost it, or the famous "she's lost her head" that is right, she lost it alright. She lost her head to another woman. The head of her household is no longer available to reason with. Therefore, she loses her mind but, sometimes revenge commands retaliation. She is then driven to commit murder.

"Only He can satisfy that which belongs to Him." Grace nodded in agreement and said "wow, say that again Abby." Yes only God the lover of our soul can satisfy what belongs to him, he created us. There is a place in our mind that only God can enter and reason with us, believe me, there is such a place in our mind that he alone can enter to communicate with us. It is there we receive the knowledge of self validation. Everyone this time whispered "Wow"

I had a vision one day of women's faces. I could not recognize anyone, it was as if they were lost in a blue type fog. I was standing in the middle of them, in this beautiful dress but I could not see my face. I was draped in a beautiful veil, on top of the veil was a golden crown with odd stones. Actually there was not a head, my shoulders were strong supporting a bloody neck. I could hear their voices clearly and words were floating around, I was able to make them out.

Their blood soaked graves screamed out to me. "We are SHE. Who HE said would be no more. He stripped us from our S. and we became He Losing our identity, we gave up our selves never finding our way back. We lacked Strength, Self esteem, and Salvation. We stopped... Being S.H.E. Seeking Holiness Endlessly... In our seeking for love, DEATH found us. Do not let our dying be in vain. Walk in strength and self esteem. Integrity is the first step of survival. We never knew how to survive." I woke up so tearful. I am still haunted by this lack of integrity, which allows us to fall apart. Integrity as we all know, means to be whole. Whoever those women were, they were not whole. I imagine some were killed and others committed suicide all because someone did not hear or see their cry for help. I understood moving the

S. from she and it was all about he. I see the S. as removing ourselves from She. We no longer exist.

All of us here today understands the suicide thought, how it first starts by making you feel like you are a total failure, then the depression and all the demonic voices are cheering you on to take your life and be done with this misery."

The room was silent, each woman was reminiscing of their moment of suicide. Montana was pacing the floor. Abigail grabbed her by the hand and said "sit next to me." Abigail continued. "I need some recipes for a book I am writing. I need your formula of how every one of you survived the bitter taste that Hell sent your way, into your marriage and your lives. How did you get the strength to turn your neck to wisdom and get back to living after the beheading of your marriage? Why do you think you survived while many bled to death during the execution of divorce? Why do think after being beaten black and blue almost to death, that you were able to look fear in the eye and denounce its hold over you? We have books to help us if we are too fat or too skinny, don't know how to do our hair and makeup, but while I was going through hell with the bishop there was nothing out there I could relate too. So many people see the axe coming but feel helpless. Oh there were books that almost touched on my problem but I wanted to read things like "what do I tell my friend if her husband is hitting on another woman or even hitting on me? What if my friend is hitting on my other friend's husband? Or who do I go too if the lust train is heading right into my life and I badly want a man that I know is not fit to be around my children, but I am burning with desire? I am as hot as a speeding train rail. Who do I tell my husband is having sex with a spirit while I watch? Why does someone feel like there is no one they can turn to, and the only answer is to allow the spirit of justification to convince them to turn to death".

# AUTUMN

Autumn, was staring into her glass of mint ice tea as if she was melting away. Expressionless, she looked up and said "that's a brilliant idea Abigail. That is why we are all here today, because you are the one we could all come too; you bonded all of us like a rich leather cover of a priceless book. We have the cover now. Let us fill the book. Every one said "Autumn, that is a great analogy." Thank you please let me go first. The women all moved from the dining room to the sofa room. There are seven different colored oversized couches, three chaise longue, and large tropical plants. Abigail will often pray in this room. With a crackling voice, Autumn began to tell her story.

"Some women get roses often some may only get them on special occasion. A tear rolled down Autumn's cheeks. With a clinched fist, she said "I would have been grateful for just one petal to hold on too. Instead all I ever received was stems and thorns; the red of the roses was replaced by my red blood that ran down the stems. If it was possible to hear tears falling Niagara Falls was in the room there was not a dry eye in the room except Montana.

Autumn went on to say "My husband had a Salome. She gets all the rose petals, his love, his tenderness, his understanding. All that was left for me were thorns of rejection; I cannot touch him without being stung by him. It was not always like that. We were like two wild animals. We could not get enough of the hunt. The Mediterranean was our playground, he hunted and I maneuvered. He had never liked getting anything easy. Our passion was electrifying, we were iron sharpening iron sparks would fly everywhere until we became one big flame that generated enough heat to melt Siberia in January. Then, the hunt was over. The kill had been performed. You know when a man and woman play those kinds of games. Unless you are grounded in whom you are, it is dangerous. The bible warns us not to awaken love before it pleases. Songs of Solomon 2:7 *that you not stir up or awaken love until it pleases.* *... swear to me that you will not awaken love or arouse love before its proper time!* Well, I must have woken it up, and I wished many times I could put it back into a coma. When I say the kill has been performed, by that I mean he taught me different ways to come out of my den [your identity] into his. Then, right when you have mastered pleasing him and him only, you are so much into the game you don't even realize that you don't matter anymore, you have alienated your friends, your family, even your favorite hobbies. Somewhere in midst of it all I disappeared, the kill was performed. I had become like a stuffed and mounted animal on his wall. Our house became a detox center, occasionally needing a fix from each other, but then that stopped. I guess I was not appetizing to him anymore. He wanted to change the venue and of course the menu. It seems like sometimes a woman gets punished for having children. He would look at me as if I was the most disgusting creature on earth, I had not lost my baby fat soon enough for him. Soon enough meant within in the six weeks, I went from being "sweetie this" and "sweetie that" to being sugar free, no sugar at all. I could not do or say anything right. For heaven sake if I knew what I was doing wrong I would try to fix it! But I never knew what.

Autumn was in tears once more, and she was not alone. Abigail kept her arms around her. "We can stop." whispered Abigail. "No, it's ok," said Autumn, "remember I survived." She continued.

"One night, he went to a bachelor party. I heard the women were wearing Victoria secrets kind of stuff. He of course confined to one of the Victoria's about our secret. That I was not desirable to him anymore, and I could not satisfy him. That information was directed to Hell, then, Hell dispatched the Salome spirit. It entered into one of the women, she then danced right into our lives, chainsaw and all. She was one of our church members, she was always smiling in my face. The most remarkable thing about her, she looked so wholesome, so innocent. I believe David said it best in Psalms 55:21. *The words of his mouth were smoother than butter, but war was in his heart. 22: His words were softer than oil, yet they were drawn swords.* While her words were pleasant to me, she had declared war on my household, sword drawn and ready for my beheading. I had found credit card receipts, roses were being sent to her work place, wide assortments of jewelry had also been purchased. He is a sugar daddy and that's all. The children and I had to do without so many times so he could support his habit with her. I should have left him, but I was scared he had become so violent. I could always tell when she had turned him down. The stems and thorns would come out of him and he would be boiling with rage. He would beat me bloody for what seemed like hours. One night, I did run and I went to a women's shelter for help. My father heard I was at the shelter, he came for me. I thought he was bringing me to his house, instead he said I needed to go back to my husband. Without hearing my side of the story, he proceeded in taking me back to the house where the tormenter awaited my return. My father said I should remember who I was in the community. Every one gasped," that bastard" said Montana. Autumn, continued. "After all, I was the pastor's wife, the first lady of the church and I could not bring shame to him or the church. I was called the "first lady," but in all honesty, I was the furthest from first in his life, but I was the first he would blame when things went wrong. My face would be the first thing his fist would make contact with, my stomach would be the first thing his feet could find to kick. So you see ladies, a petal would have been lovely. Abigail squeezed her hand to continue. They all said with tearful eyes "well, what happened?" "My father dropped me home and handed me over to my husband. After my father left, my husband had nothing to say to me so I went up to the children's bedroom. While putting the children to bed, my bruised face scared them. My 8 year old daughter said 'I want to kill daddy mummy" I told her she was safe and her daddy loved her. I went into the guest bedroom, the spirit of justification visited with me. While I was communicating with the spirit of suicide, we all had a cup of tea and they helped me justify why

I was doing the right thing by killing myself. They must have been very persuasive, because I got hold of my migraine pills and swallowed as many as I could. My husband must have come into the room to pound on me some more but I had beaten him to it, this time I was first. He must have called 911. I had slipped into a coma. While in the coma, I saw this bright beautiful light; I heard a voice in the light saying to me. *I am the rose of Sharon, my precious petal. Like a Lilly among thorns, so is my love among the daughters. I have already worn the thorns that were pierced into my head for you, dear one, So you may live. I know your pain. Just as I had to forgive them; I need you to forgive him. So I can heal you. As you walk through the valley of the shadows of death, remember a shadow cannot appear without the light. I am with you.*

Four days later when I became conscious, I noticed my husband was there waiting for me. I thought "wow, Jesus worked quickly! My husband cared and he loves me." He was here in my room waiting for me, I was so happy. Then reality checked in real quick. He said "are you awake?" I smiled and said yes, as I reached out my arms toward him, he grabbed my arms with a grip of death. It felt like my bones where being crushed. Then, he said "how dare you do this to me! You should have died." I looked at him, and all I saw was a shadow of a man, then it all made sense. I said "you know what, I completely forgive you, my husband," as I pulled my arms away from him, that enraged him all the more. Do you know that man lifted his hand to beat me in the hospital? At that precise moment, my father walked in. He must have just stepped out from the room, because they told me he never left my side. His eyes were swollen from crying. "You touch her and I will kill you with my bare hands. Whichever part of Hell that is tormenting you boy, you and it get out of here." He ran out like the coward he was. My father's voice sounded like a Calvary had arrived to take over. He fell at my bedside and asked my forgiveness. He said he had not wanted to accept the possibility that the bruises on me were from my husband, who told him I fell down the stairs.

He also thought I was exaggerating at the shelter. He knew how cruel some churchwomen can be and I would be the one the church would turn their back on if I left. Somehow I would be the one to be accused of being unfaithful. He then said, "you would have been without the head of your household, you would have been headless my dear, but now I see I was the first head God put over you, Autumn and as long there is breath in my body I will protect you and the children." I said 'thank you, but no thanks father".

My parents were at old age when they conceived me. I was only sixteen when my mother died. They said they named me Autumn because I was a wonderful change in their life. My mother said I eliminated the barren spirit from her, and I should always remember how loved I am.

Now it was my time to eliminate my pain. The physical pain goes away faster than the mental. In all the years with him, I have suffered broken ribs, internal bleeding, fractured jaw, broken nose, detached retina, and miscarried three times. He had a convincing excuse for each one. But I survived!

There were some yellow roses by my bedside, I took a petal and said "father I am like a fallen petal for now, but from this petal bushes will grow and the Lilly, him, Jesus, will be among our thorns. He sobbed, but understood what I must do. The next day Abigail rescued me from the hospital, got my children for me, and here I am my friend, to do whatever I can. **My personal 'recipe' for your book Abigail, is**:

1st. I had to acknowledge I was a battered woman.

2nd. that he did not love me, that was hard even, now it stings a little.

3rd. I had to find out who I was

4th. I had to forgive him.

5th. I had to love me more than him and allow my future to be.

While I was waiting at the courtroom I overheard these two legal clerks conversing about a similar case which they were gathering information for 'Smith vs. Long". These cases had been won on certain principles and rulings. It is all documented and filed away. So all they had to do to win their client's case is to use the information which already has been tried and proven and is available to them as a weapon. Then it hit me. I started to go to the only legal book I know, where certain things about my life have been legally documented. God vs.

Satan, it is documented in the book of Proverbs- God said *"when a man finds a wife he finds a (G.T.) GOOD THING. And obtains favor from God"*. I went into the mirror, took a good look at myself I smiled and said" hello G.T". It does not matter how I was beheaded, I am still a Good Thing, and God cannot lie. I need to know there is a WOW giver. The word says 'a man who finds a wife finds a good thing". Even with all of our flaws, like a precious jewel some of us are still waiting to be found. Autumn's voice was rising. Him who has created us has named us Good thing; Jesus himself says "there is none that is good". Ah but our heavenly father created marriage from the goodness of his pure heart. He wanted man to feel what goodness felt like by creating a wife for him to be good to. Autumn rose up and started walking around the room, looking each woman in the eye. You have to realize, first of all, you are named and called Good Thing by God, and if that is not enough for you, remember you do not come empty handed to your husband. You come with FAVOR. It is documented in the will of God. That makes God the greatest of all 'wow givers.' If God sees it fit to call you a Good Thing, I do not care what anyone else calls you or how you are treated. You just need to remember it is written and documented and available for all to read and hear. Autumn had electricity charged all over her, "Abigail" she said, "this must go in your book. Women, you are someone's Good Thing! No matter what state you are in at this moment. Maybe you are in a battered situation, or a loveless marriage. It does not change the fact that you are a Good Thing. I still have a problem doing something so simple as opening a can of biscuits, when the carton pops open I still get a little shaken from the sound. That's evidence of being battered but I am still a good thing. Don't you let a devil in Hell convince you differently because man did not name you this, God did and God cannot lie. Autumns voices elevated "Good Things hold your head up high!" Oh, let me finish before I end up preaching. Every one said 'that's alright" Autumn continued

"My problem was I tried ending my destiny, I was so consumed with self-pity. Self-pity is nothing more than us being consumed with ourselves, our rejection, our pain etc, etc. You become a one-man show. That is how I managed to shut God out from my life. Self-pity had convinced me that not even God cared about my feelings, or me. We cannot be man's complete Good thing until we find out how to first be good to our selves. To be able to finally say "I am more than my faults." Glory!! That can only come through the love of Jesus. I needed to first love myself, and have confidence in God's work. His word says "*we are fearfully and wonderfully made*". Even when you are not able to believe that you are wonderful, trust God's heart and his word. Trust him and know there is no other like you. He created me in his own image no one else has been given neither my purpose nor my assignment for being here. I am one of his masterpieces, never to be duplicated. When the afterbirth was discarded from my mother's womb, that was the same as breaking the mold. I came from her never to be duplicated. I had to forgive those that I felt had hurt me. I do not mean verbal forgiveness. Do I mean I had to go and find those people from years ago? No. I had to walk through this type of forgiveness. (Everyone looked puzzled). Okay this is what I mean. The only way you can know if you have truly forgiven someone from whatever it was that wounded you is you have to face it, if you respond to it with destructive action, God will keep that thing around until you are able to disarm its power over you with positive action. He will keep bringing it your way to walk it through. Take a journey in the word visit with David in the Psalms or his son Solomon's writings in Proverbs. Meditate night and day, the word of God will give you strength.

I met with my husband and I forgave him, was it easy? Actually by the time I went to confront him, it was. He still has his church and he has remarried. The good ole boys always protect their own. Pride would have me to try and prove to the church that he was to blame and not me, but for what? So I can deny my future its rightful place while being trapped in my past? Everyone said "repeat that!" Autumn, lifted her hands up and boldly proclaimed "I will not deny my future its rightful place in my life by being trapped to my past, Glory be to God, He is good!

From my experience came the birthing of the P.E.T.A.L ministry. (Providing Empowerment to all Ladies) I am proud to say my father works with us. In our services while we are ministering to women.

Those in need of help will slip a petal to us, we will then motion one of our warriors and they will take it from there and try to meet their needs. One evening, a woman who had heard about us brought us a blood stained stem and collapsed at the altar. She had multiple fractures and internal bleeding. She heard a message I had shared at a woman's breakfast telling women if or when you get rosés keep them, even if they are dried up, just in case you need to send us a petal which will let us know it is a cry for help. If they put a little oil and water on the petal it will not break while holding on to it. The woman is fine today we also took care of her hospital bills thanks to a secret donation. Our motto is… I am more than my pain! Our ministry is in five different countries, and flourishing. "praise God!" The women all exclaimed. They all hugged each other wiping tears and mascara off of each other's faces.

Montana got up to get some tea, she was silent as the others were asking "who wants to go next?" for Abby's book.

# PENELOPE

Penelope said "I guess God has been working with his roses all over this nation. My husband, Baxter and I always knew we wanted to be in the ministry together. We had so many dreams and we saw a lot of them come true. We were traveling all over the world ministering on prosperity. I always thought there were many ministers preaching to the brokenhearted, while the broken hearted were going poor and in some cases could not even pay their rent. During this trip, we were in Paris to do a week long seminar for a church of ten thousand members. While on our way to the service my husband received a call from his cell phone. It was a man's voice saying "he was at the Eiffel tower and it was very important he talked to him about a business deal. That was not unusual seeing we had a few business partners around world every now and then someone will find out we are in their country and will have an offer for a business that is going under and we will either buy or pass. We just happened to be one block from the tower when the call came in, so our driver dropped my husband off then he drove me to the church. He was to go back to get Baxter in one hour. We wanted to arrive early so we could set up the books and CDs, and do sound checks, so Baxter had plenty of time. But I did not hear from my husband all night. I had to do the seminar alone. They made a big deal of how my husband was out doing God's work on the streets of Paris. After three days of hearing nothing we called the police, but they had no leads. The driver was interrogated and was released. Baxter had never done anything like this before. I just knew my husband was dead, but I did not want to come to terms with it. We lived in the beautiful Basil, Switzerland, close to the borders of France and Germany. Many of our friends came to Paris to be with me, which was great, it was the only way I was able to continue the seminar. My last night in Paris, I was startled by a stranger that looked like my husband in our hotel room. His eyes looked strange, he muttered something along the lines of "he did not love me anymore and I will be better without him and may God help him" and he ran out, Just like that. I was... You know what? Neither English German nor the French dictionary had the words to explain what I felt. I went to a planet away from earth where I understood nothing. I could not recognize this place, I had never visited this pain before. When I thought he was dead I felt better than what I felt at that moment, how can that be possible? Death is a process our brain has to come to terms with eventually. However the unknown mixed with unbelief, betrayal and a self-destructive anger gives our brain a challenge for reasoning. I could not conduct the last night's service, they understood. I returned to Basil, I do not remember anything about my trip home, except when I got to the house I was thinking I was ready to walk into a building that was once my home. I left there some one's wife, the happiest woman on earth.

I have never suffered with asthma but all of a sudden, there is no air in my house. In an almost delusional state, I thought "did someone leave the gas on to kill me? Did my house somehow move to mars, a place with no oxygen and no one informed me of this? Because dear God, I cannot breathe, I am suffocating I am dying. The great interruption had arrived and I was not ready for it, and why should I have been? I thought everything was fine. I was trying to take short breaths, but my heart felt like I was having a bypass surgery and someone forgot to give me anesthetic. The pain is unbearable, there isn't anyone around to inform, to stop the operation, they have the wrong patient. My throat feels like a baseball glove that has caught a ball which had been pitched at 100 miles per hour from my erupting stomach and it is depriving me from even swallowing my own saliva. I see who I am supposed to be in the pictures, I see this happy couple all over the house. The aroma of his cologne is familiar. I thought, must be in a nightmare, someone wake me up please and tell me it is not so. I blamed God for everything; I had done all the right things all my life. I had only known one man and that is my husband. I asked God "had he abandoned me as well and run off like my husband?" Because I could not feel him, so now I am also Godless. I entered into a planet of hate I never knew existed, and I took residence there for a term. Also, something else was happening.

I went from not wanting food to trying to eat everything in sight, [every one chuckled] I went to the kitchen one night to fry an egg, I opened the carton, and the egg I chose was stuck to the carton, I could not get it out. I observed it carefully, the egg had been leaking, all the life had been slowly sipping through a crack that nobody could see, but it was there, and the egg would not budge. I was determined to move it this was the egg I wanted, not one of the other eleven but this one and I was determine to have that one but it would not budge, the stupid thing was stuck to the carton, I grabbed it and tried twisting it, but it broke. The white part of the egg had seeped through a crack and the substance clung itself to the carton, just a dried useless yoke was left, and for the first time, I cried since that horrible night in Paris. It was not a regular cry, I was hysterical, and had completely lost my mind. I gazed at that egg with so much anger. Someone had put that egg in that carton, it passed inspection I am sure, it made its way to the super market where I shopped, and no one at all noticed something was wrong because its final destiny was to torment me. I grabbed three or four eggs shell and all and tossed them into the bowl I stared at the carton where the egg I chose was still resting, the shell still stuck to the carton, I screamed at the egg, "you are the one I chose! Not those, and you are no good just as he is! I hate you!" I walked out of the kitchen and went to bed and stayed there for days. Six days later, Baxter called to ask for my forgiveness. 'Help me I am stuck" he kept on saying, I told him when hell freeze over, until then he can enjoy his vacation with Satan. (Montana said 'that's what I'm talking about)". That same night I had a strange dream, I dreamed I was in a valley and there were what seemed like hundreds of dead husbands. I was walking among them, turning the husbands over one by one and there Baxter was among the dead. I wept and held him, then I tried to drag him out of there but I could not move him, so I pulled harder and he started to break, just like the egg. I screamed and woke up. I called Abigail and all she heard on the phone was" Baxter was gone and the egg was stuck in the carton and it would not let me

135

have it and I broke Baxter" (every one chuckled through their tears). She was on the next plane to me. Two days later I met Abigail at the airport; I must have looked terrible, I saw my reflection in her eyes no matter how hard she tried to hide it. 'This kind of thing is not supposed to happen to women like me." Abigail would share stories with me in the past, I would gasp at some of the stories, even her own but I kept on existing in what seemed like my perfect world. When we arrived at my house I shared everything with her, she said "we need to know what kind of enemy we are up against" I had to tell her everything that happened before the disappearance. "No Abigail" I said "I am not taking the blame for this. I loved that man, everything he asked me to do I did. I gave him great pleasure in and out of the bedroom. The bible says" blessed is the fruit of my womb". I teach this to women, how the fruit of the womb is children, but the womb is also part of your husband's secret garden where he comes to be delighted with the love of his life and share the ultimate secret pleasures were no one else is to trespass. I excited him Abigail, I was even his private dancer, if he wanted me to swing from the dang chandelier I would, and I stayed in shape just as he wanted me to. Montana mumbled "I would have to find him to kill him". Abigail said "Montana please let her finish your turn will come".

Penelope continued. "Now I am wondering did I please him? Abigail what kind of power is this? We did everything together. When could he have had time to do this? After getting settled Abigail went into the kitchen, to the refrigerator and got the same carton of eggs out, there was six left plus the stuck broken one. She just looked at me and proceeded to beat the rest of the eggs in a bowl all the time saying not a word to me. ("That's Abby" muttered Montana) She kept on beating and beating I screamed "will you stop beating those blooming eggs! Don't you think I have gone through enough battering?" She ignored me and took out the other dozen eggs and she started to separate the white from the yellow into two separate bowls. Then she started to whisk the white with cream of tartar until it was fluffy. I am thinking I did not call my friend to come all the way from America to Switzerland to demonstrate how to cook whatever it is she was doing, I was a little upset, then

Abigail finally spoke "'so you feel battered, so what?'" Everyone is battered one way or another. What you do with it is what counts. This batter seems average, both the white and yellow is mixed in it, some will look at this as two becoming one, but I see two being unequally yoked, so tangled up that they are destroying each other, and all they can be in life is always scrambled eggs. Before eggs become scrambled, you have to put the eggs on the fire and keep beating so it scrambles, so you are being beaten in the fire.

If you choose this, then your mind will be scrambled and lost, everywhere you go and everything you touch will scramble even your prayer will be scrambled by the enemy before it gets to God's ears. Now this batter was carefully planned, she held the bowl with the egg whites to me and said there are two lives here, one white and the other yellow. They are meant to be together, but someone came and separated them. Right now, you represent the white of the eggs, and that too I will beat into the yellow batter. I am going to make a soufflé with it. Penelope when you see clearly, you can soufflé. You will rise above the situation, not scramble, but rise. Soufflés are very temperamental, as long as they are in the right environment they will stay risen or else they will fall, stay in the spirit of God, and that will keep you raised. Now darling, choose right now, what you are going to do? Be scramble or soufflé? If you do not want your other half back, that is all right, you have the biblical right to divorce him. Then learn to rise above the beheading and go on with your life. God is waiting to be your cover. Isaiah 54:5 tells us… For *thy Maker is thine husband; the LORD of hosts is his name; and thy Redeemer the Holy One of Israel;*

Now love, if you want him back then you must rise to a place where no devil in hell can touch you. The headhunter has to let your head go. Now what is it going to be? 'Penelope, I did not come all the way here to play mental house with you'. (Everyone once again, was laughing through their tears) I could not answer her quite yet. I was still slightly confused about the eggs and her batter. Abigail then reached into the refrigerator for the milk, she opened the carton to pour the milk, she was not taking any chances with my refrigerator. She checked out the expiration date, the milk had expired and had an odor to it. She just stared at me and said, "this is expired, I need to pour it out." I am looking at her and "thinking so what then? Pour the bloody thing out!" She said "if we had drunk this Pen, it would hurt us. Now, do you have a plan for when your self-pity will expire, so you can pour out the poison and make room for strength and courage so we can go to the next level and fight?!"

Something went through me, I looked at her, but this time her eyes reflected the war she saw in me. I was ready to take it on. I thought 'Afghanistan will have nothing compared to the war I am about to take on.' Hell had declared war on me, but I was going to choose my battleground. My man was a prisoner of war; I had gone from the love boat to the battleship". Abigail said "it is going to take more then you and me for this one pen. We need to call the warriors. The prayer warriors, I have five in mind. One is in Australia and another in the Lake District in England, she spends hours by those lakes praying. One in lord's France, Kenya, Africa and one in Korea. These woman for years have stood in the gap for me, I call them G.S W. God's secret weapons, each weapon stationed in a different time zone. Abigail also had a secret weapon of her own that none of us knew about, a friend who owed her a favor or two. Abigail made a call, all I heard was "I know I am the last person you expected to hear from, no everything is okay he is fine the children are fine. I have a friend in need" and Abigail told them my story. Four hours later, we got a call from a strange man, he said 'madam, it is best you tell your friend to forget the one they call Baxter, for he is as good as dead." Abigail replied 'let us make that decision. What do you know?" 'There are two women involved with him, one who only goes by De La cream, and another who goes by Madam Blanc [the white lady]. De La cream may let him go, but never will Le' Blanc let him go. They are as good as married, and if he tries to free himself from her, she will kill him." Once more, I cannot breath I felt like someone punched my stomach. I bent over and screamed. Abigail hung the phone up and grabbed me and just said" not now pen, not now, come on breath, Soufflé pen." At this point I am enraged and nothing about the little soufflé talk makes sense to me anymore. "What?! I don't want to bloody soufflé! I cannot even breathe!" (everyone laughed) Abigail made another call, she told her source what was said, they conversed and Abigail said she can take it. She stared at me with faith in her eyes; her head motioned to me, and she said "well?" I shook my head yes. She told them "We will be ready in a matter of twenty minutes." So I had twenty minutes for Abigail to deprogram me from fear struck to warrior. The doorbell rang, it was a messenger to let us know a limousine was waiting for us. We were taken to the airport where we flew to Geneva, Switzerland. When we arrived at the Hilton, Abigail got out and told me to wait in the car. Abigail met with her source; they disappeared for what seemed like hours, but were in fact only gone for half an hour. Abigail came back a little shaken, but she was not going to let me know just how much. She told the driver to "drive away"; I screamed "No, Abigail! I need to know what was in there!"

Something came over me, I knew it was Baxter, I could feel him. 'tell me Abigail' I whispered, she said "Pen, I don't think you are ready for this yet, let me make some more calls...", "No! That is my man! My husband and my best friend in their Abigail! I want him to look at me! I want to be able to look into his soul!" She said "ok, Pen maybe you are right, but let me warn you, you are going to have to go to a place many cannot get to easily to win this one Pen. You have to be able to forgive whatever you see in there for you to win this battle. I mean real forgiveness Pen, the kind that will allow you to never ever speak of this matter again. Then she said something so profound I will never forget it, "If you cannot forgive this, then you will be like that spoiled stinking milk that was in your fridge. You must have an expiration date to your torment of un-forgiveness, (aka poison.) Then comes the pouring, similar to expired milk, do not keep it bottled up, it must be poured out. Never attempt to go back and drink of this. It will harm you."

Having understood this parable, I said "let's pray" and so we did. Heaven was on alert and Hell was shaken. We went to this hotel room [Penelope stopped for a moment to give praise to God) "only he could do what I am about to tell. Abigail went in ahead of me, I could hear a man screaming, and there he was, my dignified husband, carrier of God's word. I gasped and wondered was this still my nightmare. "No, it's not Pen" I told myself, "this is your war zone." My Baxter was tied to a chair and a beautiful woman dressed in a belly dancer costume was wiping his brow. She looked at me and said in a strong Parisian accent "you are Penelope, yes?" I said "yes". I was expecting right then to be asked for a ransom, but none was asked, instead she said I am "De La cream pleased to meet you." 'pleased to meet me...?' All I could think was "whore, what the hell?" Baxter was pleading with me to get out of there, 'forget me, Pen I am among the dead. I have to have her or else I will die. Nothing matters anymore" and he grabbed de la cream and kissed her like a mad man. Abigail looked at me and opened the door for me to walk out, she said "she did not expect me to go through with this and no man is worth it". At that moment my dream flashes in front of me and I slammed the door shut!

This planet I was thrown into. I was now to become a full-blown citizen of it. I now understood the language and the custom of the people. Hell was knocking at my door and I opened it, do not get me wrong it was not for Hell to come in, but for me to enter into HELL to get my man back. (Everyone started to cheer, even Montana was engulfed in this story.)

I told Abigail "I am not going anywhere. My marriage is worth it, and I want an explanation. Where is the other woman? I demand to see her. The one you call the 'white lady' where is she, off stripping somewhere?" I had demanded, glaring at him in disbelief and disgust. I was not ready for the answer. De la cream said "madam, your husband I give back to you." Then I found myself fighting mad, this was not principalities I was facing, this was my husband's lover. I snarled at her "sorry, but you cannot give me back what was never yours in the first place." She then said "what I was trying to tell you madam, is you are right, he is not mine but at this point he is not yours either, the white lady owns him, it would be better if I did. But come to find out, he only got with me because of my connection to her, he knew as long as he kept me pleased, I would ensure he got as much as his little white girl that he wanted." I stared at her, trying to wrap my mind around what she was saying, then said, "ok then, I will wait here for her. Bring her here, I am ready for Hell's whore." She then said 'she is here madam." I was looking all round me, I ran into all the rooms, even the bathrooms. I was puzzled, I saw no one else but us. Then De La cream said, "my God you do not know what I am talking about do you?" Abigail motioned for her to stop but she did not. "The white lady, madam is cocaine, and she is in your husband's veins." (everyone gasped, except Montana). "He was just about to give away everything he owns and probably yours as well to his dealer, my brother, to keep him supplied with cocaine for a year. Trust me they would have taken everything and supplied him for a week. Then he would have to start to steal to keep the white lady's love. Something happened, they did not come and now he is going through withdrawals real bad."

Abigail checked his pupils "save my husband, Abigail! Help us!" I pleaded frantically. I felt like Baxter and myself were two great eagles that had fallen from a great mountain, and we are now broken, our wings have broken. Would we ever fly again? Only God knows. Baxter was staring at me as if I was the enemy. He started to scream at me, I will never forget the foul odor from his breath as he screamed at me. He was saying "I had never been there for him and that I was to blame and he would not give up the white lady for me." His eyes were as a mad man. I watched as hatred developed fully in his eyes. He broke out of the chair he was tied too, he charged at me going for my throat. Abigail tried to quickly put a needle to his arm, but he got past her. Super natural-like strength came into me from somewhere. I grabbed his wrist and parted it from my neck, all the while gazing fiercely into the black hole of his pupils. I screamed "Not this day devil! I am denouncing our citizenship and taking my man out with me! In the name of Jesus, loose him!" Baxter fell on the ground and passed out. I may not know much, but I know a demon when I see it. Abigail went ahead and gave him the shot to keep him under. (Every one cheered again even Montana said "wow").

"Abigail made another strange phone call for a favor, she needed a private ambulance to come and get Baxter so the media would not get to us. She got him into a private center. 'Penelope, she said I don't know what damage has been done. I don't know if he will make it, you do know Baxter is in bad shape?

Abigail owns a private clinic in Spain, they transported Baxter to it. The next day I was on a jet heading home, this time I was alone and ready for phase two. I too had to go through months of being deprogrammed from the world I had to enter to save Baxter .I had choices to make. Was I truly going to be okay? When it would be time to make love to him again will I be ok? Would I be able to look into his eyes and trust him again? Would I be able to kiss him without wondering where his tongue had been? (every one chuckled). "I am only being real." (Montana said 'you are right").

I would remember what Abby said to me in the limo. "You have to be able to forgive whatever you see in there for you to win this mighty battle. I mean real forgiveness the kind of forgiveness which this matter will never be spoken of again". She said these profound words and it stuck with me.

I read a poem once that said. "Do not awake me before my time." It was talking about awaking love before it is ready to embrace you. Previous to entering the hotel room, I had convinced myself our marriage was worth saving. Six months later I was still wondering what to do. But the worst part of this I am very wealthy, I have all the prosperity I will ever need for three life times, but it cannot buy me trust or peace.

(Abigail's maid, Heather came in to see if any one needed anything before she went home.) Heather had a glow on her face you could not miss. Pen sarcastically asked her "why was she so happy even after waiting on us all day?" Heather said, "Yes I have been here all day, and my husband Jerry just called to apologize because he ran out without kissing me. I have had this smile on my face all day long, he is now waiting for me. I really would like to be able to wait and hear the end of your story I so want to know if you stayed with Mr. Baxter or not? If you did I respect you so much, if not I understand because only we are to lie in the bed we make for ourselves. If it was me I would keep my Jerry, Jesus kept me. (Every one was quiet). Penelope looked at Heather and said "I kept Baxter. Yes I forgave him. Do I trust him? No. But I trust God with all my heart to keep him." Heather kissed Pen and rushed off home to her husband.

Pen continued. "The journey back was not easy. We took each moment one moment at a time. Baxter had a hard time forgiving himself for all the horrible things he had said and done to me."

# My recipe for your book is.

The most important thing we learned was Baxter was under a lot of pressure. He was not trusting God with his preaching. It became nothing more than nightly entertainment for him. He felt empowered by his own power. He soon found out we can only run on our own natural steam for a limited time before crashing. Baxter was not going to crash, no matter what he had to do.

It all started with him one day sharing with another preacher how tired he was from being jet lag, and he was to be on stage in one hour. The preacher gave him a pill which awakened him. From there he started popping these pills daily, until they were no longer effective. The lady in waiting was then introduced to him. That would be the white lady (Cocaine). She has never enforced her ecstasy to anyone. She waits until all else fails, knowing sooner or later her services would be called upon.

Baxter said the first time he snorted the white lady, he felt the anticipated power of her passion consume his body, mind and soul. He said the first hit is free, the second and third also. Then by the forth you realize you have been abducted. What is the ransom? Do you even want a ransom paid? You are still chasing to replicate the first high at whatever the cost, which is impossible, it is like trying to lose your virginity multiple times, you can only lose your virginity once. Cocaine is a master at deceit. It gives you the illusion that every time it can be as delicious as the first taste. It then becomes dangerous as Russian roulette, eventually the bullet will be released. When it is, will the gun be pointing at you or your family? The ransom can never be paid, you will never have enough.

Cocaine gave him an imagination that he had never experienced before, so he became much more creative with his preaching, intense would be a better word. People were drawn to him like moths are to flames. I never saw it coming, maybe it is because I did not want to see. I noticed our lovemaking was different, more erotic if that was possible. 'What do you mean?" Asked Montana "well we went from lovely, intense passion to a painful, pornographic style. Her passion needed to be fed, that is when La Coco entered the scene. She came with the kinky sex, she was the dominatrix of the two women.

Baxter was a lover of food, he was a great chef in our house. His appetite was not what it used to be, he was beginning to lose weight. He could have stood to lose a few pounds, so I also ignored that. There wasn't a more gentle man than my Baxter. So when he would get irritated with me I thought maybe he is tired and is in need of rest. I feared the truth. But now I know fear of the truth will strengthen a lie, fear of being alone would have you to embrace everything; fear of what society will think will cause you to be a people pleaser. At the end of the day our marriage was in the palm of my hand do I close my hand and keep it or do I drop it and let it go? I could not make such a decision until I put P and S in check. Pride and self-pity these two are first cousins they are always the first on the scene of Crime and Passion.

We promised God we would not let yesterday problems contaminate today's blessings. Baxter remembers hearing the nurses and doctors saying he would not make it he will not see tomorrow. He remembers looking at the clock it was five minutes past midnight. He knew yesterdays doom thoughts had been pronounced on him even though it was only five minutes past midnight, It was still tomorrow whatever strength he had left in his body he looked at that clock and said "hello tomorrow I am honored to be in your presence".

He mentioned to me something so insightful I still get chills. He said "Pen all tomorrows come in two parts, light and dark even in the darkest hour it has no doubt light is coming because it is so. Now every morning when he awakes he says "welcome tomorrow! They said I would not see you but here you are to awaken me hello my gift". Abigail here is a poem that blessed Baxter

*Arise my son, Arise It troubled me that sorrow caused you to Sleep with their garments last night. I took the liberty to undress you while you slept I removed your garments of mourning and grief, Oh your sorrow and disappointment was exceptionally heavy my son.*

*These garments with the tormenters of the night tried to persuade your faith that there is no hope of tomorrow and the bright glow of the sun shall not appear in your presence.*

*I overheard the conversation between the Moon and the Sun in the early dawn as the*

*Moon told the Sun of your brokenness. How your tears sparkled as it passed by your window last night. Hurry sun hurry to pass by me so you can burn yesterday's dilemma and fear from his atmosphere as you rise" Pleaded the moon for you my son.*

*I then clothed you with Gladness and Laughter dancing skipped right into your heart because your faith fought its way to my ears and whispered to me "here I am"*

*I then attached the spirit of Joy and healing to the beams of the morning sun.*

*Arise my son Arise*

## JOY COMETH IN THE MORNING
## FROM THE LOVER OF YOUR SOUL *copy written Contessa Emanuel*

Did I get my Baxter back? No. I received a new man, which the ashes of Hell had been washed away from him with cleansing power of our mighty savior. Today we now run an addiction center, not just drugs but any type of addiction. Our staff is made up of 80% delivered and trained "EX" addicts, the other 20% are intercessors and spirit filled businessmen and women.

Our mission statement reads. "Tomorrow is promised to no man, if you are blessed enough to be greeted by tomorrow, treat it with reverence and it will return to you with blessings of Joy." As Penelope reached out to Abigail's hand she said "my friend, the grasshopper became a giant through forgiveness."Abigail said "Penelope, you did more than forgive to be a giant, you forgave and accepted restoration."

There was not a dry eye in the room except for Montana of course, but even she was touched by Penelope's strength.

The women took a break and wandered around the rose garden. It was wonderful, the dawn of day was setting, the time when the grass is all the greener it seems. Some in silence, some praising God for what they have just heard.

# FRANCIS

The women came back in and wanted to continue. Francis was to be next.

"I was a television newscaster, I reported the nightly news; we are always ready for interruptions, for special reports. I remember exactly where I was when the program we were watching was interrupted. I was getting ready to go to work while watching the special report that announced that an airplane had just flown right into the twin towers, killing everyone aboard. Our country was under fire, we were getting ready to enter into a terrorist war. The country and the world was numb and in shock. I was at work when I heard Farah Fawcett had passed away from her long battle with cancer. I was in my driveway when I heard from my daughter on the phone that Michael Jackson was dead, an undeceiving moment. I am sure it is a similar impact for thousands of women when it is their turn to be beheaded by the headhunter. They will never forget the moment that Hell sent its terrorist to try to kill their marriage. The six o'clock news in Hell is always waiting to interrupt our programmed lives with a special report of our destruction. I know when it was that the special report came into our lives. The world's great interruption comes through our radio, and we hear the announcement. I did not hear mine, I saw it. Hell had assigned me to a headhunter. This one did not have a chain saw, it was equipped to break my neck. Clayton would come to the television station every day and bring lunch to me in a picnic basket. I was the envy of the station. I was covering a story at his church when we first met, for me it was love at first sight. I thought how any man can preach that well and still look that sexy. The most wonderful thing was when others saw me as overweight, Clayton would say "just more for him to love on." We were married in six months, a lavish wedding, one fit for a prince and his princess. I never felt guilty about it being church money because his CD'S, books and his talk show was extremely lucrative. The only time we were not together is when we were working or when he went to one of his two studios to do his recordings.

It was a beautiful summer day. I had a doctor appointment because we were having problems getting me pregnant. That day I got the best news in the world, I was pregnant. The studio gave me the rest of the day off, I wanted to celebrate with lobster. I stopped at the fish market to purchase a couple. I knew Clayton was supposed to be coming in from Europe the next day. I decided to go to Hilton head to our summer cottage and leave a pair of booties on the microphone to surprise him. I first I went to the kitchen and put a pan of water on for the lobster. The studio is down stairs in the basement, it is very much sound proof, therefore you could not hear anyone coming in but you can see everyone from the TV monitors in the studio. I was never heard or seen coming in. I went into the bedroom to change my clothes while the water was boiling. I could not find the belt to my linen pants, I then remembered the last time I wore my pants it felt tight, so I took the belt off in the studio while listening to one of his tracks. I was taking the booties downstairs, as I got down the first flight of steps, I was surprised to hear music, *Marvin Gay, 'let's get it on."* I thought Clayton must have left the stereo on, but then I heard groaning. Every one gasped.

(Abigail took hold of Francis's hands while she composed herself, all the while holding back the tears). I looked around the landing on the stairway, through the banister, I saw Clayton naked on his knees and he had hold of someone's hips. My eyes were not ready for what sight was about to violate them.

My man, my holy ghost filled man, was having sex with another man. (a lot of gasps and "oh my Gods" were echoed). My brain shifted into gear to help me by blinking, and hoping it was a horrible vision, but it was not and the image was now in high definition. I dropped the booties and ran back up the steps. In retrospect, I do not even remember how I made it up the steps after what I saw. I was deaf and dumb. I started to run out of the house while catching my vomit in my hands, then, the lobster pot caught my eye. Hell challenged me to an invitation on Hell's six a clock news. I accepted the invitation, spewed the rest of the vomit on to the floor, wiped my mouth and walked into Hell in slow motion. When I entered into the kitchen I emptied a bottle of West Indian hot pepper sauce into the pan of boiling water. They were still too busy getting off to hear me coming back down the stairs. Aretha Franklin was singing at this time, R.E.S.PECT. I stooped over the balcony and threw the boiling water on them. Hell, I did not even see two men, I saw two dogs in heat stuck together. I sure did not see a man of God. Now let me say, I have nothing against gay men and their life style that is between them and God, but when you trespass into my life, I call it breaking and entering. He stole my heart and broke it; I had to enter into Hell to get justice for Breaking and entering. I said not a word while they were screaming, and felt not a bit of remorse I just watched in disgust and hatred as they writhed in pain. Aretha was screaming 'R.E.S.P.E.C.T.' in the background. I got into my car and called 911. "Operator I just poured boiling hot water on my husband and his male lover you can find them at..."

They both suffered with third degree burns. The pepper sauce, I heard, was just as painful as the burns. Walter got it worst. His body protected his lover's, his lover must have turned his head around while the boiling water was searching for somewhere to land. It landed on Walter's face, the cornea of both his eyes were damaged. Walter lost his church, and I lost my life as I knew it. My sentence was three years in prison. There was a reception so to speak waiting for me in prison by many women who felt my pain. You'd be surprised how many women have been imprisoned because of crimes of passion. In any event, Abigail heard what happened to me and got me out of prison in one month. She was at the gate waiting on me. Her first words to me were (everyone again said it together) "THIS SHALL CAUSE US TO SOUFFLE. Come on G.T. let's go home."

She would never tell me her secret weapon, but now I know it could not be anyone but you, Francis said chuckling as she looked at Montana, "Montana, thank you for my life" (the two women laughed and hugged one another.)

(Montana actually had tears in her eyes) Montana said "you shouldn't have done even one day." "It's ok" said Francis, "because of my experience, I got involved with prison ministries for women. Many of our sisters are in prison serving time for crimes of passion. Public defendants just see them as crazy, deranged women. The few prisoners who could afford legal advice, well most of them were just being robbed by their attorneys.

They say it takes many years for sand to cultivate to a pearl while resting in an oyster shell. Prison turns many of our pearls back to sand, coarse and rough. Even though I was out of prison, I was behind the bars of un-forgiveness. Bitterness had sentenced me to life without parole. The stress was too much, and I ended up losing my baby. Why do we say we lost a baby any way, as if it can be found again? The wonderful life that was growing inside of me miscarried. I should have walked away and thought about my baby, but I could not. Rage had set in. My problem was I tried ending my destiny. I was so consumed with myself that self-pity came to visit. It is nothing more than us being consumed with ourselves, our rejection and our pain etc, just like Autumn said. Restoration is what I needed. I felt like I stole life from my baby, Walter stole life from me, and Walters's lover stole life from my marriage and our lives.

It is bad enough when a man leaves you for a woman, but something deep down in us women feels so in adequate as a woman when he leaves you for a man. To say I felt used was an understatement. The bible says 'blessed are you when men despitefully use you.' Let's get it right, I was despitefully used on so many altitudes. I felt like a rag that was used up and thrown away.

A man's Good Thing, is the furthest thought from our mind. How do you fight another man for your man? The head of your house hold? I was not embracing any W.O.W Words of wisdom; I was embracing W.O.D. Words of Destruction. It did not matter what was the reason Walter did what he did. "Reasons waiting to be explained are nothing but delayed seasons of forgiveness." "Say that again! Said Abigail" Reasons waiting to be explained are nothing but delayed seasons of forgiveness. Some men are so good at betrayal that they have learned to beat the system, finding loopholes in our formula. Walter and his lover went under the radar for a while never being detected because we women pride ourselves in 'having the formula,' knowing when a man is lying, cheating, and all of the rest of the stuff they do to allegedly attain us. If you stay true to God, whatever is done in the dark will come into the light. He will not let his faithful women or men be made a fool of for long.

## My recipe for your book

I, Francis, had to 1st find out how to forgive. When a prisoner is up for a parole hearing, the family member of the victim has to be informed so that they can oppose the release of the prisoner if they choose too. Satan, as we are told in Jeremiah, is our opposer. Every time I went for a parole hearing into the spirit world through prayer, my release was always blocked by the opposer. Who rightfully accused me of not having a forgiving heart? I got tired of my bars, I cried out to God to help my unbelief.

My unbelief, that God could help my bitter heart. I heard from the Lord. 'If you don't forgive, I cannot forgive you." So I made arrangements to visit Walter. It was not easy preparing to go back into the enemy's camp. I had to remind myself I was already victorious, yea right, easier said than done. Pride would come in and tell me you did nothing wrong, don't forgive those dogs. I went to the mirror, and took a good look at myself. I allowed my thoughts to journey back to that dreadful day. My breathing got rapid, my lips had become stiff, and my jaw was trembling. I recognized the real enemy, it was rejection. I thought ok, this can work both ways I decided to do some rejecting of my own. I rejected Satan's plan for my heart, and said to the Lord ok pour your antidote in me, I cannot do this alone. I felt His power running through my body like a smooth healing tonic. I was now ready to do my part.

Walter's body had healed, but his heart was not. He still hated me for destroying his life, for publicizing his secret life. I looked into his scared eyes and told him I forgave him, and I meant it sincerely. He spat on my face and told me that for a while now it had made him sick every time he ever touched me, the very sight of me disgusts him, but he wanted a baby and I was nothing more than a she-dog for breeding. What happened next was hard, but necessary. I felt the warm tonic run through my body again and I walked up to him, grabbed the tail of his shirt and wiped the spit off my face.

I repeated "I forgive you Walter" you are not worth me doing any more time in this prison of hatred. With tears racing down my face, I said "Walter it is written I am a Good Thing with favor." As those words came forth from my heart, my freedom was right behind it. Parole had been granted to my heart, I was free. (Glory! shouted the women.)

While driving back from visiting Walter, I drove past a hospital. I could see the emergency sign. The lord impressed me to park in the parking lot of the hospital. I thought maybe someone was on the way and God wanted me to minister to him or her. No, that's not what it was. He had me stare at the EMERGENCY sign "what do you see?" He said, "Emergency" I thought. God spoke once more, "Look into Emergency and find my message" and there it was. Francis paused briefly "Wait, someone give me some paper, I have to write it how I saw it. EMERG, EN, CY. That's what the Lord showed me. I had been taken down to the depths of Hell, not knowing if I would ever come out. 'Emerge' He said, 'and see' what I have for you. Angels are sent out every day like ambulances on an emergency run. They are dispatched from heaven, seeking for those of us that are ready to emerge into forgiveness." The women started clapping in excitement, exclaiming praises to God.

"That was ten years ago, I moved back to the Virgin Islands and applied into law school with the financial help of an unidentified person. I have done well, I will be taking my bars soon; I delayed it to be here with Abigail in her time of need. My source has also created a trust fund so I can help women in need free of charge. This has cause for us to soufflé. As usual, it was said in unison. Hey Autumn, I became more than my pain, more than rejection, I became whole! There is one thing else, Abby for your book.

My mother would always recite in difficult times what her mother recited to her. "Every disappointment is a blessing." And now I understand what my mind was rehearsing for all these years.

You may have made appointments for your life, but if it was not God's appointed time for you, he will discharge the plans whichever way he sees fit to do it. So we can enter into His appointed plan for our purpose. It was purposed for me to be an attorney, not just any attorney but one in God's army. Walter disappointed me, but God reappointed me and it is surely a blessing. (Every one clapped for joy). Abby hugged Francis and added "So what you're telling us, I believe, is to look deeply into our disappointments and see if this was appointed by God for us." Yes that's right Abby, we all know it takes practice. Grace said, "ok, I see a T-shirt with that saying on it 'disappointments are God's reappointments.' Everyone was excited at the idea. Montana replied "whatever."

It was getting late, everyone spent the night with Abigail. Montana went home and promised to be here early. Montana knew the woman would be up early to have prayer. She will deliberately be late.

# JANE

The next morning the doorbell rang. Montana arrived just when prayer and devotion was over. Abigail smiled and said "missed you at prayer" to an annoyed Montana. "I am just joking, Montana." laughed Abigail.

The doorbell rang again, at the door was a young woman, her name is Jane. "Hello, is Dr. Monroe here?" Abigail came to the door. "Hello, Jane." "Oh, Abigail, I heard what your husband was trying to do to you. I don't want to disturb you. I just wanted to encourage you. I know God has all of this under his control. I would not be alive and functioning if it was not for your love and kindness. Abigail hugged Jane and thanked her. Come in and join us Jane. Abigail took her to the table and poured her some hot mint tea, then, they sat down with the rest of the women. Abigail introduced her to everyone. Jane had come directly from work. She still had her uniform on, as she was a nurse.

"Jane, we are sharing with each other our diverse ways we have overcome the attempted or actual execution of our marriage and/or lives and embraced integrity. I have an idea for a book of 'recipes for how to overcome.'" Jane said "that is great, integrity is priceless but is not cheap!" Montana turned around in her chair, looked at Jane and wondered was she at the meeting with Contessa. "Would you like to share your story, Jane? If you have time that is, and if you are not tired, I know you just got off your shift." said Abigail... "Ok" she sighed. Everyone was excited to meet another woman that had been touched by Abigail's love.

Jane began. "I was a runaway child, turned out by pimps to be a prostitute. I became a junkie for many years. I had always been mature for my age, I thought I knew it all; no one could handle me, disobedience reigned like crazy in my veins. I was dying on the streets of Hell, which had used me up and had no more use for me. I had gone from being auctioned to the highest bidder to the lowest bidder's passing me by. I was in a dog eat dog environment. I depended on whatever fragment Hell had scattered on its streets to feed on. I did whatever it took to chase my next high, but never catching up with it. I always wanted more. I did whatsoever it took so that crack cocaine could make love to me, trying to re-live the feeling of the first time I was seduced by it. My body did not need food, sex or even love, just the cocaine. I lived in abandoned houses, like rats fighting nightly for a corner.

If I got to bathe once a month, I was doing well. The junkies who stole from the other junkies to pay to have sex with me smelled as bad as I did, so it did not matter to them how I smelled.

One day, as I was coming down from my last high and getting ready to search for my next high, I heard a voice from the past. "Jane? Hey, Jane! How have you been doing?" I stared at him in confusion, he asked "you don't recognize me, do you?" His name was Paul. He said, "I use to shoot up with you for years" "You did?" I asked, "I don't recognize you at all, well anyways, I need a fix do you have some spare change?" I kept my eyes on him "I knew a Paul, he doesn't look like you though, so if you really are that Paul, then show me the scars. let me see the tracks on your body then I will believe you." So Paul rolled up his sleeve of his white oxford shirt. He took his shoes off and showed me his needle marks up and down his arms and his feet. I screamed and broke down crying, because I remembered a Paul who I had helped to shoot up because he was shaking so hard. He could not get his veins to act right, so I helped him out. "Show me the scars" I said again. Then Paul took my hand and slowly moved my hand up to his neck. I was searching for a certain scar, because I had tried to use a vein in his neck, and punctured a main artery. My hand was not steady, and it ripped his neck. Blood was spewing out everywhere, I ran screaming for help. It looked like he was bleeding to death. A customer came to buy sexual favors from me, and I was so deep in my addiction," she paused as a look of pain and shame came across her face, it was clear that it hurt her to even recall this story. She composed herself and continued. "I could not turn him down, I needed my next fix or else I would lose it, I would die. That's the way I felt. I had an opportunity to join the chase again, maybe this will be the one. I needed it, so I went with the john (customer) and left Paul to drown in his own blood.

I had no conscience, but I used to know someone who used to have a conscience, the Jane before crack. I had been hijacked and silenced, nobody cared I was not important enough to be ransomed. Who could afford to get involved with me? How many friendships, how many family members did I need to destroy before that thing that had completely taken me over could be satisfied? I did not know at the time, but now I know HELL can never be satisfied.

(Penelope had tears streaming down her neck, remembering Baxter's ordeal). "As my trembling hands went to Paul's neck, my eyes were in over flow. The torment that had tormented me for so many days and nights when I was coming down from a high was returning. My fingers met with the scar. I quickly moved my hands away and started to run. I thought he was a ghost, that had come to repay me back for that I had done to him or should I say what I did not do for him. As much blood as was spewing out of his neck that night, there was no way he could be alive. Paul ran after me, when he caught up with me, in with a vigorous, breathless voice I said, "I cannot look at you, I would feel better if you came with revenge in your eyes. I see no revenge. Paul, are you a ghost? You died, I know you did." Paul said "you are right, Jane. I did die." "Oh Heck no," I started screaming, in my drug induced state I had theorized that he was a ghost, come to get vengeance and drag me to the 'other side' with him. I screamed for someone to help me "I don't want to die! help me!" no one was around but Paul and myself. Just like that fatal night, here we are again, alone.

I remember him looking at me wide eyed, more than likely in disbelief at how delusional I was being. He firmly placed his hands on my arms and said "Jane, I am not a ghost, I am alive. Listen, I have been born again. I am not dead. You have felt me, even my scars. Is my blood not warm in my veins?

I shook my head in disbelief as the tears flowed again "who saved you that night Paul? Who came to your rescue? I remembered hearing the ambulance that night before I left you, I had just kept saying "I'm so sorry, my friend Paul, I'm so, so sorry" Paul said, "A man came by that night and saw me dying in my blood. He said to me "young man you are dying, do you know Jesus Christ?" I said no, he told me how this Jesus died for my sins, and that he had paid the ransom Jane, so I could be set free and live and that he arose with all this power in his hands, and that he cheated death, he then said he would like to pray me through to the other side so this Jesus could receive me when I got unto the other side. "You know what Jane?" He asked laughing, "When you are dying in your own blood, you will do or say anything for help. There was something different about this man though, he wanted nothing from me Jane, he wanted to give me something, he wanted to give me life. I accepted his Jesus and passed out.

Next thing I know I am waking up four weeks later in a hospital, and this man is still there. I opened my eyes, he smiled at me, and I closed my eyes for what seemed like a few seconds, then he was gone. I was told if I needed blood he would have given me his blood that night to save my life. I received the power of the blood of Jesus. I became born again, his love is powerful, let me introduce you to him Jane."

I told Paul, "no, not now, I have just finished servicing a man for my next fix and you know how it is. It's getting harder to find a place to bathe, I stink. I have not bathed in 4 days Paul, so I am sure you will understand if I do not want to meet him looking and smelling like this. I need to find a place to bathe Paul. Then, said the most surprising thing to me. "He cannot smell anything Jane, he has a sinus problem. Please come visit him with me: I looked at Paul, wondering what other excuse I can give him so I can get rid of him. It did not matter what I said, he had an answer for it, so I thought what the heck? Maybe I can con this man into giving me some money for a meal, then I can get a fix. Okay, I said if you promise he cannot smell me. That was on a Sunday morning while Paul was on his way to church when he ran into me. I gave in and went to church with him. The preacher was awesome, it was as if he was talking directly to me. He made this Jesus sound like everyone's best friend that you cannot live without, next thing I knew I was at the altar weeping to this Jesus. I felt the power of God in such a way that no drug had ever made me feel. It is a high I did not have to chase. It was always with me when I needed it.

(Jane was filled with tears the women came one by one, embracing her. Montana could not move. Jane went on) "Jesus accepted me, but not that church. They did not know what to do with me. The women in the church wanted to know which class is Jane to be placed in, I was not just a number on a row, but a child of God. Paul had done the hard work. He had got me into the church, and now here I am belonging to this institute with a group of women. The closest they had been to a woman like me is seeing my life style on the movies. Only one woman was able to let her facial expression not smell me. We can only really know if someone can smell our odor, it is by the expression on their face. Only one woman could be Godly enough and not smell me. I am standing with this group of women thinking, ok, "I am loosed, now what?" I will tell you what, I wanted out of there and to go and get drunk and high. Whatever I could get, my hand would do, but that feeling I felt at the altar came back. So I calmed down.

While living the life of a prostitute, I remember a young girl who had not made her nightly quarter. She was so petrified that a beating was inevitable from her pimp. I serviced a couple more men so I could help her with the money she needed, we did things like that for each other on the streets of Hell.

I felt more love on those streets than in that church. What I really wanted to do is find out who their husbands were and see if I had serviced them, or worst still, I wanted to seduce their men at their home and leave my panties as a calling card.(Montana said "amen to that") instead, I got with Paul and studied the word day and night. I kept on getting stronger. I read about the prophet Hosea, who God had him to marry a prostitute. I prayed for God to send me a Hosea. I thought he did but it was an imposter, a very good one that was able to fool me or should I say I allowed myself to be fooled by him.

We were very prosperous for sixteen years. Then one Christmas Eve, he decided he did not want to be married to me anymore. Yes

Christmas was bad timing, but maybe it would not have been that bad if I had not just completed marinating the turkey It was pull out the chainsaw cut down the timber and tie her to the bomb fire painful, the ovens alarm were buzzing sending the signal to let me know the oven has met the appropriated heating time and it was ready for roasting. I felt like some great mistake had taken place. The turkey is who should be in the oven roasting, not me I somehow managed to grab my keys and some clothes, and drove all night through the snow covered mountains of the Carolina's and Tennessee to Indianapolis, Indiana to be with my children. I don't even remember the drive but I remember the heat of the bomb fire that hell had started that was racing through the forest of my mind trying to burn any love I had left for the human race, I was cold and angry, and the heat felt good. I was like the beautiful ornament candle that you never light at Christmas, it just stayed pretty all year round, but the sparks from the bomb fire found me and now my tears are like running hot wax, there is a flame on top of me.

There would be an executive board meeting every morning in hell, about what they are going to do next in my marriage, the word states Satan is the father of lies, then if that is true Satan was my father in law because my marriage was a big lie. I should have been glad it ended, but at the same time, I did not want to be defeated.

He wanted younger. I guess whoever the headhunter was, she did a good job on him. Any man that will end his marriage on Christmas Eve had to be overcome with extreme lust. The intercourse he engaged in with her took us from our course that we had both been on for years. Even the first four letters in passion (pass) tries to warn us if this passion does not mean us good, but harm to keep passing. Do not stop, do not enter. I asked the Lord why? All I heard was "I was Chosen and Empowered to survive". (The women all started rejoicing).

If the truth was to be told, our marriage had been in trouble before she came along. Let me put it this way. I was so wrapped up in being religious, I did not really give the marriage what it needed to grow. Neither one of us did. I came off the streets, got saved, and indulged myself in religious ritual. There was not anyone to direct me on how to be a wife. It is important to find out what all is needed to help a woman with this walk of salvation. I knew how to satisfy him in the bedroom, but I failed everywhere else.

I came from a world where I thought that's all a man needed to keep him happy. I could not cook, I did not know how to dress a home. (Something was happening in the spirit realm that no one could contain except Montana.) Jane stood up with a glow that could be seen by all, including Montana. Jane looked at Abigail and said to her in a prophetic voice Abigail stood and walked towards Jane and looked into her eyes. She knew the spirit of the living God was resting on Jane. "Abigail Monroe, know this, Just as God parted the red sea for Moses, so he has parted all your red seas. Satan has lost. You were never your father's wager to begin with. You have suffered in a loveless marriage just as Abigail did with Nabal of Carmel. (1st Samuel: 25). Integrity reigns on you as it did on Abigail of Carmel. Nabal will die and a David will come to you. As it is written for your sake, we are killed all day long. We are accounted as sheep for the slaughter. Yet in all these things Abigail, you are more than a conqueror through Him who loved you. For I am persuaded that neither death nor life, nor angels nor principalities nor powers, nor things present nor things to come, nor height nor depth, nor any other created thing, shall be able to separate you Abigail from the love of God which is in Christ Jesus our Lord."

Abigail started to cry, salty tears were rolling. Abigail was getting weak, no one else was seeing what she was seeing. This was no longer the face of Jane, but Gabriela. Abigail collapsed, her spirit overwhelmed by it all. Montana rushed to her. "No" Penelope said," let God talk to her". Montana was motionless, with a cautious look on her face. She was suspicious of everybody. Poor Montana, she just cannot handle too much more of this spiritual world. She was ready to pull her gun out and tell those women back away from my cousin but she couldn't.

"Abigail it is I Gabriela". Abigail was again at the pond with her. "Walk with me" said Gabriela they walked to the edge of the pond. Abigail said "this cannot be real" I don't have much time Abigail, please listen said Gabriela. Do you believe you are the salt of the earth? Asked Gabriela, "Yes" said Abigail. Then what I am about to tell you will make sense.

Do you remember when you first came to the pond and asked the pond to send the ripples to take your tears to the heart of the pond? You have often wondered what made that pond so especially blessed. The pond, my dear has been here for centuries, and for centuries women who have been chosen to survive have made their way to this pond, for centuries their tears have been pulled to the heart of the pond. You're salty tears and those before you have created a reservoir of salty water to salt the earth. When we cry, God reminds us as we taste our tears, that we are the salt of the earth; your tears have not been in vain. The women in your house now can have a better view about God because of your tears that entered into the pond. The pain you were allowed to feel was nothing more than an S.O.S, a message to your destiny that you are on your way, and purpose is coming with you. Abigail, You kept your promise. You have ministered to others in need, and now you await your fate of your future with your husband. Now look into the pond Abigail" said, Gabriela. "Are you sure?" she asked, "yes, dear I am" Abigail remembered the last time she looked into the pond, she saw herself beheaded. This time it was different. The ripples did not come to cover her vision. The pond was as clear as a mirror. Abigail knelt down at the edge of the pond and slowly stretched her swan like neck over towards the pond, her heart was racing. The pond reflected her friends in a circle with their heads intact, her daughter's heads also all intact. She was happy, but still a little disappointed. Gabriela knew what was going on. "Look a little harder" she said and there in the center of the ladies in the pond, a figure was emerging up from the bottom with outstretched hands, she emerged with tears streaming down her face, shouting praises to God. It was Montana. Abigail cried some more 'salt' into the pond, but this time it was tears of joy.

Gabriela then said "know this Abigail Monroe, Nabal will die and David will send for you." Abigail opened her eyes, and the ladies were all around her praying. Montana was standing over her, you could tell she was concerned for her cousin, but she was in an arena that she could not control.

Abigail smiled. She was concerned for Montana. She hugged Montana and whispered "it's ok, I know you must have been scared"

Montana said "Hell, Abby I need a drink, I cannot stay here. It's all too much for me. I can't process all of this."

At that moment all the women walked towards Abigail, it was not planned, but they ended up in a circle. Jane looked at Montana, who she had never seen before today, and said to her. "You mighty woman of the law you are addicted to lust and allergic to the spirit of God." Montana got offended and growled at Jane with that lioness growl of hers." What do you or your God know about me?!" Montana was getting unusually shaken by Jane, but Jane was on a mission, and she was not backing off. Jane walked up to Montana and whispered something in her ears in a way that no one else could hear. Montana lost the feeling of her legs; she started to walk backwards towards the ladies.

Montana grabbed her hair, she was trying to stay glued together, but it was not easy, she was falling apart. Who is this Jane who knows her secret?

Montana had successfully redirected the attention from her as she does in the courtroom every day. She glanced at one of the women, Grace. Grace had a sober look to her all day long. Montana was very curious about her. Montana said "you know what Grace, you are not moved by all of this "my man done me wrong stuff" now are you? I have been watching you, your not easily moved. Some of this might have moved you, but not much. You are wearing that "please, spare me the drama" look, you women have not been through nothing compared to me look". Abigail scolded Montana. "Stop this Montana, torturing this poor girl! Stop now!"(*Satan said 'finally some action from my girl I wish I could persuade her to get her gun out and blow the whole bunch away, but that cousin of hers and that overrated love thing has her delusional for now"*) Abigail knew what Montana was doing, that she was steering the situation away from her. After all, that's what she does well in the court room. Abigail glanced at Jane to see if she was ok, and she was

Abigail looked at Grace to give an assuring look. That it was OK, and she did not have to share. She was just happy to have her here for support, and that was enough.

Jane said wow, ok. Abigail, I guess my formula for your book will be the same as Francis's. I believe I was reappointed, and my future and my destiny has been pre-appointed by my Lord and savior. But I feel I need to add, Mothers, love your daughters. Fathers, love your daughters. Someone is out there waiting to give them fake love, make sure they know the difference between fake and the real thing.

Do not keep them isolated, their mind needs to be full with positive thoughts, minds that are left alone can get real creative to do wrong.

"It's Ok" said a softly spoken Grace. "I don't wear the look you are referring to, Montana, for the reason you think. Montana what you saw was a women that wished she was the one that had got hurt first, and not her that had done the hurting. I was not beheaded, I did the Severing. I was married to a wonderful man of God. Actually we were a powerful team, we traveled the Globe preaching and delivering. He preached and I was used by God as an instrument to deliver many from demon control and whatever else they were bound to. I loved a man who loved God more than anything else. Kingdom living was our purpose. We worked towards getting everyone to see the love that God had for them. I thought I was happy, I would sometimes think of him and pinch myself to see if it was all real. So I understood Pen for her love for Baxter. (Montana rolled her eyes)

1ST Corinthian 7-9

THE FALL FROM GRACE

*Looking carefully lest anyone <u>fall short of the Grace of God</u>; lest any root of bitterness springing up cause trouble, and by this many become defile; Lest there be any fornicator or profane person like <u>Esau,</u> who for one morsel of food sold his birthright (Hebrew 12:15-16)*

The worst part of this story is I fell from his grace, while at the height of the ministry the Lord had trusted with me. While I was so busy taking care of everyone else, my flesh (carnal mind) was very busy taking care of itself. My flesh placed a phone call to Hell and turned me in; I never saw it coming, when it arrived I immediately felt the flesh burning inferno. Even the humidity in the air had ceased to be around me. The morning dew also refusing to rest on me. A mighty wind blew, a spark to the severe drought of my life and turned my dried lustful flesh into an inferno.

While in a state of sin, I was Grace Moran, an undeniable sinner with no conscience. After accepting salvation, I was born again, I had taken his name, Christ, and became a Christian. I was in two binding contracts, or one could say covenants; one with God and another with my husband, so I really committed adultery against Jehovah, the true lover and cover of my soul, and my husband. The pain, the hurt, the shame was unbearable at times.

*If they fall away, to renew them again to repentance, since they crucify again for themselves the Son of God, and put Him to an open shame.*
*(Hebrew 6:6)*

Even today it hurts to talk about it, I almost feel like crucified Jesus all over again, putting him to an open shame, disgracing his name, but when I think of his goodness and mercy, my soul cries alleluia!

It all started Autumn of 1988, led the brutal winter of my life; my daughter had just turned five years old. Jimmy Swaggart, and Jim Baker, had both fallen from grace, and the Christian world was taking a big hit. I had only been saved eight years, the ministry, F.I.A, faith in action, was being prospered by the Lord. Souls were being saved everywhere we dared to tread on, which included prisons, streets, teen shelters, God had blessed with a powerful deliverance ministry. Demons fled and hell trembled, but I did not want to travel any more, I wanted to be a stay at home mom for a while and enjoy my baby girl's school days.

There was a dark side to my husband. Somehow, he thought I was more popular than him, and the ugly spirit of jealousy sprung his head up and took root, I could not take all the arguments. I called Joyce, our sectary and told her to cancel all my engagements and give them to him, but they did not want my husband, they wanted me. I wanted him to be happy, so I was willing to step down and go to work, so I convinced myself I did not want to travel any more, I never consulted God about that which was mistake #1.

I was going to do things my way, which would put me into a winter that made it seem spring would never come again in my life.

Nature gives signs of when it will rain or storm, and we prepare and take precaution. We will listen to the voice of the weather person more than we listen to the voice of our savior. All the warning signs were there, even dreams were sent to me more than once. The heavens had put out warnings, and I chose to ignore them. When things are not going right with our marriage, even with our lives period, we seem sometimes to stop talking to God, and that's what I did. Praying and studying, it all ceased. The very marrow in my bones were drying up, Satan sent a message to me in the Sunday news paper in the classifieds, there it was, a Cincinnati group had an ad in the paper

DO YOU WANT TO START A NEW LIFE? COME WITH US, NO EXPEREINCE NECCARY WE WILL TRAIN.

I applied and got an interview, they were extremely impressed with me, but why shouldn't they have been? Lucifer had cast a blinding spell that was going to put me in a whirlwind of misery for seventeen years.

I had a dream that same night, I was trying to get out of a burning building, and I got to the window where the fire escape was, but did not make it any further, and I stayed in the room. Then I was sent another dream, the next night that my boss would seduce me, in the dream the man resembled one from the Mediterranean. I didn't see any Mediterranean men around when I was being interviewed, so I dismissed the dreams and accepted the job.

I was at the job for two months when they announced to us our store manager will be with us on Monday, and the temporary manager, which I did not realize was a temp, would leave us. Yes, the new boss was Mediterranean (the ladies were shocked, including Montana) I did not care, because he was nothing I would look at twice. The total opposite to what I liked in a man. My husband, who was already paranoid, claimed to see the signs, he told me "that man will take you from me, Grace. He is smarter than me and a man of position." I told him he was crazy, even if I was not saved and married, my boss was too short and balding. We laughed, and I asked why would I want a George Jefferson when I had a Denzel? But in reality my husband had spoke damnation over me. Don't get me wrong I am not blaming him. It would not be long before the inferno would consume all my strength, the joy of the lord had been removed from me, I thought of how it must have felt like when the ark was removed from the Israelites, and they the lost all the battles

It was all so puzzling to me because my sexual desires had all but diminished.


There he was, clothed in a wonderful navy silk and cotton blend Italian suit. He walked into the office as if he was a Gladiator and we, the spectators. The boss was announcing to the staff that we needed to pair up for training. There were 31 of us, not including him. He chose me as his partner. Part of this exercise consisted of him fitting me with several pairs of frames, demonstrating to us how to fit the spectacle frame to the patient's face. He slowly placed the glasses on top of my ears while all the while his beautiful brown eyes were pulling me into his soul. I never saw a soul needing to be saved or delivered, something else was happening.

The unquenchable thirst from the flames of Hell produced a powerful course for me to follow. The Un-forbidden fruit of Hell was both producer and director, Satan being the agent, always waiting for his wages. The script is always ready to be rehearsed, it just patiently waits on the characters. I was doing a good job of auditioning for the part. While un-forbidden was making its way on the scene, my boss said "this frame is called rapture" I smiled nervously. He leaned in towards my face, I could smell his sweet peppermint breath. He gently placed the glasses on my ears, he was feeling that the temple of the glasses fit right on to my ears. He moved his fingers gently around the back of my ears, all the while looking directly into my eyes. Our lips were just millimeters away from each other's, so close I could taste the sweet peppermint from his breath. It was like Hell's flames had rested on my ears, moving rapidly to the rest of my body. My dried lips searched for a moist relief from my tongue. His eyes glanced down to my tongue just as it was pulling in my bottom thirsty lips. My lips parted as my eyes fell unto his well-trimmed mustache that rested on his chocolate lips. I wanted that peppermint chocolate kiss so badly, I did not care that we were in the optical shop with thirty other people, because I surely was being tempted into Hell's play ground. Our eyes met, he was moving in for the kill. Our lips almost brushed against each other's when he whispered, 'no one's eyes so beautiful should be covered with glasses." I was safe for now, my husband who came to take me to lunch interrupted us.

The optical occupation is a place where you cannot accuse any one of "touching your ears." It is a close contact occupation. My husband never saw, the flames of Hell quickly diminished in his presence. This dance between my boss and I went on for months. I fought a good fight, I was exhausted in prayer but it seemed like my prayers were ignored. I could not understand why God was allowing this to happen to his servant. I didn't understand why He would allow me to be miscast in the play. This man was not even physically my type. He was short. I do not like short men. I called on my best girl friends that I could trust to pray me through, she did try but nothing happened.

February the 15th, the next year was when I disgraced the lover of my soul. My boss invited me to his house to pick up a book that would help me with the American board of opticians test I needed to take. I nervously knocked at the door, he answered and asked me in seconds before I crossed the threshold of HELL. JUSTIFICATION came on the scene. I had a legitimate excuse. It had been justified for me.

I thought, because my husband and I had been at each other's throat to the point that he moved out and we filed for divorce that it was not a problem; me coming over here to get the book which he seemed to always forget to bring to work. I was not yet divorced when I went into his house. He had some news to tell me. He was getting ready to be transferred, and he wanted to know was there a chance for us. I said no. The next hour, I was in his bed consumed by a third degree burn from the flames of Hell. The very act was consumed by so much passion. I could not see any wrong. It just felt right. The very moment it was over I screamed with such pain "My God My God, what have I done to you"?

My boss ran into the bathroom petrified, he had never had an ending like that before. It was also an ending to my life as I had known it before, to begin my life sentence with Pharaoh. I was not the only one in trouble. Jimmy Swaggart is on the news, crying "I have sinned." I thought, what, is burning passion an epidemic going around?!

I blamed God for years. I felt like he did not hear my prayers. However, I did not stop there. When you have tasted the sweet poison of adultery, you are never satisfied. I had now become the proverbs 5 woman.

Let's rewind a little. My biggest fear was I would not stop with the boss. Hyena's only go after what is already dead, they are lead to their meal by the odor of decomposing flesh. My flesh must have been rotten to have awaken the old spirit that was once dead [your old life style.]

While I was engaged to the boss, I thought, well I have already sinned so why not explore other possibilities before heaven's bloodhounds find me?

I met Mr. Cray when he came in for an eye exam. He is the type of man that exists to accommodate a woman with the pleasure of sinning. Cray I could call anytime, and if he was available, he knew exactly what I needed. This one session he called C. B. C. night: candles, bubbles and champagne.

Montana sat up with much curiosity with an interested smile on her face. Cray would have the bubble bath drawn, and the champagne chilled and placed by his black Mediterranean marble tub, which is surrounded by mirrors. The flames of the candles created an essence of amber in the room. The tub was accented with two forest green swirled with black onyx, majestic roman pillars. There was a fan above the tub, just in case it got too warm. He was a creature of comfort; he would even drape the towel around the onyx pillars, everything is so detailed with him.

Whatever you needed, he had. I mean anything. I once opened a drawer and found women feminine monthly needs.

Now, Mr. Cray came with a set of rules, which were not up for bargaining. You knew he was not a one woman's man, ah, but he would treat you as if you were the only woman on the planet for the night. He took great details in knowing your favorite music. I always requested the three tenors. Cray would sit at the foot of the tub and just say, "speak to me", as he massaged my foot. I would pour out my soul to him as he poured the champagne.

Mr. Cray made love to a woman's mind. Even though he knew the rite of passage was extended to him, he never entered the port. Without fail there would be flowers in the morning at my office, the card would simple say *"whenever you need me, you know where to find me"*, signed Cray. I became a Cray junkie. I could not get enough of this man's pleasure. One day, I sent him a note stating without U. pleasure is misplaced and spelled (pleasre) without the U., (every one awed, except Montana of course, rolling her eyes and commenting on how corny it was.)

He begged me not to go through with the wedding. He said I was going to have my spirit imprisoned, and I needed to be true to myself, but I didn't listen. One night as I was leaving Cray's house, another woman was coming in. she said "you must be Grace, I am so pleased to finally meet you" and kissed me on the cheeks; Cray rested his lips on mine right in her presence. He knew I was falling for him; he just had to remind me that there could never be just one woman for him. Even though there were rumors of this one woman that he could never obtain. It was said he lived for the moment, she would accept his heart. It was as if his heart had been put into protective custody where no one else could touch it. He had a nude portrait of her on his bedroom wall, not her face, only her body from the rear. I secretly envied her. A few days before I got married, Cray called to tell me "you are a trophy that is going to be misplaced on the wrong mantel." Actually, he might as well have told me I was being miscast for this role. (Recalling the story started to become too much for Grace, she started to cry). Heaven's bloodhounds did find me, so what else was there to do but to beg for God's forgiveness and give myself back to God? I was thankful that he said he was married to the back slider. It happened on a Good Friday, now the next thing to do was to marry. I was safer doing that, I thought at the time, then letting the enemy use me with different men.

I had my dream wedding. I took God's most holy covenant and tried to cover my lustful disorder by getting married to the one I committed adultery with. We even had the nerve to take communion at the ceremony. I thought it would make everything holy and we would live happily ever after, it was not to be. Once more, God tried to get my attention. While trying to light the unity candles, not one of them would light. It was embarrassing. I could hear my mother muttering from the front row "that is not good, not good." We walked away from the candles, into the darkness and walked into a new life without the light.

Just as Eve was ordered by God to obey Adam, my punishment was now to obey and honor a man who ruined my life, now the birthing pain of misery begins. My joy went into a state of impoverishment.

Yet, the love that God had showed me through his forgiveness was overwhelming. I knew that I would never cheat again, the price was too high, but I did not realize the price I was about to pay to receive God's anointing back on my life to do his will. It would take seven years before God reinstated me to go back and preach in the prisons.

I did imprison myself into an unloved marriage. Worst still, my twin daughters had to enter into a miserable house and lived where love died. I stayed faithful to the man I was unfaithful with. Don't get me wrong, I was not that strong or a great martyr, I did it all unto God. But some days I must say, I did suffer with the martyr syndrome. So you see Montana, it's not what you thought.

Now what did I learn from sleeping in the bed I made in hell? The bible tells me: "Even though you make your bed in HELL, I am there" Psalms139-8 *If I ascend up into heaven, thou art there: if I make my bed in hell, behold, thou art there. ... Wherever I am, there art thou; and where I cannot be, thou art there.*

Before we enter to the bed that has been custom made for us, the Lord gives us many chances to repent and walk away, but when we don't, he allows the mind to be reprobated, so we can come back to the lover of our soul.

I slept in that custom-made bed for many years, fitted sheets and all. I thought I was using satin sheets but there was nothing smooth about the sheets I laid on. It turned out to be more like burned polyester, rough and sharp enough to cut.

I understood the 'wow' that was given to me by the Lord. Same one Abby got. "No one can satisfy that which belongs to God, no one at all."

I use to think I was not able to go on, until one morning I opened the bible and let my eyes wander on where ever it would open at. It opened at Genesis, the story about Cain and Able. Most of us know this story very well, but for the first time while reading it, I was giving a rhema word, Montana interrupted, "a, what?!" Grace answered, "Montana, Things which are being revealed to us from the Lord." I looked up the name Able. One of the many meaning in Webster reports... *Able: being put in a position to do something.* Wow, I thought that is powerful. But Cain came along and put a stop to him. The question came to my spirit.

Who or what was the Cain in my life that wanted to kill 'the Abler' in me? For a while every time I thought I was Able to succeed, here came Cain killing my dreams, my purpose, and even my will to please God. My middle name is Mable, I have always hated the name, but that day I saw the name differently. I saw it as me being a carrier for the word. *Able, being put in a position to do something,* so I did something with my life, I am Mable St Claire. Everyone asked in amazement "Mable St. Claire, as in the author whose books are now movies Mable St. Claire?" Yes, that is me." Grace answered laughing. Love did come out of a deep sleep and visited me one more time. I am married to an amazing Hosea. He does not care about my past, just my future. Actually, he always said "Our past is our passage to our future, paid in full."

"He knows I owe so much to Abigail who came to my life while I was scrambling, and showed me how to soufflé and rest in my situation and arise in God. Penelope smiled and said "now look at how eloquently she put that, I sure didn't pick up on that at first" (everyone laughed)

Autumn walked up to Grace and hugged her and said "thanks for the monthly check to the PETAL ministry," Grace was shocked and so was everyone else. Grace asked "how did you know?" she answered, "Because every check you sent has, *"you are able",* stamped at the bottom." Grace responded "that is nothing compared to what you women have to deal with every day. I feel like I am part of your work by funding your ministry and praying for you and the women you encounter with daily."

The women were crying again, this time it was so overwhelming to be meeting the woman who believed in them and their work. Montana could not take it, so she had to break the moment up.

Montana stood up and said "if I had to choose who I would feel comfortable with hearing about your God, it would be you Grace. All the others have been betrayed, including Abigail. Wow, you have tasted the flames of Hell got burned and lived to talk about it."

Everyone looked at Montana with astonishment. "For a while, I thought maybe it would be Jane, but drugs were directing Jane's acts. Grace's Act's were the true battle of good and evil, even though evil won the battle, but not the war. Grace said "Montana I don't get it, I have not been beaten raped or cheated on I have surely not escaped death. You have been listening to us for two days now, why are you so bitter? Montana replied "I am not bitter, just being cautious." Abigail walked towards Montana and said "it is time to let go. I know you have spent thousands of dollars to your therapist" Montana replied "Yes and I also ended up seducing one of them." Grace then said, "No one is asking you to be saved, just to share." "Ok." sighed an irritated- Montana.

# FRAGILE, HANDLE WITH CARE

"Abigail and I went to an all girl catholic school, so we never were in contact with boys except our best friend Wellington. Believe it or not, I wanted to be a nun Just like most catholic girls did. But it was not to be. I found out my father was cheating on my mother with out of all persons, a nun. She did not want to be in God's service anymore because of my father who took her virginity before she became a nun. He threatened to scandal her name and the church if she did not keep sleeping with him. She did it only to keep the church from such a scandal.

They did not know my mother had seen them, but I did because I was there. We were going to the weekend cottage at the Lake District to air the cottage out. We saw father's car and decided to sneak in on him and surprise him. We were the ones to be surprised. I will never forget the pain of death that visited my mother's face. Two days later, my mother killed herself. After the funeral, I got drunk for the first time. I wanted to know what power that sex held that it could rob me of my mother. My father kept on apologizing, I told him if he ever came near me I would cut his dick off, and if he threatened that dear nun again I would tell everyone he raped me. (everyone gasped) oh no, he didn't, but it would have been my bloody word and my mother's dead body against his word. He looked into my eyes, he must have seen Hell or something, because he turned white as a sheep. At the reading of my mother's will I saw a sealed envelope addressed to me, it was not be opened until my eighteenth birthday. I was only fourteen at the time of her death.

It was not hard to find someone to help me with my quest of this sexual power. I did not enjoy it, I was clumsy, but I could not get over how much pleasure the man would have in his eyes, it made me feel powerful. He was twenty. By the fifth time, in a matter of a month, I got the hang of it. I even thought I was in love, not knowing exactly what it is I am supposed to be feeling in the first place. What do you compare it to? With nothing to compare it with, you are convinced that it is love. Well any way, I moved in with him when I was 16, because clumsy me got pregnant, but I miscarried. One of my best friends came to stay with me, she was still a virgin so she had many questions. I was awakened one evening to the sound of pounding flesh. Abigail walked over and put her hand on Montana's shoulders and said "you do not have to continue, Montana." Montana said "it's okay." I opened my eyes to the horror of my best friend, not being raped, but having sex with my man, in my bed, while I was asleep right next to them. It is a feeling I cannot compare to anything else in this world, the innocence of my mind was being assaulted, violated and brutally raped. They never noticed when I slipped out of the bed. I was in a trance, it felt like I was having an out of body experience. I went to the kitchen and got a knife and stabbed the both of them in their legs. The knife was still in his thigh while he chased me. He grabbed me and said "I just wanted to prove to you she was not your real friend!" The stench of her was still on him. She was screaming, I rushed over to kill her but the smell of the two of them over powered my mind, so I passed out. I don't know how I got there, but I woke up at my aunt's house. They survived, but the person I was before that night did not make it. She died. The person you see today is the one that cultivated from the soil of pain that buried me. I moved in with Abigail's parents, but that did not work out because of her crazy father. But we escaped and came to America.

Grace, I am the woman in Cray's portrait. He taught me the art of passion. (Grace gasped in shock) Other women came to him to be pleased, I went to please him. I evolved into the female Cray. He trained me well, I'm the one that taught him about C. B. C. nights. It's because of him that I stayed in law school. He was my law professor. "Master and embrace the law, Montana and it will serve you in time." He would always quote this to me.

I did not open the letter from my mother, it stayed sealed for years. My therapist urged me to read it a few years ago, and I resealed it." Montana opened the letter and began to read.

*"Dear Montana, if you are reading this I must be home with the lord, hopefully I went at a good old age. I have wanted to share this secret with you for years. This is so hard, I wanted to be with you when you found this out. I hope Abigail and Wellington is with you, you three have been un-separable for years. I think of the times you would fight Abigail's battles for her, a lot of Yorkshire lads can say they have had a 'Montana shiner' (black eye) and when one got lucky and gave you one, Abigail would be there to bandage you up. Then, you would argue with Wellington, why you had to do what you did. I chuckle now at those memories, but poor Wellington, he could never out argue you. "Montana," he would say, "this is a man's world…" and run for his life.* (Every one chuckled) *yes dear, as usual I am beating around the bush, you would always remind me of that… Montana, darling my precious one, you were left in the cold next to the rubbish bin by your biological mother. Your mother was a prostitute, and your father her pimp. He told her to abort you, but she could not kill you. (Abigail and the women are numb with tears) She hid her pregnancy for months while still selling her body. One day, your father beat her so severely that she went into premature labor. She gave birth to you in an alley and left you there, wrapped up in newspaper like an order of fish and chips. My housekeeper was taking a short cut to go home when she heard you crying. She did not know what else to do but to bring you to me. I was barren, my dear. You were my blessing. The moment I heard your first cry, I began to live, I was useless and of non existence until I held you in my arms, I began to live. I cleaned the blood off you and cut your cord. You must believe, I loved you more than life. If you are thinking you are from bad blood, you are not. I do not know what ever happened to your biological parents, rumor was they were dead. God saved your life that night, Montana and you saved mine. That night two more babies were born Abigail and wellington. You three are bonded forever. I pray Abigail is there to help you heal, and wellington is holding the three of you together as always. I love you so much my little scrapper, I hope you are living for God, my dear he saved your life, Your loving Mother.*

You could hear a feather fall. Abigail said "Montana, how could you have hid this from me?" Montana snapped back, "What was I supposed to say Abby?! I am child of a prostitute and a pimp who abandoned me?! And maybe that is why I am so evil? I have paid thousands to my therapist, and yet I never left out of that office experiencing the amazing feeling I am feeling now. I think I am now ready to forgive, to forgive everything." At that moment the phone rings.

# CONFESSION OF A DOUBLE AGENT

The phone rang. Everyone just looked at each other, waiting for the housekeeper to announce who had just interrupted the moment. "It is Mr. Monroe for Abigail," Montana said "No, you cannot talk to him, let me do it." Montana answered with "whatever you have to say, you have to say it to me." Madison's voice on the other line Shocked Montana. "We are on our way, Montana." Click. Montana said, "I guess they are coming over." Abigail asked "Who is they?" Montana replied "Madison and Sean I guess." There was not much time to say anything else when the doorbell rang. Madison and Sean walked in, the women ran and hugged Madison. Montana was confused because Madison is supposed to be the enemy. It really troubled her when Madison and Abigail embraced each other. Sean was slightly confused as well. Then he said "Abigail, your attorney made an enormous impression on the bishops the other day." Abigail replied "I am quite sure Madison will be just as impressive addressing the panel on your behalf." Sean interrupted "Abigail, please let me finish." Montana said "this is so illegal at so many altitudes". Sean yells "Please Montana! For once, shut your BIG mouth! Abigail as I was saying, I am dropping the annulment. Madison has brought the divorce papers for Montana to look over." Montana smirked. "What is wrong, Madison? You convinced your man to drop it so your name would not mingle in the mud?" Abigail said, "Montana, enough. I will sign the papers."

Abigail turned around brushed her hair from her face as she stared at the papers which she is to sign, knowing the moment the pen hits the paper the beheading will be final. She gave a faint smile to Sean and Madison and said, "I am sure you will do the right thing." She gave the papers to Montana. Sean replied "that's right, now just sign the paper so we can be on our way".

After going over the document Montana gave the papers to Abigail, the room was silent, the same deafening silence that appeared in the hall of the beauty contest before the disappointed announcement of the winner. They had hoped for a different ending, Abigail deserved a happy ending. she had helped so many of them to put their lives back together. Once more Abigail stared at the document, she was not prepared for this. 'I need a moment" said Abigail. Autumn looked at all the women and they said. "This too shall pass"... Madison asked to speak with Abigail in private. Both Sean and Montana protested, but Abigail had her way. The two women left the room and walked out into the rose garden. It was very uncomfortable for Sean being in the midst of six of Abigail's closest friends. Sean excused himself and said "tell them I will be in the car." Montana was so preoccupied trying to figure out what was going on in the rose garden that she did not even hear what Sean had to say.

Penelope said "those two have been so close for so long in this strange relationship." Autumn replied "Abigail knew. With Madison's connection with the CIA and British intelligence, and do not forget the French Intelligence, Abigail would not let her personal feelings interrupt with our well-being. It had to have been hard for her at first." Penelope said "yes, but we know her firm stance on forgiveness. She has not told us anything that she herself has not put into practice." Francis said "I would have done every bit of my six years, maybe more for bad behavior if Madison didn't get one of her colleague's to take my case." Montana heard that part and said "what are you talking about, Francis? I took your case." Francis comes back at her "That is right Montana, but I beat a guard up real bad. Abigail could not get in touch with you, so Madison represented me that day, so really you both helped (. Montana did not like what she was hearing). And Pen, madam Coco and company would still have your Baxter wrapped around that chair. So what do you all think will happen if Madison said she does not want Sean? Do you think Abigail would stay married to him?" Jane said "yes, of course. She has never thought of a life alone." Montana sharply replied "I hope not, Abigail has been in love before Sean, with a scrumptious English man. His name ladies, is Wellington. As my mother stated in her letter, we were all friends as children. "Well, what happened with him?" inquired the women"?

Abigail walked away from him, it was a very thick foggy day. You barely could see your hand in front of your face; she had a massive fight with her father, lost a beauty contest that should have been hers, it went to a tart (loose woman) that slept with the judges. Abby always looks for the good in everyone. So when she was robbed of the contest, it was devastating because she wanted the money to escape from her father. If she stayed with Wellington, it would mean staying around the same city as her father, she could not do that. So she sacrificed her love for Wellington for her freedom. It was not a very good chapter in her life that day. Wellington came to give her support, but she did not want his help. Actually her exact words were she did not want to ruin his life. Now, my best friend and cousin have to deal with her father, whom she just buried. Her daughter Jordan is not sure if there is going to be a wedding, after all, the veil did try to choke her. If that was not enough, her husband's lover, who really is not his lover because a so called evil spirit used her body to seduce Patrick in his dreams, confronts Jordan. We now know she might be her half sister? Then, there is my Aunt Mona, Abigail's mother. She is taken over by grief for a man who tried dehumanizing her every day of her married life. She may say she is not, but I know better. Abigail's husband is trying to erase twenty-five years of her life, like it never happened, and now his lover is locked up in a room with Abigail. So, right now I do not think Abby cares who has Sean. All she wants is closure and her daughters to be safe and happy. Wellington, I am sure, is married with many children running around his mansion. Ladies, I am sorry but bump this. I need a drink! I am not handling this too well." The ladies Replied, "No, Montana."

Montana says "listen, I thank you very much for today, but if you think I am accepting your Jesus today, it is not happening! I am not ready for angels, demons and whatever the heck else! I know the law, I know who I am, I love my cousin and no man loves me, but lusts after me. Those are facts that are real, and I can deal with that, but all this other stuff…

I am going to my car to get a drink! Any one want to join me? …I am joking. Ok, I am going, I will return in a moment if Sean and I don't kill each other outside." Right when Montana was to leave, Madison and Abigail came in from the rose garden. Sean must have been looking out for the women, because he was right behind them. "Ok, Madison can we wrap this up and leave?" She said "I am not leaving with you, Sean." Madison walked over and held Abigail's hand and said "this woman is now my friend, my sister in Christ whom I love very much." (Montana, was thinking "oh hell, what are they lesbians now?!)

Then Penelope stood up and said "I could not expect any less from the woman who came to our entire rescue at the request of Abigail." Montana said "blooming heck! This is the person you would have all the secret conversations with all these years when you went to help these women?!" Before Abigail could answer, a shocked Sean replied. "What are you saying Madison?!" Madison replied "I love you Sean, but I love God and me more. Sean, God has made me realize I am more than my past failures. I do not know where to start. Sit down Sean. I am only here because Abigail and I thought it was best if I represented you, and not one of your good ole boys. I apologize for the deceit.

I really thought I was dying when I asked you to join me in the Seychelles. I knew you had a wife, but I did not know your wife. I made everything sound ok by convincing myself I knew you first. I was the one to be your wife. I did not care that you were a Bishop of a church or that you had sheep to attend to. I needed you. Your father never liked me, but he owed me. He had other plans for you and you did not want to disappoint him, then he lost a lot of money and you were conveniently dropped into Abigail's, with the wealthy cousin's lap.

Anyone who knew of me knew I was a deadly She Dog. Get in my way, and whatever it took to move them, they were moved. Many coffins were used as transportation. I was a Free agent, the gods of good or evil… neither one had my vote. (Montana smiled, she understood well.)

My mother warned me of your family Sean. The elders of our city knew of the pact that was made with the underworld for the soul of their first born.

# DEATH BY TRUTH

*(S*atan looked in) *"Whoa, whoa What the Hell is going on?! I just listened for a while, they were boring us. I was on my way to the Middle East to check out some of my collateral. (The women's confession was beginning to be too much for Hell.) I have, one might say, been regaled (entertained) long enough, from every one of those wimp's, "death stories!" do me a favor; please kill those people for me! Just wipe all of them out! said Satan."*

*Gabriela intervened: "Satan, shut up! No one is touching anyone that belongs to us. Now it is going to be my pleasure to watch you as you listen in, and watch your evil schemes being brought to the light. Now, let us finish, or as you so eloquently put it Satan, let us be regaled." said an amused Gabriela, as her angels laughed mockingly at Satan alongside her.*

Sean, the soul of the firstborn would bring power and riches. For decades they have met secretly at Stonehenge. When you would call me and tell me of your erotic dreams... and you thought it was me coming to you as a spirit? No Sean, that was not me. That is all part of the gift from the underworld. You have been sexually tormented for years. I witnessed those spirits in our bed. You do not remember do you, what it was you were running from? The plane crash erased all of the horrible mess you were guilty of. Sean, you were being accused of raping your half sister. (Everyone gasped). Sean blurted out "that is a damn lie Madison! A damn lie! Why are you doing this?! Are they blackmailing you or what?"... They made you do it, Sean during one of their drunken rituals they made you do it. Your father and the whole bunch of them... "Sean, Abigail knew nothing of this. I motioned her to meet with me outside to fill her in first. I thought she should know the truth. They are deranged men. They would mix alcohol with human blood and called it a "bloody Mary." Those men are powerfully connected.

You would be surprised if you knew just how far their tentacles reach. From the government to the music industry, satanic rewards are being distributed hourly, and so is Satan's collateral being cashed in hourly. You being one of his collateral Sean, he claimed your soul that night. You came to me horrified of what you did because your sister's screams was tormenting you. She pleaded for you to stop, and all those damn bloody jerks watched as you disgraced your virgin sister. She committed suicide two hours later. She took a knife and split herself open from her gut to her abdomen. It is said she went mad and was trying to cut out her private part. God had mercy on her and took her quickly. (Everyone was in tears and angry) Her father who was not in debt to the Monarch of Hell, came looking for you with a gun and found you at my house Sean. He had the gun to your head, but your biological father got to my house in time; I am the one who rang him to get here quickly. He promised your step father he would make you leave England for South America if he would only let you live. I am sure there was a threat or two thrown in to help his persuasion of letting you live. So you were put on a plane to South America, we don't know where you were going when you crashed in America.

I flew here to see if it was really you… You really did have amnesia about the whole thing, but I took it on my own to make sure you stayed in America. You asked me why were you here, I told you some rubbish about you were here to go to divinity school. You believed me and went all the way top of your class. I really don't think you would take it seriously, but you had amnesia, so you didn't know what you were running from. But your demons followed you. I told you it was best for you to forget me, it was too dangerous, so you went on a 'wife hunt' and Abigail was it.

Sean, you know the life we led. I was a cold bitter she dog, and you a low life demonic wolf in sheep's clothing. I loved you so much, I told myself none of this was your fault and that you were a victim of your birth. I played on Hell's playground with you. Nightly orgies were our way of life. Both of us entertained male and female whatever our appetite was demanding… (Montana lifts her eyebrow…) Hell, served it to us and we had our fill of it. Until death came knocking on my door, and I met Gabriella while in a coma. She is the one who sent me to Abigail. (*Satan: "Well that answers that question, the meddler as usual."*)

She told me Abigail would help me; her job is to save lives. How do you say no to an angel Sean? An angel! I could not believe God would send something so pure and clean in my presence. Abigail met with me, I told her as much as I could about us, without her knowing all about you, but you better believe I had my people watching your girls just in case, but Gabriella assured me they were safe. Even though Abigail knew I was the love of your life, she put all of that aside knowing one day she would be asking me to help these women with my international resources. I have had to use even your father's Parliament influence a time or two to get assistance for some of the women. A little blackmail goes a long way. Sean, our child belongs to your father's satanic group, and your first child with Abigail is getting ready to be a virgin bride." I talked you into dropping the annulment. I was worried that Montana would find the truth about you and expose you. She is better than I ever imagined and she has some powerful connections that warned me she will move hell for Abigail.

It was all too much for Sean. His head started to pound, he was having flashbacks of that horrible night with his sister. His other thirty percent of his memory was coming back. Satan had rapidly released it back to him. He had Total Recall in slow motion. He grasped at his heart, his heart exploded. His face twisted to the left side as one having a stroke. His blood shot eyes locked into Abigail's eyes. He reached to her and collapsed. Jane ran to him "he is having a heart attack! Call the ambulance!" Montana replied coldly, "why? Let the dog die. Please, if there is a God, let him suffer first." Abigail scolded Montana. Sean never regained consciousness and died on Abigail's lap. The silence was deafening, while she is fighting to keep her unfaithful husband alive. She cried out "No God! No, he is the father of my children!" Montana screamed "is he going to turn to bloody maggots as well Abigail?!"

*(Satan sighed "No, he is not worth my energy, by now I'm worn out, trying to get rid of this blooming family." He motioned towards his demons, "just bring him home boys." Then glanced at Gabriella. "Well Gabriela?" She answered, "He is rightfully yours, Satan. Take him. We have no use for him.")*

"I do not think so, Montana" said a somber Abigail. Then, Montana did something that shocked everyone. She walked up to Madison and said "thank you for being there for Abigail and my nieces. I misjudged you. I hope we can work together one day." Madison opened her arms and embraced Montana. It was awkward for Montana, but she embraced her back. Madison said "I would love that." Abigail embraced both of them and said "we are going to be a force to be reckoned with." Every one left out of the room, including Madison, and gave Abigail time with Sean. Gabriella appeared to Abigail. "Do not waste your tears on him, dear. Do you ever wonder why God never granted you a son? This son would have raped your granddaughter's that was yet to come into this world." Abigail threw Sean's body from her lap as if maggots actually were eating at him. Right now, the curse dies with Sean. It is over Abigail Monroe, widow of Sean Monroe. You were not to be beheaded; your daughters are safe, the curse is over. You were Chosen for this task, you served well. Integrity has served you well and broke the curse. You are now whole.

The women came back into the room; Abigail was feeling sad for the soul of Sean, a man she never really knew. "I feel sad for his soul, but to think I rested next to that monster all these years, and had children by him. How can that be possible?"

One week later, Abigail buried Sean. There were tens of thousands that attended Sean's funeral, his secret with Madison and his curse went to the grave. Not even the children knew. The women stayed for the funeral. Pen said "Abby, a few days ago which seems like a lifetime ago, you were to be a divorcee, and now you are a widow." Abigail said "I guess death decided to behead me."

Sean and Madison's daughter did not attend the funeral, she is roaming somewhere in the Middle East was the last report given on her. Three months later, Jordan had her dream wedding. Everything went off as planned. All the ladies returned this time to celebrate Jordan and Patrick. The happy couple are away on their honeymoon. The bishops are deciding who will replace Sean at the church, Abigail has been asked to help with the search.

# LOVE AWAKENS

Abigail is finally home alone with her thoughts. She has moved into the mansion. She had the ground worked on, so she can have a view of the pond. She goes to her favorite room facing the pond. It is beginning to rain, Autumn is making its way in. Summer is preparing to end its season. Autumn is pond's favorite season. Abigail's heart is heavy, she pours herself a cup of tea and sits on the antique dusty rose camel back sofa. The maid has lit the fire, it has become a little chilly. Abigail caressed the cup and wept. "Why, God? Why? Do you hear me Jehovah? Why?" I loved him all these years, and only now you decide I need to know I was not loved, even by a monster. I do not do 'Leah' well, I want to be Rachel. I want to be loved for me. I am of age. Who will want this old woman? Yes, ok I know it will be ok, but please father let me have a weak moment. I have to be strong for everyone else. I just feel so dehydrated. I am always pouring out into others. I hurt, like hell it hurts. "Awaken not love before its time," you said, but I think right now, father love has slept in and forgotten me and I have been toiled with its imitation. Abigail fell asleep on the couch. When morning arrived, Abigail went to the pond to pray. She asked God to forgive her for last night, she interceded for all the hurting women who are still struggling with their pain. Abigail's phone rang, it was Montana. "Are you ok love?" I am in Russia with Madison. We have tracked Manuela here, oh and guess what? I think I finally ran into love." click. "Montana, Montana." Said Abigail, smiling and shaking her head.

Mean while, at the house the doorbell rang. The maid went to the door. The stranger simply said "I am here for Abigail, is she in?" Heather rang Abby on her cell phone "there is a visitor for you." "Send the person to the pond," said Abigail, "No, second, thought give them a cup of tea and sit them at the table, Heather. Let me finish down here first, Montana might be trying to get in touch with me. It is all on my time from now on." Heather smiled "yes ma'am, I will." Twenty minutes later, Abigail rang Heather to see if the stranger decided to stay or did they leave, "they're still here ma'am" Abigail responded "Well, Montana has not rang back. I hope that was a deliberate hang up and not her in trouble, but knowing her she was probably just in a hurry to cause trouble for someone else. Send the person down, Heather."

The stranger walked down to the pond. The early morning mist had not totally lifted. The mist covered Abby like a beautiful veil. A tall handsome gentleman, Abigail did not know who he was until his eyes got close to hers, he simply put his fingers on his lips then gently released them on Abigail lips and said, "Your mother rang and said you may be willing to greet an old friend." Abigail smiled "Wellington, is that really you?" She was so happy to see her childhood friend, but with everything else that had happened, she wasn't sure if it was really him or a hallucination. Abigail wiped her eyes and asked again "is it really you, Wellington? Is your wife with you? Wellington caressed Abigail "I never married Abby. You left me in the fog, Abigail. The fog never lifted, and no one else has been able to burn it away. I tried to forget you Abby, but each spring your smile would return with the forget-me-nots and the blue bells and my hope would be like a rare rose bush whose rose only blooms every decade. It a waits the rose to appear again, making the bush complete. It has been two and a half decades now Abby." Abigail touched Wellington's lips to silence him. You could see by the rhythm of her chest, at last, her irregular heartbeat was on its way to be regulated. She reached into his arms, her rapidly beating heart rested on his firm chest. The two hearts were beating similar to the drums of Africa. Their lips slowly parted. He would taste the mint from her tea, and she the honey that sweetened his tea. He has waited so long for this moment. Wellington inhaled the fiery passion from the touch of her lips. At last, the fog is being burnt away. They closed their eyes and the tears exploded out and met with passion on their moist lips. Sweet and salty, the kiss it became. Wellington pulled away and said "Accept the invitation of my heart, Abigail; allow my passion to heal your wounds.

You are to bleed no more. The loveless axe shall never visit your neck. I am your head, your lover, your cover. Oh Abby, what shall we say of this love? How can it be constrained? Our Father shall guide our steps and teach us the truth of a love that is pure and undefiled." Passion over took Abigail and she fainted into the arms of Wellington.

Abigail was once more with Gabriella. "Your true head has come to take his rightful place by your side, my dear."Abigail could not hear a word. All she wanted to do was to touch the pond, and so she did. The ripples came, but this time, to give her back her heart. She will be able to trust her heart again, with the one who awakened her love. As a well-orchestrated symphony, the ripples stood still and then parted, leaving only behind the mirror of the pond. Abigail looked into the pond and there it was, her head was back on her neck. Her tears once again contributed to the pond.

"Go back Abigail" said Gabriella as she embraced Abigail. "You are to live a long prosperous life with Wellington. Integrity has made you whole."

Abigail opened her eyes and was scared. It was all a dream, but she was still in the arms of Wellington. "I trust you with my heart Wellington". Abigail hugged Wellington; she lifts her head to the heavens and thanked her heavenly father for her being a Favored one of God.

# CONCLUSION

"Thank you readers, I hope you were blessed by this journey and you were able to take something from it. I hope something was said to ease your pain and you are feeling empowered and you really are on your way to stop denying your Future its rightful position in your life, by not being trapped to your PAST. No man is worth that power over you. Let's pray that if we are lucky to love again, we will be wiser.

None of us are perfect. We suffer at times from what I call the L.O. K. syndrome (lack of knowledge). We think we know what we need, but do we? Or are we on a Hollywood type of scavenger hunt. Hollywood has done a great job brain washing us of how the perfect man or woman should look like, and deceiving into thinking that love is all about looks in the first place. You know "Tall dark and handsome," what does that even mean? God made us all in his image, so we must all be beautiful to him. One thing for sure, our looks have been duplicated for centuries. When God seeks us out, there is only one thing he looks at, and that is our heart. What if you were asked "what type of 'heart' are you hoping to meet?" how would you answer? That is something to think about, right? Maybe we can add it to our vocabulary. Five Heartbeats said it best *"is there a HEART in the house tonight? stand up"* we should be searching for the heart that will stand with us during a storm. The heart that can recognize we are having an 'irregular heart beat.' Our hearts should beat as one. The heart of man is in our mind, so in theory, the head is the carrier of the heart. It comes in different packages. If the eyes are the window to the soul, then if we look deep enough, we should be able to see when the heart is in trouble.

There a few men in I believe God placed in the bible that represents the heart of God to model after, so when the heart of Mr. Right manifests, we will know him. One thing for certain, many imposters will come before the true husband that God has chosen for you appear.

The question is "how do you recognize the great imposter?" Sooner or later, he will try and might even succeed for a season, to impose his ways and will unto you. He is always making life better for himself, never considering your feelings or needs. In other words, an imposter is mindful of himself. He has mastered the art of deceit. He lacks a very important ingredient of being human. He has no conscience. A man without conscience is capable of inflicting unimaginable pain.

If by chance you have caught on to him, but he has already INFECTED your heart, he may already be playing the rejection game with you, trying to push you over the edge. Remember it is an IMPOSTER that is rejecting you. Also, if you have children, I must say, the imposter who has entered into your household with your children will NOT be in harmony with you on the raising of your children. He will always impose his ways, mostly when it is time to chastise your child without ever showing true love to the child. He will impose into the love you have for your children, always secretly competing for your time. Your true husband will love you and your children, it will not be a competition. If you cannot tell if a man is pretending to love your child, then just ask your child! Most of us come into relationships with bad emotional credit. We left a lot of relationships without closing our accounts. Then we ourselves become imposters. The man who encounters with us for the first time is not sure who he is meeting, if we are pretending to be emotionally debt free, when in reality we are almost emotionally bankrupt. Because our time spent in a relationship was not spent wisely.

Our precious time is just like money. Invest it wisely, and it will multiply and give it back to you. Be irresponsible, then most of the time you will be bankrupt. The next time someone asks "how you will SPEND your day" remember to SPEND it wisely.

Now here you are, an emotional wreck. You are attempting to piece back together your wrecked ship and sail into to the calm seas of someone else's life. Your ship will not hold it together and you will drown in your own deceit. If you are a wreck, let him know you are a temporary wreck, along with all the other things that just naturally come along with you which have made you the unique person you are today. The right man will love you just as you are, and you will love him just as he is. So what type of heart will accommodate your past? Remember your past is what has cultivated you into the person you are today.

Leah in all her pain or should we say in her storm of being unloved was still a chosen woman to carry Judah the seed, which our Lord and Savor Jesus would come through. Are you a Leah? Do you feel like you are unloved or even hated by the one you love? Why do you think such stories of pain are in the bible? It was because it shows that Jehovah is aware of every detail in a woman's life, and knows our pain that we suffer of being unloved. Rachel on the other hand, was loved and worshipped.

*Genesis 29:30–31 and he went in also unto Rachel, and he loved also Rachel more than Leah, and served with him yet seven other years. And when the LORD saw that Leah [was] hated, he opened her womb: but Rachel [was] barren.*

Wow there it is. In my opinion, here are the two women in the bible we can totally compare our situations with. Are you one who suffers the 'Leah syndrome?' being unloved, or worst still, hated by your husband, or the 'Rachel' who is unconditionally loved by your husband? If you are a Rachel that is completely loved by your husband, you are a blessed woman. Treat him like the king he is. You might be one who started off as a Rachel, only to end up as a Leah. (Very common)

Leah was a victim of her environment and culture. Please read the whole chapters of Genesis's 29 through 33. It is great study for the questioner listed below.

The character (heart) of the men I am going to mention have all played a great part in God's plan in the lives of certain women. We can still benefit from the character of these men today. Also, the work book is being provided for you to use in group settings like a book club or a bible study group. Please include the teens.

I need you to honestly answer the questions that we have prepared for you. These questions are for women of all lifestyles; again I suggest

191

you do this in-group setting. I pray that some of you do not take offense to the sensitivity of some of the questions.

We suggest that the questions you may feel most offended by, that you will pray for strength for the woman who will answer yes to that particular question. Let's build new ships! Let us see where our reappointments take us too.

*Heavenly Father, who is in heaven, please help these women, your daughters to be honest to their heart and minds just as you have helped me to be. Send the spirit of truth to help them, and please send the comforter to rest on their hearts as they process where they are in their lives today. Let their truth, no matter how it hurts, be seeds for tomorrow's success... In Jesus, name Amen.*

# WORKBOOK

Let us start

1. Are you honestly a needy person?

2. Do you have a shameful past?

3. Are you looking for a "daddy figure" (one to completely take care of you) in a man?

4. Do you think others may see you as a "Head Hunter?" Have you been one in the past?

5. Have you been in incarcerated?

6. Have you been battered?

7. Have you been mentally abused by anyone including family members?

8. Have you been made to feel like you cannot do anything right?

9. Have you brought the hireling, (the boy friend) into your children's lives?

10. Have you encountered the Incubus or the succubus? Did you get pleasure from them?

11. Which character in the book do you identify with and why?

12. Have you been raped?

13. Do you feel ugly?

14. Do you think you are overweight and unattractive to men?

15. Are you or have you been a substance abuser?

16. Do you think you are a victim of a generational curse?

17. Are you saved now?

18. Has your trust in men and marriage been shattered?

19. Are you a jealous person?

20. Are you a control freak?

21. Do you have a problem forgiving?

22. Do you know the difference between love and lust?

23. Do you think you recognize when breaking up is best for you?

24. How far will go on in a relationship, knowing that you are being used?

25. Are you in a habit of telling yourself, "He cares" When he treats you like yesterday's left over's, cold and tasteless

26. Do you 'stop existing' until he calls? Are you having a hard time processing, why he does not totally want you, especially when you 'have the entire right package?'

27. Are you holding on because you cannot handle rejection?

28. Are you willing to have part of a man instead of none?

29. When rejected by a man, do you want him back, just to dump him?

30. Would you change your religious beliefs for a man that loves you?

31. If your man were flirting with your best friend, would you want to know? And would it be ok if your friend told you?

32. What if your husband tells you it is a lie, who do you, believe?

33. What if her husband was flirting with you, would you feel comfortable enough to tell her the truth or would you just put him in his place, then does it becomes yours and his secret? (Blackmail material he can use later)

34. Have you ever put your fleshly needs before your children's needs by bringing a man into your household that does not care about your children, but the catch is he loves you? If so what came of it?

35. Would you side with your friend's husband while he humiliates her in public in a so called fun way, even though what he is saying about her is the truth?

36. If you were hospitalized would you feel comfortable to have your best friend stay overnight at your house to look after the children with your husband?

37. Would you share with your friend that your man was physically abusing you, knowing she is the type that would call the cops?

38. How will you react if the friend he is flirting with is skinny and you are full figured? Will you blame yourself for his indiscretion?

39. What if he tells you, "I was only trying to prove to you, that she was not your friend"? (Guilt factor)

40. Can you forgive the person who called herself your best friend who engaged in sexual acts with your man? (much prayer)

41. Do you think you have the right to ask your friend not to come to your house dressed provocatively?

42. Can you share with your friend, how your man has demoralized you. By saying things like, "you are fat and ugly". "You are so skinny you look like a crack head". "The very sight of you makes him sick." Would you be praying she does not use this info for her advantage?

43. If your man has caused you to be addicted on drugs, can you share with your friend and ask for help, or would you destroy yourself, worst still, die trying to protect him...

It's over. It was a little heavy, ok a lot. I hope that it was enough to make you think and apply sound knowledge to you and your situation.

There is no right answer to any of these questions, only the truth. Combine your answers in groups of what you think each answer should be listed under. (Example): if you answer yes to the questions, which would indicate you have a shameful past, then you would be a woman that needs God to send a Hosea in her life, or a David. After you study the chapters on these men, you will know where your answers belong. Not every man can handle a woman with a past, or one that has been battered and has become a strong independent woman. You, woman of God will need a Barrack.

I am hoping you will have 'G.T.' group discussion in your homes or churches. Choose the question you think most fits your group. Some of the questions are more provocative than others, we don't want to offend anyone, so choose wisely in what is a very sensitive matter when putting your questions together.

So are you ready to see some of the men in the bible that have been chosen? Try comparing the authentic you with their character. I personally needed a Hosea, Boaz or a Barrack in my life.

Have fun reading about these men and their heart, ask a true friend which character of these men they think you should be with. But remember, you have the last say. Please repeat this… "I am a GOOD THING!!!" Ok G.T. lets pray

*I pray heavenly father for those that you have chosen to read this book and those that need to get to know you in a more intimate way. Please strengthen those right now and may the grace and mercy from your throne run deep into their lives. Some need to feel your presence right now father, please send the Holy Spirit to touch them so they can handle the truth about themselves. I thank you for your healing that is flowing from your heart right now into their broken hearts. Love your chosen ones father. Amen. Your servant…*

## David

2nd Samuel chapter11

A David will understand one that has committed adultery; he will understand that passion that drove you, seeing that he committed adultery with Bath-Sheba. Nevertheless, he will love you as long as you really do have a repented heart. There are a few different Davids, the David that rescued Abigail from her wicked husband and would not leave her as a widow. The David that loved Sheba, but realized he loves God more. David knows the way to God's heart. He will know if you are playing with him or God.

## Hosea

Hosea (chapter 1: 2) The Lord commanded Hosea to take a prostitute as his wife.

A Hosea will be the stronger out of the entire bunch. He will love you, even though you have been a prostitute or have lead a life of that nature, maybe many partners. A man with the heart of Hosea will love you in spite of your past, because he is driven by the love of God. That kind of man is sent to the most hurting women and those who have a hard time loving themselves. Hosea will be patient because God himself will send him to find you.

## Jacob Genesis 28th

Jacob will work hard to prove his love to you. Jacob understands the fear factor, He understands being put into a situation you have no control over. He will also understand your drive to get what God has for you. Jacob will pray you through any situation. Just as he prayed all night and told the angel of God "he was not letting him go until he blessed him" genesis 32nd verse 24-26. Jacob understands how important it is to full fill a void. Jacob understands how to humble himself and ask forgiveness.

## Isaac. (The virgin with the virgin wife Rebecca) Genesis 24

Isaac the son of Abraham and Sarah

You virgins out there, find your Isaac, the only patriot not to have shared his bed with another woman. Also, it is very important for the Isaacs that you love and respect his mother. He will love you first, and provide for you, but you must respect his mother. He comes from a strong woman, Sarah. She taught him well, how to love and love deeply. He will understand your strength.

### Boaz *(his mother is said to be Rahab the prostitute)*
Ruth chapters 2 thru 4

Boaz is a man that is not in any way threatened by a woman's strength or her past. He understands when God has ordained a woman with hidden and noticeable strength; he will stay in the background and watch you shine. Please, I would ask that you respect him, and it is up to you to make him feel like the great man that he is.

Boaz is the one that will stand up to his family for you. He will seek you out, then he will observe your ways. He watches from a far while you are struggling, you may think no one this world cares about you or your struggle, but the heart of Boaz does. Be yourself. Follow the good your heart is telling you to do. He will find you in your greatest hour of need. Boaz in a way, has some qualities of Hosea. He will love you in spite of your past, as long as you have a spirit of Ruth. It is rumored his mother was Rahab, the prostitute that helped the spies in the book of numbers.

### Barrack Judges 4:

*Barak said to her, "If you go with me, I will go; but if you don't go with me, I won't go." "Certainly I will go with you," said Deborah. "But because of the course you are taking, the honor will not be yours, for the LORD will deliver Sisera into the hands of a woman." So Deborah went with Barak to Kedesh.*

You strong, independent women you know who you are. Maybe you are a threat to a lot of men you come in contact with, you need a Barrack. His and Deborah's story is remarkable. Barrack is not stupid, he knows when Gods anointing is on a woman and he will let her lead when God says so. There is situation sometimes when a man has to let a woman lead the battle and he will not care if she get gets the credit, as

long as it gets done. But don't confuse his submission with weakness...
*I pray the book helps you on this journey called life...*

*A P.E.T.A.L. providing empowerment to all Ladies...*
*Don't forget, disappointments are God's reappointments.*
*Be empowered until next time, Contessa Emanuel, a Petal.*

CPSIA information can be obtained at www.ICGtesting.com
Printed in the USA
LVOW040205170712

290318LV00002B/1/P